Advance prais

"Readers, prepare to meet the real M... ...ng leading lady who will both delight an... ...prise all who feel they already know the story of the fabled von Trapp family. As immersive, heartbreaking, and ultimately redemptive as the musical for which Maria von Trapp is so widely known and loved, this one is not to be missed. Brava!"

—Allison Pataki, author of *Finding Margaret Fuller*

"In *Maria*, Michelle Moran has revealed a fresh view of a beloved family's story, the glamorous world of 1950s New York, and a fascinating peek behind the curtain of the writing and production of Rodgers and Hammerstein's masterpiece *The Sound of Music*. This is pure delight from start to finish."

—Erika Robuck, author of *Sisters of Night and Fog*

"Michelle Moran is back! In *Maria*, Moran makes a triumphant return in offering readers a captivating and fast-paced journey through the life of Maria von Trapp. A must-read for fans of *The Sound of Music*, presenting a fresh perspective of a legendary figure. It's also a clever book, going meta by illuminating the musical's creative choices, thereby exploring the interplay between history and historical fiction."

—Stephanie Dray, author of *Becoming Madam Secretary*

"For anyone who loved *The Sound of Music*, Michelle Moran's beautifully drawn portrait of Maria von Trapp will add multiple dimensions to your understanding of the beloved classic. With meticulous research and a fine sense of style, *Maria* evokes the real miracle of the incredible singing von Trapp family and brings their story vividly to life. Getting to know the real woman behind the beloved story will only make you love her more."

—Elizabeth Letts, author of *Finding Dorothy*

"Alternating between the life and experiences of beloved heroine Maria von Trapp in the 1940s, and the perils of adapting her story for the silver screen years later, Moran adds new dimension to a story that has captivated hearts and minds for decades. The hills truly do come alive with the sound of music in this deftly crafted tale."

—Aimie K. Runyan, author of *The School for German Brides*

BY MICHELLE MORAN

Maria
Nefertiti
The Heretic Queen
Cleopatra's Daughter
Madame Tussaud
The Second Empress
Rebel Queen
Mata Hari's Last Dance

MARIA

MARIA

A NOVEL OF
MARIA VON TRAPP

MICHELLE MORAN

DELL ❦ NEW YORK

A Dell Trade Paperback Original

Copyright © 2024 by Michelle Moran
Book club guide copyright © 2024 by Penguin Random House LLC

All rights reserved.

Published in the United States by Dell, an Imprint of Random House,
a division of Penguin Random House LLC, New York.

DELL and the D colophon are registered trademarks
of Penguin Random House LLC.
RANDOM HOUSE BOOK CLUB and colophon are trademarks
of Penguin Random House LLC.

Library of Congress Cataloging-in-Publication Data
Names: Moran, Michelle, author.
Title: Maria: a novel of Maria von Trapp / Michelle Moran.
Description: New York: Dell, 2024.
Identifiers: LCCN 2023058402 (print) | LCCN 2023058403 (ebook) | ISBN 9780593499481
(trade paperback; acid-free paper) | ISBN 9780593499498 (ebook)
Subjects: LCSH: Trapp, Maria Augusta—Fiction. | LCGFT: Biographical fiction. | Novels.
Classification: LCC PS3613.O682 M37 2024 (print) | LCC PS3613.O682 (ebook) |
DDC 813/.6—dc23/eng/20231222
LC record available at https://lccn.loc.gov/2023058402
LC ebook record available at https://lccn.loc.gov/2023058403

Printed in the United States of America on acid-free paper

randomhousebooks.com
randomhousebookclub.com

2 4 6 8 9 7 5 3 1

To my mother, Carol Markstein-Moran. There is no one who embodies the spirit of *The Sound of Music* more than you. At eighty-two years old, you still believe that any mountain can be scaled, and that's such a beautiful thing.

MARIA

PROLOGUE

Dear Mr. Hammerstein,

It may come as a surprise that I am writing to you, as it appears that the theater industry believes I am dead and can now make up whatever they wish about me. Although I appreciate a good yarn as much as anyone, I would ask if the following summary truly seems to be an accurate representation of my life, about which your new musical is supposedly based:

There was once a young woman from Austria who wished to become a nun. She prayed and sang her devotionals, until one day she managed to sing her way into the heart of a dashing young widower with seven children. Though she was nervous about becoming a stepmother, it turned out that all seven children adored her. And though the young woman and her new family were forced to flee their homeland, everything turned out just fine in the end (so fine, in fact, that a musical was written about her life).

I am given to understand that although the musical is nearly complete, the lyrics you are writing remain to be added. I am therefore reaching out in the earnest hope that you will remove the most egregious errors in the script before it is too late. In January, I will be fifty-five years old. If statistics are to be believed, I can anticipate living another twenty years. It is my deepest wish not to spend those remaining years explaining how I never escaped from Austria by crossing the Alps into Switzerland (a magnificent feat, given that Salzburg has never bordered Switzerland), or how my eldest stepchild, Rupert, has never been a sixteen-year-old girl named Liesl. And this is to say nothing of all the other fanciful changes throughout the script.

I know that someone of your renown would not wish to promote a work that has taken a person's life and altered it so dramatically. For this reason, I am requesting a meeting at your earliest convenience, as I have several ideas on how the script can be fixed.

Sincerest regards,
Maria von Trapp

CHAPTER ONE

FRAN

The Hamptons, New York
1959

B Y SEPTEMBER OF 1959, Fran can spot the hopefuls from a mile away. Usually, they're men with manuscripts tucked away in their bags, working the room until some industry notable asks to see what they have. But tonight it's a woman in a low-cut dress. She's Monroe to Fran's Hepburn, the perfect hourglass with four-inch heels and overbleached hair.

"You seeing this?" Eva asks from her deck chair, using her wineglass to point to the window. The darkness frames an interesting scene inside the house: the famous lyricist, Oscar Hammerstein, standing next to the piano singing while Fran's boyfriend, Jack, plays, the two of them entertaining the crowd by composing funny limericks on the spot. Marilyn's look-alike has squeezed onto the piano bench, and while she's laughing at Hammerstein, her eyes are for Jack.

"It always seems to be someone, doesn't it?" Fran asks. She

leans back and inhales the salty air of the Hamptons. It reminds her of home and she wants to drink it all in: the beach, the chatter, the breezy wraparound porch.

Eva leans forward and raises her brows. "You really aren't bothered by them, are you?"

Fran laughs. "Why? It's not like Jack can help these girls in any way."

"And what makes you think all they want is help?" In the light of the porch, Eva's face looks angelic, haloed by perfect honey-blond curls. For the last four years she's been cast as one young ingenue after another on Broadway, and she'll probably still be playing them ten years from now. Whereas Fran's mother says that someone with her coloring—brown hair, blue eyes, and freckled cheeks—will be a prune by twenty-five if she won't keep out of the sun.

They both watch as Marilyn scoots over on the bench until her thigh is brushing Jack's and Eva lets out a disapproving, "Hmmm. Peter avoids girls like that," she warns. And to make a point, she looks across the room to where her beau is standing in a circle of men. He's the tallest of the bunch, with loose brown curls he never slicks back and a giant smile. As usual, it looks like he's doing all the talking while the other guys laugh.

Now Fran takes a sip of her wine and shrugs, unconcerned about what's happening inside. "Guess I should be thankful she's not Jack's type."

But Eva lowers her glass. "Franny, easy is everyone's type."

Fran's not sure about that. Still, she's secretly pleased when Hammerstein takes Jack's place at the piano and Jack starts to sing. Three years ago, he'd been the most intelligent student in her seminar on James Joyce, with deep, intense eyes and an answer for everything. She'd pegged him as the snobby East Coast boarding-school type, and while she hadn't been wrong, she'd been surprised to find him singing at the campus bar one evening, part of a college a capella group. After their first set the group fanned out across the bar asking for requests, and after a long sip of her Old Milwaukee, Fran had offered a suggestion.

"How about 'Mona Lisa'?"

Jack's dark eyes had lit up. "You mean, Nat King Cole?"

Fran had smiled. "Who else?"

The group was good, their baritone voices mimicking the bass notes of Cole's piano, and for a few minutes Fran was transported back to Norfolk, where her father was probably still listening to Cole belting out this same tune on their old phonograph.

When the group had finished, Jack returned to Fran's table to ask if he could buy her a drink. They spent the next three hours talking. She discovered he was the son of some hotshot politician. And he found out she was the daughter of Frank Connelly, the man who'd made the one-stop-shop grocery chain famous.

"So it was *your* dad who was responsible for putting all those butchers out of business," he'd teased.

Fran had taken another sip of her beer and shrugged. "Actually, it was me." Then she told him about the idea she'd had to build a grocery store with both a butcher and a bakery inside. *Why go to three stores when you could shop at one?* she'd asked her father. And he'd trusted her enough to try it out.

Jack had fixed her in his gaze, lost in the idea that she'd been the one behind this revolutionary change. And Fran recognizes it as the same look he's wearing now while he improvs near the piano as the same one he'd had then: like a man completely transported by the moment.

Jack continues to sing until Hammerstein is finished, then everyone claps wildly and they both take a bow. A moment later Jack and Hammerstein appear together on the porch and the blonde is back to making her rounds.

"Fantastic," Eva says, fluttering her fake lashes as she approaches the two men.

"Well, thank you, Miss LaRoche. That's very kind." Hammerstein smiles, and Fran doubts that anyone would ever pick him out as someone who owns Broadway. He's a funny-looking man, with a great big face, broad shoulders, and strong arms. He looks like the sort who would carve meat instead of words for a living. He casts around for his wife, and as soon as he spots her, the broad shoulders relax. "Well, fellas, you know the old saying . . ."

Early to bed, early to rise. Everyone else at the party will stay until one or two in the morning. But Jack, Peter, and the rest of Hammerstein's assistants are filing out the door, trying to look cheerful about abandoning the fun at nine o'clock. And it's not because it's Tuesday. Hammerstein's wife once told Fran that he never stayed later than ten o'clock at any party. And, of course, what's good for the goose is good for his staff.

Jack slings his arm over Fran's shoulders and pulls her to his side. At twenty-three he feels as solid as he did when he was crew captain back at the University of Virginia. "Ready?"

She settles into his embrace, enjoying his light touch in the buttery warmth of the evening air. She had been right to go with the cap-sleeve sheath instead of the blue cardigan and skirt. The sweater would have been too warm, even with the breeze. Walking with Jack back to their car, their shoes crunching over the gravel, Fran thinks of how, when they first began dating, she'd been learning to drive and Jack had offered to help. He'd been the only student on campus with a convertible, and later, when she learned what it had cost, she took it as a sign of devotion that he'd been willing to teach her in a car that was worth more than her grandfather's house.

Fran slides onto the cool leather of the passenger seat, waiting for Eva and Peter to join them. Rolling down her window, she breathes in the last of the salty air. Jack seems quiet. They normally exchange gossip from the evening, but his eyes are pinched shut and she assumes he's thinking about the work he'll need to do for the new musical. It's supposed to be something sweet and pastoral. A true love story straight out of the hills of Austria. So it surprises her when he opens his eyes and asks, "You catch that blonde tonight?"

Fran doesn't miss a beat. "The one with the dress?"

"That was Freddie's girl."

"*Really.*" Freddie is a quiet guy from the office. "I didn't think he had it in him."

Normally, Jack would laugh, but his mind is somewhere else. "I couldn't believe Hammerstein on that piano tonight. I mean, sixty-four years old and still on fire. That's the kind of staying power I want someday, Fran."

This is different and Fran tries to make out where it's coming from.

"I just can't stop thinking about the new musical," he admits. "I don't know if I'll ever be able to write like that." But as Eva and Peter reach the car, Jack's stream of self-doubt is forced to take a break and he bangs his fist against the wheel. "I left my jacket inside." He jogs back to the house as the car fills up with laughter.

"You should have seen him," Peter says, and Fran turns around. Peter has ditched his jacket and his shirtsleeves are rolled up to his elbows. "He was doing an Elizabeth Taylor impression."

"Oh, be serious," Eva says, fishing through her pocketbook.

"What? It was great."

"It was juvenile," Eva rules, pulling out a fancy gold cigarette case and snapping it open.

Peter shrugs. "Well, he had everyone in stitches."

Eva lights up a cigarette and takes a long drag. "I'm just glad he's not working with you again." She exhales and the first tendrils of smoke curl toward Fran's window. "So, what are you boys doing at the office nowadays?"

Peter fans the smoke away from his face. "A new play."

"I had a copy on my desk and was tempted to read it," Fran admits.

"You should have," Peter tells her, rolling open his window.

"Why?" Eva wrinkles her nose, trying to imagine wanting to read for fun.

"Because she has a degree in English lit," Peter points out the obvious. "Plus, aren't you working on a book, Fran?"

Jack returns and starts the car. "Who's working on a book?"

"I hope you're kidding," Fran says, elbowing him in the side, since she's been writing *A Northern Wind* for the last two years.

"Oh, yeah. Yeah, she's gonna be the next Agatha Christie, right?" He slides his arm around Fran's waist.

"Well, I was telling her she should go ahead and read the play," Peter says, sitting back.

Jack glances at Fran as he backs out of the driveway. "Really? You want to?"

She can't believe he's asking her this. "Of course I do!"

Peter leans forward, his forearms propped against the leather headrests. "You said you liked *South Pacific,* didn't you?"

Jack frowns. "When did she say that?"

"Last week at lunch," Eva says dryly.

"Well, this play is even better," Peter promises. "There's only a few songs in there right now, but they're the catchiest lyrics Hammerstein's ever written."

Fran finds this hard to believe. "Better than the ones for *The King and I*?"

Peter nods. "Yes."

"How about *Show Boat*?"

"Definitely."

"So what's it called?" Eva asks, patting down her hair.

"Well, the book is called *The Story of the Trapp Family Singers.*"

Eva flicks a long ash out the window. "Now that's a mouthful."

Peter agrees. "The producers wanted to change it to *The Singing Heart.* But Hammerstein convinced them to go with something else." He waits, just like a little kid, making Eva ask.

"Well, what?"

A grin spreads across his face. "*The Sound of Music.*"

Eva and Fran listen as Peter describes the script to them, from Maria von Trapp's time preparing to become a nun to her fortuitous meeting of the very wealthy and practically single—well, except for seven children—Baron von Trapp. The way Peter tells it, God Himself arranged for their meeting. Two lovelorn birds finally alighting on the same empty branch.

"Come on. You're telling me this girl was about to become a nun but—*oops!*—a wealthy Baron fell in love with her, and then look at that, now she's a Baroness?" Fran gives Peter her best I-don't-think-so look and Eva laughs with her. "And where'd he get all those kids?"

"I know. It sounds ludicrous," Peter admits. "But she's not what you think. Just read it for yourself."

He seems pretty convinced. And now Fran has to admit, she's curious about what kind of a woman finds herself married to a Baron after almost marrying herself to God. So Jack makes a detour by his apartment and returns with the script and the book that it's based on. "Just read the script," he prompts, probably not wanting to take up too much of her time. But the moment she's back in her apartment, she snuggles under her blanket and lingers on the book, running her hands over its cover. She knows what they say, but the look and feel of books are important to her.

The cover is nicely done. It's been published by J. B. Lippincott & Company, so she's not surprised. In the center is a photo of Maria sitting outdoors at the head of her family, her children arranged neatly behind her in traditional Austrian outfits. Fran imagines that if the image were in color the hills behind them would be emerald green, but she's left to wonder about their hair and eyes. The write-up inside is compelling:

> With more than 1,000 concerts in the United States and Canada, the Trapp Family Singers are in the second decade of a career that has brought them far since their almost penniless arrival in this country as refugees from Hitler.

So after marrying a wealthy Baron she lost everything. Yet still remained married. Fran admits that the cynic in her is intrigued. She puts away the book and starts on the script and by two in the morning she's turning the last page. She must look terrible when it's time for work, because Jack takes a step back as soon as she opens the door to her apartment.

"When did you go to sleep?" he asks.

She tries to remember. "Two? Three?"

He comes inside and slides his briefcase across the kitchen table. "Well, we have ten minutes to get to the office." He makes his way to the kitchen and Fran sees him wince at her package of Bushells instant coffee. *Not everything can be Greenwich Village's fancy espresso, Jack. Not on a secretary's salary.* Four years ago, when Fran's father surprised her with this apartment, she had told him it was far too fancy for her. "It's in such a nice part of the city," she'd protested. "Maybe you should just rent it out."

"We bought it for *you*," her father had said.

But she had two younger sisters who'd be off to college in another few years. Were they going to buy them apartments, too? What about their retirement?

Her father gave her one of those big Connelly smiles.

"You worry too much, Fran. You think I haven't been saving for all these years?"

"Sure. But *look* at this place." Fran turned around, taking in the expansive windows and high French doors opening to a terraced view of the park. "And the furniture—"

"Yes," her father said proudly. "Your mother picked it out."

So Fran had moved in and, a few days later, Eva's parents bought her a place in the same building. "A full-floor aerie," Eva had gushed, showing off her new apartment on the twenty-second floor.

Now Fran hurries into her bedroom and shuts the double doors, putting on the first dress she comes across in her closet. It's a miracle she's able to get ready in time. She pauses in front of the mirror just long enough to adjust her usual pillbox hat—a gift from her sister when she was eighteen—then they're both out the door, her black stilettos clacking down the hall to the elevator. In the cab, she dashes on some lipstick, then waits.

"*Well?*" Fran asks as she settles into her seat.

Jack frowns. "Well, what?"

Her voice rises. "Aren't you going to ask me what I think about the script?"

He stares at her, a real-life Captain America with his chiseled jaw and head of blond hair. "Fran, I'm actually kind of busy in my own head this morning." He must realize how this sounds, however, because immediately he apologizes. "Look, I'm sorry. What did you think about the script?"

Fran is quiet for several moments. Then finally she allows, "It's good."

"That's it?"

"He could have changed a few lines in 'My Favorite Things,'" she adds testily.

Jack is surprised. "Like what?"

"'Pink satin sashes.' It would sound better if he changed it to 'blue.'" She shrugs. "It's a longer vowel."

It looks as if Jack wants to know more, but they've reached Sixth Avenue and the cab is pulling up to the curb. In front of them is the high-rise where Hammerstein has his office with Dick Rodgers. Over the past four years, Fran has become increasingly impressed by the empire Rodgers and Hammerstein have built, made possible because they realized early that their work was as much a business as an art. They no longer simply compose and write. Now they produce, publish, market, publicize. And all of it requires an army of clever assistants—young men like Jack, who secretly hope to become the next Rodgers or Hammerstein.

Fran opens her own door and steps outside. It's one of those perfect September days: the air is crisp and the trees are just beginning to turn. But there's no time to appreciate the scenery. She hurries into the building, where the bellman is all smiles this morning, making her feel terrible that she's probably still scowling. "Morning, Mr. Mayer, Miss Connelly." He punches the button for the fifteenth floor.

"Good day so far, Mr. Jones?" Fran asks.

"Any day I wake up is a good day, Miss Connelly."

Fran chuckles, because this is what her grandfather used to say. He'd been a shoemaker by trade and used to tell his sons there were two things a person would always need: shoes to wear and food to eat. Which was probably why her father ended up in the grocery business. Twelve chains later, each one bearing the name Connellys, Fran figures it was probably solid advice.

When they reach the office, there's a hum of activity already going on. Rehearsals on the new script started on Monday even though Hammerstein's still finishing the lyrics. It's taking him longer than usual. With *Flower Drum Song* it was a song every few weeks. But it's different this time, and Fran wonders if maybe there's something wrong. It's not just how long it's taking him to write. It's the fact that it's nine o'clock and there's no one behind the giant mahogany desk. Usually, he's there two hours before everyone else.

"Well?" Peter says as soon as he sees her. Jack has already disappeared into his own office and shut the door. But Peter perches on the corner of Fran's desk, completely at ease with himself. "You read it last night, didn't you?" he asks.

"Until two A.M."

"I knew it!" He laughs at his own certainty. "*And?*"

"You were right." She slides her pocketbook into the top drawer and takes out the day's schedule, smiling up at him. "It's simple and sweet and impossible not to like. Makes you wonder how much of it is actually true."

The office door opens and Hammerstein appears, carrying his lunch in a paper bag. "Good morning, Mr. Rickman." Peter slides off the desk. "Miss Connelly," he adds brightly. "Still working on your book?" There's no underlying hint of amusement in his voice. Not like when Fran's mother asks the same question.

"Just editing now," Fran says. "But I did have some good news last week." Hammerstein stops to listen. "*The New Yorker* accepted one of my stories."

A slow smile spreads across Hammerstein's face and she

can tell how genuinely pleased this makes him. "From the very beginning you've surprised me, Miss Connelly. Yet for some reason this doesn't surprise me at all. Well done. I'd like to read it when it's out."

"Of course," Fran says. "Thank you, Mr. Hammerstein."

Hammerstein continues to his office and Peter gives her a secret thumbs-up behind his back, following him inside. It's Roundtable Wednesday, when all of the assistants give advice on the current script. If Hammerstein's written any new material, this is when they'll go over the placement of those lyrics in the script.

Fran makes her way to the ladies' room and hangs her jacket on the rack next to her hat. Richard Rodgers has his own assistant, a girl named Rhonda, but she hasn't come in yet, otherwise one of her fancy pillbox hats would be perched on the rack as well. Fran pats her hair back into place and returns to the desk. It's just after nine o'clock and the phone is ringing.

"Rodgers and Hammerstein." She cradles the phone against her ear, freeing her hands to type up the press release she didn't finish yesterday. The voice on the other end nearly deafens her, but Fran just rolls her eyes. Another crisis at the Lunt-Fontanne. *So what is it today?* she thinks. *Missing prop, angry talent, sick actor, locked dressing room?* But when she hears the words "Maria von Trapp," she snaps to attention. "I'm sorry. What? Can you say that again?"

Richard Halliday draws a long breath on the other end of the line. "The *author*—as in the woman who wrote the book this play is based on—is standing here demanding changes to the script!"

Now this is a crisis. Fran glances at Hammerstein's closed door. Nothing is to disturb Roundtable Wednesday short of a flood or a fire. But it could be a third type of disaster if Mrs. von Trapp goes to the press with her concerns. "I'm calling in to Mr. Hammerstein and sending someone over," she says.

"No."

Fran leans back against her chair, surprised by Mr. Halliday's vehemence.

"Maria's not going to listen to just anyone. Oscar needs to come."

Not happening, Fran thinks, but tells him, "All right. I'll see what I can do."

"And if he can't come, Fran, it needs to be you."

Hammerstein picks up on the second ring and Fran can hear the Roundtable voices go quiet on the other side of the door. She quickly explains the situation unfolding at the Lunt-Fontanne.

There's a moment of tense silence.

"Take her to the St. Regis for lunch and find out what's bothering her," Hammerstein says. "Bring a pad and write it all down."

"And if she insists on seeing you?"

"It's the first week of rehearsals. You can tell her we're still working things out."

Fran is tempted to ask if this is true, then realizes it doesn't matter. She retrieves her pocketbook from the drawer and grabs one of the steno pads that Hammerstein keeps in large stacks around the office. Then she nips back inside the ladies' room for her jacket and settles her hat back into place. A moment later she's out the door again.

As she makes her way down Sixth Avenue, Fran rehearses what she's going to say to Maria. Summers spent working in her father's store have made her comfortable with confrontation. There was never any shortage of irate customers. When Fran is sure how she's going to approach the woman, she lets her mind wander.

It's an easy game to guess where most people are going. This is because New York is the only place she's lived where fashion can be so accurately decoded. Take the men from the financial district, for instance, in their expensive suits and dark felt hats. Or the men going to their pub jobs dressed in casual trousers and oversized sport coats. There are young guys ambling late to class in their Converses and jeans, and your typical high school girls in twinset sweaters and ballerina flats. But Fran doubts anyone would be able to pinpoint where she works. The robin's-egg blue of her dress complements her eyes, but otherwise she's unremarkable. Just another one of the thousands of women headed to a typewriter somewhere.

When Fran first arrived in the city, she had tried to find a job in the publishing industry. But it turned out no one was excited about a girl with a southern accent at their front desk, and all the desks that really counted—the ones behind closed doors—were reserved for men. But that was four years ago and things are changing. She thinks of her acceptance letter from *The New Yorker* back home, lying open on her bureau beneath her father's fountain pen. When it arrived she ran her fingers over the fancy stationery, the embossed letters moving like puffy clouds across the page. Perhaps by the end of the year her book would be ready for submission. Maybe sooner if she stopped going on so many trips to the Hamptons.

Fran is so lost in thought that she almost walks past the Lunt-Fontanne. She backtracks a few steps, then takes a moment to pause and look up. Last year the sprawling building had been a movie theater. Today, the rows of wide velvet seats and sparkling chandeliers host some of the best shows on Broadway. Her eyes rest on one of the long red banners with a picture of the actress Mary Martin. She's dressed in a traditional Austrian costume, her hair braided and pinned back to look like a young Maria von Trapp.

Fran has met Mary Martin half a dozen times since working for Hammerstein and knows that the actress is admired throughout the business for the extraordinary dedication she has to her work. If Maria is inside fuming about her portrayal, it will absolutely crush Mary. Not to mention derail the entire production. Because it's Mary Martin and her husband, Richard Halliday, who have the rights to the story.

A red-suited man with white hair opens the door for Fran, then shakes his head.

"Trouble?" Fran asks, and Gene just whistles one of the tunes that she's been hearing around the office. She recognizes the song as Hammerstein's, the one with the lyrics that ask how a problem like Maria should be solved. "Great," she mutters.

"Good luck, ma'am. 'Cause you goin' to need it."

Fran braces herself as she crosses the lobby and enters the theater. It takes a moment for her eyes to adjust to the dimmer light, but nothing unusual seems to be happening inside. The stage is crowded with actors preparing for a scene in Nonnberg Abbey, where the Mother Abbess is seated behind an austere desk, surrounded by nuns who have come to talk about Maria. She can see the costume designers pinning and tucking the robes of several of the nuns and a group of technicians adjusting the lights. But there's no sign of anyone causing trouble.

Fran crosses the theater and continues looking around. She doesn't spot Mary Martin, but Richard Halliday, who is not only her agent but her husband and the show's producer, is there, tugging at his mustache as he paces the stage. A faint hope springs up that maybe the storm has already passed. Then a group of nuns disperses and Fran sees her.

She's standing in the middle of the action, dressed as if she's just wandered in from an alpine meadow. Her gray hair is held back by a dark green kerchief and her dress—the same traditional Austrian costume pictured on the front of her autobiography—stands out among all the black robes and mantillas. She's been giving directions to a group of nuns and has now turned her attention to the set designers.

"Nonnberg looked nothing like this," she pronounces. "You have a fountain over there and I have no idea why. There were no giant fountains!"

Fran reaches the stage as Halliday is actually beginning to turn purple.

"Fran!" he cries. Then he tells Maria, "Look," drawing the woman's attention away from the offensive prop to Fran.

Fran stands at the bottom of the stage and smiles up at the older woman in the white apron. A large cross dangles from her neck and the pendant is nearly blinding in the stage lights. "Mrs. von Trapp?"

The woman straightens. She's tall, with piercing blue eyes and cheeks like little red apples. "Yes?"

"I'm Frances Connelly. Mr. Hammerstein sent me to find you."

Halliday places his palm on the small of Maria's back and ushers her off the stage. At the bottom of the stairs, Fran holds out her hand.

CHAPTER TWO

FRAN

Manhattan, New York
1959

"Y OU SAY YOU COME from Hammerstein's office?" Maria asks. Up close, her eyes are more gray than blue.

"Yes." Fran nods. "He heard you had suggestions and thought we could discuss them over lunch."

"I've already had lunch."

"Well, that's no problem," Halliday says. Behind him, the nuns are taking their places and rehearsal is about to continue. "Just order yourself a drink and Fran here will take notes on everything."

Maria stiffens. "I want to be clear." Her Austrian accent is strong, but there's no mistaking her words. "There is almost nothing I like about this script."

A knot begins to form in Fran's stomach. It's possible she won't be able to smooth this over. "Well, perhaps we can focus on your biggest concerns," she suggests.

"There are too many of them. But I can tell you this,"

Maria says, clutching the pendant in her fist. "There is no scene with the Captain that's acceptable. Those German writers turned him into some strict Prussian officer and I see you've simply gone and copied them. He wasn't the disciplinarian. He never was. That was all the Baroness."

"Make sure to write this all down," Halliday says. "Word for word."

Maria looks shocked. "You're not coming?"

He gives a helpless shrug. "Rehearsals. But I leave you in capable hands."

Conflicting emotions cross Maria's face and Fran squares her shoulders, trying to look capable.

There's a moment of silence, and when neither Fran nor Halliday fills it, Maria sets her jaw. "I will visit the powder room first."

The second Maria is gone, Halliday turns to Fran. "You know, I can still remember Maria's face when she got off that boat from New Guinea. Took me months to track her down, and when I finally found her, you want to know what she said? 'Mary Martin? Who's Mary Martin? And why should I give a fig about her wanting to play me?'" Halliday laughs, as if nothing could be crazier than someone not recognizing his wife's celebrity.

The story has practically become lore throughout the business. After searching for Maria von Trapp for the better part of a year, Halliday and Mary arrived to discover that she'd already sold her rights to a German company for a paltry nine thousand dollars. In perpetuity. It took months of negotiating with the Germans, but eventually they got what they wanted: the rights to produce a play based on Maria's life with Mary Martin as the lead.

As soon as the play debuts on Broadway, 20th Century-Fox will be allowed to film a movie using the same script. Apparently, Hollywood wants someone younger than Mary for the lead, and the last Fran heard the most likely candidate was Audrey Hepburn. She thinks it says a lot about Mary that she doesn't mind that. It was also Mary and Halliday who decided to give Maria three-eighths of a percent of the profits, simply as a gesture of goodwill. It's not a sizable figure, but if the play does as well as Rodgers and Hammerstein's *Oklahoma!*, then it should turn out to be quite a tidy sum.

This all transpired over two years ago, and now Fran fixes her gaze on Halliday.

"Oh, don't look so cross," he says. His breath is already sour with alcohol and it's not even ten o'clock. "You'll take her to the St. Regis, enjoy a Bloody Mary—"

"With all due respect, I don't believe she's come here to enjoy a Bloody Mary. This is her life story and she's *upset*."

"Which is why we'll get her a nice dress for the premiere and a matching handbag. Then she'll be right as rain."

Fran stares at Halliday. "You knew she'd hate the script."

Halliday leans so close that his breath is hot on her cheek. "Of course," he whispers. "What do you think the three-eighths of a percent was for?"

Fran's not sure when she became one of those despicable Broadway types who smiles too much and talks too fast. But as she and Maria step, blinking, into the perfect weather outside, it occurs to her that she's no different from Halliday.

"I don't know how much your lawyer's told you about the

production," she begins, "but the Lunt-Fontanne is one of the best theaters on Broadway."

Maria looks down at Fran and ignores her olive branch. "How long have they been working on the script?"

Fran leads them along the street past the Radio City Music Hall marquee. "Six months?" she guesses.

Maria's voice tightens. "And they're hoping to open in November?"

"Yes."

"Then we'd better hurry," Maria says, quickening her pace. "I have quite a few suggestions."

Fran practically has to run in her heels to keep up with Maria in her loafers. She figures if she can just get her to talk—about the city, about her singing, about anything really—she'll have to slow down. But Maria is on a mission. They race up Fifth Avenue past Rockefeller Center and Saint Patrick's Cathedral. And it's only when a group of four women exiting the cathedral stop and begin pointing excitedly at Maria that she finally slows down.

"Maria!" one of the women calls out. "Maria von Trapp of the Trapp Family Singers!"

Maria stops and the women immediately react. "It's her!" they squeal, and Fran can actually see Maria's sharp edges beginning to soften. The group rushes over and surrounds her, peppering her with questions and compliments. One of them likes her dress and another is running her hands over the frills of Maria's apron. All of them have been to one of her concerts and several want to know when she'll be singing again.

"Oh, I'm afraid we retired three years ago," Maria says

sadly. "But we run a lodge in Vermont. And we now have a music camp."

Within moments, the women are reaching for their pocketbooks to write down the address of the Trapp Family Lodge.

The same scene is repeated on Fifty-Third Street. And Maria is happy to answer questions about everything: Austria's mountains, its church bells, the best sausages in the city. She's glowing by the time a tuxedoed waiter escorts them across the dining room of the St. Regis and holds out a chair for her.

"It must be wonderful to have so many fans," Fran says, settling her napkin across her lap. "I can't remember ever reading a story about someone who's led such a charmed life."

Maria's lips thin into a very straight line. "It does come across as charmed in the script, doesn't it?"

Fran recognizes immediately that this was the wrong thing to say. "Well, yes. Your love story—"

"With Georg? My dear, that wasn't a love story."

Fran can feel herself gaping.

"Oh, it's all in my book." Fran doesn't want to admit she hasn't read it. "But no, my life wasn't charmed." Maria swats away this idea like a gnat. "I was an orphan," she says. Then she lowers her voice. "When I ran away to the State Teachers' Progressive Education College, I didn't even have five *groschen* to my name."

"You were a teacher?"

She nods. "That's why the nuns sent me to Captain von Trapp."

Fran is flooded with relief. "So you really were a nun." At least this part of the script is correct.

"I was a postulant," Maria corrects, instinctively reaching for her pendant. "And not a terribly good one at that."

CHAPTER THREE

MARIA

Salzburg, Austria
1926

I WATCH AS SISTER JOHANNA fights against her billowing skirts, crossing the rooftop one unsteady step at a time. "Maria!" she exclaims. She's only twenty-nine, but her voice sounds so much older and shriller. "Maria, what are you doing up here?"

She comes to stand next to me as I turn in circles, taking in the view. "Have you ever seen anything like it?" I ask. The entire world is stretched out before us, gilded beneath an amber sky. I squint as the rising sun catches the water of the Salzach and imagine the river is a string of diamonds.

Sister Johanna is incredulous. "You came up here to see the mountains?"

I take a deep breath of the mountain air. "I came up here to commune with God."

"The purpose of entering a convent, Maria, is to commune with God from within."

But that's ridiculous. "According to who?"

"According to the person who founded this abbey twelve hundred years ago!" Johanna frowns. She only wants the best for me, I know, but she doesn't understand. "You've missed breakfast," she says.

"That's fine." I point my chin to the sky, enjoying the warmth of the early-morning sun. "I don't care much for breakfast."

"Well, you're about to miss class."

"What?" I search her face. "What time is it?"

Her voice is clipped. "Ten past eight."

My six-year-olds will be waiting for me on the first floor of the abbey. "Why didn't you say something?" I gather my skirts and take the steps two at a time.

"All right." I clap my hands as I reach the landing. "All right. Into the class." There's tittering from several of the boys, but I herd them inside and have them find their seats.

"That was great, Miss Maria. It looked like you were flying! Can we do that?" Johann asks from his desk. He must have seen my slide down the banister to save time.

"Absolutely not," I say, taking attendance. I review the list and make a checkmark next to each child's name. All twenty-five students accounted for. But as I put down my clipboard I hear a little sniffle from the back of the class. The students motion me to Ilse's desk and I make my way over.

"Ilse." I squat down so that my eyes are level with hers. "Is everything all right?"

She shakes her pigtails.

"Would you like to tell me about it?" I ask.

She gives a little gasp. "I forgot my lunch," she whispers.

I smile. "Well, that's easily fixed," I say. "You can have mine."

Her eyes go big. "Really?"

"Of course." I straighten.

"Can I have some of yours, too?" Rupert asks from behind her.

I laugh. "Let's all share lunches today!" I suggest. "It can be a picnic." The cheer that goes up in my first-grade classroom squeezes my heart. "Everyone on the rug!" I tell them. "We're going to learn a new song."

The classroom door creaks open and Sister Lucia's wrinkled face appears in the crack. "A word?"

"We were about to begin!" I protest, reaching for my guitar.

She opens the door fully and a second figure steps inside. "The Reverend Mother wishes to see you. Sister Helene will watch the students."

In the two years that I've been here I've never once heard of a postulant being summoned to meet the Reverend Mother. I push down the panicky feeling rising in my stomach and put down the guitar, then turn toward my students. "Something important has come up," I tell them, "but I'll be back in two shakes of a lamb's tail!"

The children have already arranged themselves on the rug. "But what about our new song?" a little girl asks.

I try for a confident smile. "I won't forget."

I follow Sister Lucia into the hall and she leads me down a flight of stone stairs. "Did the Reverend Mother say why she wants to see me?"

Sister Lucia only shakes her head. Lay sisters don't speak

with candidates. In fact, there's no speaking at all among the nuns except between the hours of one and two. She walks as far as the bottom of the stairs. I'm expected to make my own way up to the Reverend Mother's parlor.

When I reach her door, my pulse begins to race. I hold my breath and knock.

"Ave," I hear her call. *Come in.*

I push open the wooden door and peer inside. The room is dark. Heavy furniture fills the chamber and a little old woman sits at a desk three times her size. I expect to find her scowling, so it surprises me when she smiles kindly and says, "Please, sit down."

I settle into a wooden chair, taking a moment to study the Reverend Mother from across her desk. She's old, probably in her sixties, but her dark eyes are still bright and none of her teeth are missing. She folds her hands in front of her and begins.

"Maria Kutschera," she says, "is that right?"

I nod, my throat full.

"Tell me, Maria, how old are you?"

"Twenty-one."

"Twenty-one," the Reverend Mother repeats. The place is so dimly lit and cold that I wonder if she even knows that it's summer outside and the geraniums are blooming. "And you came here when you were just nineteen, is that correct?"

"After I graduated from the State Teachers' Progressive Education College. Yes, Reverend Mother."

"And how do you like it here?"

Is this all she's looking for? "Oh, I absolutely love it," I admit. "The children I'm teaching have become like family to me. And this convent—well, I consider it my home. It's where I want to spend the rest of my life."

"Wonderful." But the Reverend Mother clasps and unclasps her hands in front of her, and I notice that her smile has faded a little. "And what would you say this convent has taught you these last two years?"

I feel like it matters very much how I answer this question, and my breathing quickens. My entire life I've wanted a home. To have it taken away now when I've come so close . . . "I've learned many lessons at Nonnberg," I begin, reaching. "But the most important lesson has been . . . to discover the will of God and then implement it."

"And what if the thing God wishes is hard?" she asks.

"Then surely He will provide the strength."

The Reverend Mother nods. "That is absolutely right."

I begin to jiggle my foot, worried.

The Reverend Mother watches me, and it's as if she's puzzling out what she wants to say next. "The sisters tell me you spent much of your youth climbing in the hills. Coming here could not have been an easy transition for you."

I think of all the infractions I've been reprimanded for over the years—giggling in the halls, speaking before one o'clock, sliding down the banisters—and I'm not sure what to say. The Reverend Mother saves me the trouble by opening the desk and producing a familiar sheet of paper.

"Your resolutions from last year," she says, and I'm sure I've turned pink from my neck to my ears. "Would you care to read them to me or shall I?"

"Oh, no. You can," I mumble.

"All right. 'I will not whistle. I will not skip over the last steps. I will not go up on the roof and hop over the chimney.'"

"Reverend Mother—"

"'I will not tickle anybody and make them laugh in a time of silence. . . .'"

"Reverend Mother, I believe, since then I've mended some of my ways."

"Yes." She looks surprised by this. "It has taken a great deal of time for you to become adjusted to our world. Which is why I am about to ask something you may find exceedingly difficult."

My heart feels as if it's banging against my ribs. *Please don't tell me to leave. Oh, please don't say I'm not fit to enter the novitiate and take my vows.*

"Yesterday, a very famous naval captain paid a visit to our abbey. Are you familiar with the name Captain Georg von Trapp?"

I stare at her and wonder why she would think I would know anything about some ancient sea captain. "No. I'm afraid not."

She nods slowly. "Well, he is a war hero. A widower with seven children and the last one too sickly to attend school. The mother died of scarlet fever and the little girl is recovering from the same illness. She's too fragile to make the long walk to the schoolhouse, and apparently the dirt road cannot be traversed by car. So he came to us."

I still don't understand what this has to do with me. "But what does he want?"

"He wished to know whether we might lend him a teacher."

The full horror of what's happening suddenly becomes apparent.

"Maria." The Reverend Mother unfolds her hands and her dark eyes steady me. "You are the best teacher we have."

"That isn't true," I say at once.

"I am told you taught your students forty-seven songs between September and Christmas."

"Yes, but—"

"And when the superintendent came to inspect our school the sisters say he instructed all of our teachers to follow your example."

"That is true," I say feebly, sinking back into my chair. The room feels oppressive, the dark wooden furniture crowding in on me.

"The assignment would only be for ten months."

"What?" I cry, forgetting myself. The Reverend Mother's eyes widen. But I don't care. "Please, Reverend Mother, there are other postulants," I say. "What about Sister Angela?"

The Reverend Mother shakes her head.

"I can't do this. I don't want to go out there!"

"Maria, we are not asking you to leave forever."

"It's almost a year. It might as well be an eternity!" The feeling of losing control spins around inside of me. Tears fall onto my robes and the Reverend Mother holds out her hands across the desk. When I take them, the skin feels papery and thin. We sit this way for some time as I will myself to be calm. But the tears keep falling.

Eventually, the Reverend Mother rises from her desk and comes to stand next to me. Her voice is soft and soothing when she says, "Tell me why you became a postulant."

"To serve God," I say, wiping my tears.

"Well, God is calling you now to this Captain. We've never had this sort of request. Just as we've never had a postulant like you."

I look over to see if this is a criticism, but there's only kindness in the Reverend Mother's face.

"You were an orphan before you came to us, is that right?"

I wipe away my tears with two quick swipes of my hand. "Yes."

"So the idea of leaving another family must make it even harder for you."

I don't want pity, not even from the Reverend Mother, but I respond, "Because I know what happens when people are sent away."

The Reverend Mother sits back and considers this statement. "And is this what you think is happening?"

My eyes are drawn to the only window in the parlor, and I realize that it is hung with the same lace curtains Mutti used to have. I trace the scalloped edges in my mind and hear her voice. All of their voices. But especially his. Loud and violent and threatening.

CHAPTER FOUR

MARIA

Kagran, Austria
1913

H E'S YELLING AGAIN. I creep to the door and listen, drawing my knees up to my chest, then tugging the nightgown over my feet. Because Mutti is not allowed to spend money on me, the fabric of the gown is stained and wearing thin.

"What do you mean he now lives in the city and doesn't want her back?" Downstairs, Uncle Franz's voice is full of rage.

"Perhaps it's a matter of money," Mutti offers.

"A man who travels the world studying *music*?" I can imagine Uncle Franz's enormous face swelling up in anger at my great-aunt's suggestion. "Then how about all those letters filled with money? 'Greetings from India,' " he mimics. " 'Tidings from Brazil!' "

"I don't believe it's a matter of money so much as it is temperament," Mutti's daughter says. But my uncle doesn't care for his wife's suggestion.

"I don't give a damn what it is!" he thunders at Anni. "If he has the money to rent an apartment in Graben he can pay us more for that child or take her back!"

I can hear the audible gasps from around the table and panic grips my chest. *Don't send me back. Please don't send me back.* I remember almost nothing about my father. I know only that it's been five years since he cradled my sickly mother against his chest, convinced, I am told, that if he held her body tight enough her soul could not escape. But escape it did, slipping away in the middle of the night when I was only two. A few weeks later my father deposited me with his cousin, the same woman who had raised my half brother fifteen years before. It seemed my father's wives had a habit of dying and leaving him with children.

I shiver in the attic of Mutti's farmhouse. It's small and cold, but it's the only home I've ever known and I don't want to go anywhere else.

"I'm sure he'll provide for whatever his child requires," Mutti says. I have known her as Mutti, meaning *mother* in German, my entire life.

"We'll see," I hear Uncle Franz respond. "You say he's coming in three days?"

"Yes. I've asked him to tutor her," she replies.

Uncle Franz's laughter echoes throughout the house. "A tutor. As if that child will ever amount to anything more than a *schlampe.*"

At the long wooden table the next morning, when Mutti tells me about my father's visit, I pretend I haven't overheard them. I push the eggs around my plate and hear the word *schlampe* again in my mind. I don't know what it means, but I'm afraid to ask.

"Well, aren't you excited?" Anni asks. She's Mutti's older daughter. And the prettiest one, with thick blond curls and soft green eyes. When Anni was just out of school she caught the attention of Uncle Franz and her father thought it would be a good match. Possibly because he'd been having trouble with the law and Uncle Franz was an important judge in Salzburg.

"Gusti, this is a wonderful opportunity," Mutti continues, wiping her hands on her apron. Her gray hair is swept back in its usual loose bun and her cheeks are red from cooking. "Think of all the stories he can tell you." She knows how much I enjoy stories. "Like the one about your birth."

I've always loved hearing about that. How my mother went to visit her family in Tyrol before I was born and gave birth to me on the train ride back to Kagran, where she lived with my father. I'd been too stubborn and impatient to wait until we were home and the train conductor had had to stop the train while my mother delivered me. I was named Maria Augusta Kutschera after my mother, Augusta. And by the time I was one, my father began calling me Gusti, the same as her. That's how much we looked alike.

"And though you may not remember this," Mutti continues, taking the wooden chair across from me, "your father is a very accomplished musician. In fact, he's going to become your tutor."

I stare into Mutti's kind, wrinkly old face, confused. "Why?"

"Because music is his passion," Mutti explains, gathering our chipped porcelain plates. Uncle Franz says a few missing pieces don't mean you just throw something away. "And now he wishes to pass it on to you."

But I've seen fathers at the park with their children. Why wasn't he coming to play ball or take me to the zoo? Why did I need to study music?

"There's nothing to worry about," Anni promises, but I don't believe her. Then, two days later, just after dinner, I overhear her in the kitchen with Mutti. "There's something wrong with Gusti," she says.

Mutti isn't concerned. She's baking *Sachertorte* for tomorrow and it requires all her concentration. She's not a skilled cook.

"Have you noticed how quiet she's been?" Anni persists.

I press myself against the cold stone wall outside the kitchen, straining to hear how Mutti will respond. "I suppose she has been rather well behaved."

"It's not normal," Anni says, filling the washbasin and starting on the dishes. "No muddy shoes, no climbing trees, no picnics with her imaginary friends."

"Sounds like the child is finally learning!"

"Maybe." But I can imagine Anni's face. God hasn't blessed her with any children of her own, possibly because He hates the thought of Uncle Franz being their father. So Anni treats me as if I'm hers. She never minds when my dresses come back torn or my hair sheds seeds and flower petals during my bath. Now her voice grows so low that I have to really strain to hear it. "Or perhaps she's worried about her father's visit."

"Well, she should be. But not for the reason she might think, poor *liebling*."

When they don't say anything else, I tiptoe up the creaky

wooden stairs to my room. The late-autumn sunshine that spills through the window almost makes the bare walls and wooden planks look beautiful. I wrap my heaviest blanket around my shoulders and perch on the edge of my bed. I have no desire to meet my father. I'm eight years old now. If he'd wanted to see me so badly he should have come years ago.

I lay down, intending to be angry about this for a while, but I must fall asleep, because the next time I open my eyes the sun is up, illuminating a thick line of dust across my windowsill. I put on the outfit Anni has carefully laid across my desk. A simple green dress with a white apron. I know Mutti's hands will be in too much pain to brush my hair, and Anni is always busy with the tasks Uncle Franz has set out for her, so I part my own hair and braid it myself. One braid on each side tied off with a green ribbon.

When I look in the small mirror above my desk, I decide that I look like a good girl, the kind who doesn't bring frogs home in Mutti's pickling jars or keep rocks in her pockets. But when Uncle Franz passes by the parlor and catches me waiting on the couch, he goes still.

"What are you doing on there?" he demands.

"Aunt Anni said I should wait here for my father."

"You've been waiting six years." He laughs. "What makes you think he's really coming now?" But just as he says this there's a knock on the front door, and in spite of my nervousness, I'm secretly pleased that Uncle Franz is wrong. Mutti hurries to answer it. A distinguished-looking man in a long black coat and a gray bowler hat is waiting on the other side.

"Karl!" Mutti exclaims, pulling him into her big embrace.

He smiles uncomfortably and takes off his hat. "Well, come inside!" A few leaves trail in behind him as Mutti shuts the door. "Gusti," she calls. "Your father is here."

I rise from the couch. "Good morning," I say stiffly.

"Gusti." My father steps inside the parlor and studies me for a moment. "My God, you look just like your mother."

I stare back at him.

"Well, come in, sit down," Mutti says, and Anni bustles in with a tray of tea. But my father continues to watch me, even after everyone is seated and talking. My aunt Kathy and her husband, Pepi, have arrived from across the village and they all want to know what he's doing now. Is his apartment really in Graben? What's it like? Has he come to stay?

"Yes," he answers, giving me a meaningful look, "I've returned for good."

"Well, that's wonderful," Uncle Franz says, grabbing the largest slice of cake. "I suppose that means you'll want to take Gusti with you."

"No!" I cry, and everyone looks shocked.

"She's just nervous," Anni explains, pouring Uncle Pepi's tea.

"Well, there's nothing to be nervous about," my father assures me. "I'm not here to take you away," he promises. "My apartment is filled with delicate instruments—it's really no place for a little girl."

The invisible band constricting my chest begins to loosen.

"But now that I've returned"—he glances at Mutti—"I do feel it is my duty to teach you, at least. Do you like music?"

I have always liked the music they play at church and the sound of the bells on Sunday morning. But I'm determined to be difficult, so I shake my head. "Not really."

"Gusti, that isn't true!" Mutti scolds.

I take a sip of tea.

"Has she ever played an instrument?" my father asks, and I wonder what sort of life he imagines I lead here.

"And where would we find an instrument?" Uncle Franz asks. He's a very important judge, but I've heard Aunt Kathy say that all of his money goes to drink, which is why we live in Mutti's old farmhouse.

My father looks deeply concerned by this. "Well, would you like to visit my apartment?" he asks me. When I keep my silence, he continues, "Perhaps if you come I can show you my birds."

I lower my teacup. "In your apartment?"

"Oh, yes. Dozens of them."

I glance at Uncle Franz, certain he'll have thoughts about something as outrageous as birds living in an apartment, but he is actually grinning. "I think that's a wonderful idea," he says through a spray of cake crumbs.

My father smiles, and for the first time I realize what a handsome man he is, even if he's older than the fathers of most of my school friends.

"Well, then, that's settled," Uncle Franz announces. "She will take the bus on Saturday mornings and stay the weekend."

"What about church?" I cry.

"Oh, yes, she must come with us to church," Mutti puts in.

Uncle Franz nearly chokes on his cake. "A waste of time!" he rages.

"It doesn't matter," my father says. "I'm afraid I can't keep her on Sundays. I teach."

Uncle Franz's cheeks have gone red. "Saturdays then."

And just like that, it's decided. I'm to be sent every weekend to the apartment of a man I hardly know. And he will teach me about music.

My father stays the remainder of the day, talking about things that don't interest me—his travels through China, Austrian politics, art. Then he stands and I'm expected to go and embrace him. I give him a stiff hug and he pats my back.

"We'll meet again in a few days," he promises.

On Saturday, Anni walks me to the bus station, where an old double-decker is loading its passengers. It's my first trip alone.

"You will return before dark," she says, nervous. But there's no question of her coming with me. Franz wants her home where there is housework to do. "And no stopping in the park or finding someone to talk with." My two favorite pastimes. "Also," she adds, tucking a loose curl beneath her straw hat, "be sure not to touch anything in your father's apartment."

"Why?" I ask.

"Because your father has traveled around the world collecting musical instruments. I doubt any of them are replaceable."

I clutch the small sack of food Mutti has prepared for me and twist the burlap ends in my hands. I haven't had breakfast, but my stomach is so full of dread that there's nothing in Mutti's bag I'd possibly want to eat. "But what if I don't go?" I whisper.

Anni reaches out and caresses my face. "It's only one day. You'll be back in your own bed by tonight, *liebling.*"

I take a seat at the top of the open-air bus and give a small wave as it lurches down the road, leaving Anni in a cloud of dust. Tears are beginning to cloud my vision, so I distract myself by counting the cows. Kagran is a small farming village, so it isn't long before the old farmhouses and wooden fences are behind us. I've only left Kagran once, to attend a church service with Mutti in Vienna, and I remember now the feeling of the buildings crowding in on me and the oppressive crush of people. Except, for some reason, it's different this time.

We cross the Danube and as we approach the city the entire world seems to come alive. The cobbled streets and squares are teeming with people in their weekend best, the men in waistcoats and top hats, the women in traditional Austrian skirts. It's such a pretty day, with the old white buildings of the Landstrasse clustered like pearls beneath a turquoise sky. I inhale the warm scent of freshly baked bread from a *Bäckerei* where a long line of patrons curls out the door, making me wish I had the money for a pastry.

The bus jerks to a stop outside the Kaisergruft, the church where Austria's most important royalty is buried. I hurry to get off, then stand on the pavement for several moments, looking up at the old, tall buildings. There's something about being on my own that feels exciting. I ask for directions half a dozen times before I reach the address on Mutti's scrap of paper. My father's apartment is in a cream-colored building with fancy scrollwork and high, arched windows. A black-suited man holds open the door for me and I step inside.

"Is there someone you wish to see?" The man frowns.

"Karl Kutschera."

The doorman's suspicion deepens. I'm not carrying an instrument, and perhaps my clothes could be finer. "Are you a student of his?"

"No. He's my father."

At this, the man goes very straight. "Does he know this?"

For the first time that day, I laugh. "Of course. He's expecting me."

I'm not sure if the doorman believes this, but he nods and points to the stairs. "Third floor, the only door on the left."

I take the stairs two at a time, enjoying the sound of my footfalls on the polished marble. It's like being in a palace. The sunlight, the space, the columned walls. But as soon as I reach the third floor, my mood darkens. I don't want to be here. My father hasn't cared enough about me for the last six years to visit even once. Why should I care about seeing him now?

I stand in angry silence on the landing outside his door. From here I have a view of the stairs and I begin to count them to calm myself down. I reach twenty-one before the door opens and my father, blinking, steps into the hall. For a moment, the sun turns his eyes a dazzling shade of blue. Then they darken and narrow.

"Gusti? How long have you been here?"

I don't answer him.

"Well, would you like to come in or do you plan on staying outside?"

I consider the question without moving. It's not a bad landing. It's bright and sunny. Plus, I can watch the comings and goings of the residents below. Right now, a woman with a small white parasol is making her way down the stairs, her small, gloved hand gliding along the polished wooden banister.

I turn to my father and try to make out the apartment beyond. It looks nothing like our farmhouse. I can't imagine who hauls the buckets of water all the way up here to the third floor. Or the pails of milk. I can hear his birds, chirping from some mysterious place behind him, but I can't see them. I take a tentative step forward and my father smiles.

"There you are. Put down the sack and come have some tea."

The carpets are nicer than any I've ever seen, thick and soft with vivid patterns in orange and blue. I leave my sack on a table near the door and follow him inside. The apartment smells like paper and leather and I immediately understand why. The first room we enter is a library.

In Kagran, the only books we own are my uncle's law books and the Bible. But here they rise in tiers to the ceiling, surrounding us on all sides. A pair of wooden ladders that roll along a bar must allow him to reach the very top shelves. I have the sudden impulse to climb one, then remember my aunt's warning and continue to look around. The room is filled not only with books. There are papers as well, rising in tidy stacks from every corner. But most interesting of all are the instruments hanging from various places along the walls, just as Anni predicted.

My father must catch me staring at them because he says, "When Mutti heard I had returned to Vienna she insisted I find you and give you lessons."

I press my lips together to keep something hurtful from spilling out. So he didn't visit Kagran because he missed me. He came because Mutti had asked him to.

"Mutti believes you have some talent for music. Is it true that you sing while doing your chores?"

I look around the room without meeting his eyes. "Doesn't everybody?"

"Not well. She also thinks you might take quickly to an instrument."

There's nothing I can say to this. I've never held an instrument in my hands, and the only one I've seen up close is the organ at church.

"Now, I've not taught a child in many years. So if I'm going to tutor you in music," he begins, "there will need to be rules." I turn and pay attention. "No eating in this room, no shouting, no running." I wonder what sort of occasion he imagines I might have to run and shout in a place like this. "If you wish to touch something," he continues, "you must ask. And always, always, move carefully among the instruments."

The sound of birds calling to one another from the next room is almost deafening, and I suppose my father can guess which way my thoughts are tending because he says, "All right. One peek at the aviary and then we start."

I follow his footsteps down the hall to a room that's been separated from the rest of the apartment by a net. The smell is so overwhelming that I cover my nose with my apron. When I realize what I'm looking at, however, I gasp. A tree is growing from an enormous pot in the center of the room. Dozens of birds flitter around its branches, chirping happily and eating from feeders. My father parts the net and offers me the chance to step inside.

"It's unbelievable," I whisper. "Where do they all come from?"

"India, China, England," he rattles off. "There are two from Brazil."

There's a red one with a large, curved beak and quite a few green ones that make a lot of noise. I want to spend all afternoon in here, but after a few minutes my father looks impatient. "Ready?"

"Oh no! Not yet." The tree stretches past the high arched windows and practically touches the ornate ceiling. The whole room is too wonderful to be believed.

My father smiles and we spend another ten minutes inside. One of the green birds lands on my shoulder and I scare the other birds by shrieking. "Ow, their claws are sharp!"

My father cups the little bird in his hands and it flies away. I brush a dropping from my dress and he laughs. "Ready now?"

"Yes."

He takes me back through the net to the library where all the instruments are arranged, then points to a fancy silk cushion on the floor. I sit while he takes a funny-looking guitar down from the wall.

"This is an oud," he says. "Do you think you can remember that?"

I nod obediently. "An oud," I repeat.

"I brought it from Egypt because I liked the fact that it has eleven strings. Listen." He plucks out a tune and looks up to make sure I'm still listening. "We're going to go through each of these instruments," he says, "and write down what we like best about their sounds. Where is your paper?"

I look around. "What paper?"

"How are you going to write without paper?"

"You haven't given me any."

He stares in exasperation. "All right. Then play this instrument and see what you like best about it for yourself." He hands me the oud and I struggle to position it comfortably in my lap. "The same notes that I just played," he says.

I pluck a few notes and look up. "I'm sorry. I can't."

"Why not? Weren't you listening?" He takes the instrument and plays the notes again. Then he hands it back to me.

When I fail to mimic them, his face grows red. "Like this!" His hands fly over the strings and produce sounds I will never be able to make. When my eyes brim with tears, he shoves the oud back into its carrying case. "I don't know what she was thinking," he mumbles.

"Please, if you can teach me—"

My father straightens, the gold of his cuff links catching the light. "Teach? You either have an ear for this or you don't." He closes his eyes briefly and sighs. "Perhaps we'll start with an easier instrument," he says. "One you can take home to practice on."

He leaves the library and I try to imagine what he's going to fetch. A recorder, I think. Or maybe a tambourine, like they have at school. I remain sitting on my round silk cushion, wondering if I should touch a giant violin that's propped against the wall. I decide against it, but when my father returns I ask him about it.

"The cello?" He shakes his head. "Definitely not. Try this," he says. "This is a guitar."

It's the most beautiful thing anyone has ever let me hold. I lay it flat on my lap and begin plucking the strings until my father sits down on the cushion next to mine and shows me how to hold it. Sitting like this, I can smell the lavender from his clothes and I wonder where he washes them with no river nearby. And then I wonder if my mother smelled like this, too.

He goes and fetches another guitar, then begins to teach me how to pluck the strings. There are six of them, each with a different name, and I'm supposed to memorize these and practice something he calls chords. We go on like this for a while, then my father stops and asks if I'd like to sing while he plays.

"What should I sing?"

"Whatever you wish. How about a lullaby?"

I choose "Der Mond ist aufgegangen." I don't know why. In English it's called "Evening Song" and it's very simple. But when I'm finished my father's face has completely changed. "Sing it again," he says, so I do, and at the end he claps his hands together and jumps up. "Gusti, you have perfect pitch!"

Of course, this means nothing to me, but it seems incredibly important to my father, so I smile. My perfect pitch must kindle some hope in him that I'm not such a failure after all, because he spends the rest of the afternoon working on my voice. Apparently, not everyone can sing the very high notes of "Der Mond ist aufgegangen."

"Well, Gusti," he says wonderingly, "it turns out Mutti really was right about you."

"And what is that?" Uncle Franz asks at dinner when he sees the giant case propped against the wall.

"My guitar!" I exclaim. "Papa got it for me."

"I hope you don't think you'll be playing that in here."

So I play whenever my uncle isn't home, and after a few months my father starts teaching me how to read music. As soon as I enter his apartment with its floor-to-ceiling books and birdsong we begin. And I discover in those long hours how similar we are. We both like the same food, we share the same laugh, we even have the same hatred of carrots.

One winter evening, as the snow is falling slantways, I look at my father in his chair by the fire and have a sudden yearning to stay. What's the point of going home? Uncle Franz doesn't want me and I only cause trouble for Anni. Besides, what if I get lost in the snow?

"Papa," I begin. He looks over the edge of his book at me and I'm sure he's wondering why I'm not already in my mittens and coat. "It will be a long walk to the station in this weather," I tell him. "Do you think that maybe—just for tonight—I could stay here? In your apartment?"

He blinks several times, trying to process my request, and I know just from the tone of his first few words what the answer will be. "Gusti, my apartment's not fit for a little girl."

"But I stay here in the day," I protest. "It can't be any different at night."

"I don't think it would be a wise decision." He closes his book and balances it on his knee. "What about Mutti?"

"Oh, she won't care!"

"I think she would." He rises and goes to fetch my coat. Then he holds it open for me. "Shall I walk you to the end of the street?"

The lump in my throat is too big for me to speak, so I shake my head.

"Then good night," he says formally. "Rhythm and note reading next week."

CHAPTER FIVE

Maria

1914

I'M SURE IT COULD have gone on this way for the rest of my life. But a year later, Mutti calls me from the kitchen table as I'm hurrying down the stairs with my guitar. There are tears running down from the corners of her eyes and her face is red. "Gusti," she begins, "I have terrible news."

My first thought is for her health and a sudden panic wells up inside me. But she's twisting her hands in her apron and shaking her head. "I know he seemed like such a healthy man for fifty-two. He was always eating well. I don't pretend to understand." Her watery eyes meet mine and she sobs, "Gusti, your father passed away yesterday."

The shock of it is so great I don't know what to say.

"There was no suffering," she promises. "He simply went to sleep and made his journey to the Kingdom of God."

This can't be happening. "I don't understand." He was supposed to teach me today.

"I know, *liebling*." She reaches out to draw me close, but I pull away.

"I want to see him."

"You can't." She takes a white square from her sleeve and dabs at her eyes. "His housekeeper discovered his body and they've already taken him."

This is the news that breaks me. "Where?"

"To the *leichenhalle*." The mortuary. She sobs again. "I'm so sorry."

I'm nine years old and for the first time I am really, truly an orphan. I think of his instruments lying silent in his library. And his beautiful, happy birds. "What will happen to everything in his apartment?" I ask.

"The birds will be taken care of," Mutti promises.

"But what about his books? His papers? His diaries?"

"Uncle Franz will take care of it. He is to become your guardian now."

As long as my father had been alive he had been my guardian, even if he lived a thousand kilometers away. But without him my guardianship must pass on to another male.

"He's making the arrangements right now," she says softly, then takes me in her arms. "It's all right," she promises as I cry. "We will always look after you."

The entire family is arranged around Mutti's dinner table, some in wooden chairs, others in the cushioned chairs dragged in from the parlor. There's Uncle Franz and Anni, Mutti and her youngest daughter, Kathy. Even Mutti's sons Alfred and Gustav are back from the city. Mutti has gone through a great deal of trouble to cook *tafelspitz* with minced apples, but I have no stomach for food. Uncle Franz, however, is already on his second plate when he begins to discuss what's to become of me.

"I sent word this morning to Karl at the university to tell him of what's transpired."

My heart leaps. Perhaps my older brother will become my guardian.

"Of course, he made no mention of wanting to oversee the raising of a half sister." I only have to take one look at Uncle Franz's face to know what he thinks about this. My older brother is obviously useless and now I am a burden. He chews the edge of his white mustache and fixes his eyes on me. "So I will take it upon myself to become this child's guardian."

Fear, like a giant hand squeezing my heart, makes me completely immobile. I want to protest, to ask if Uncle Pepi or some other distant relation might be able to step in. But there's a sad hum of agreement around the table and it's clear no one wants to disagree with Uncle Franz. Besides, if he is offering to take on this burdensome task why should anyone else fight to do it?

"I believe her father left her with a substantial sum," Mutti says.

Everyone at the table perks up at this.

"Yes. And it will be used to feed and clothe her until she can be married," Uncle Franz says firmly.

"But I don't want to be married!" I cry.

Six faces turn to look at me, as if everyone has forgotten I'm here.

"What you want is of absolutely no importance," my uncle rules. "Your father was a fool to raise a daughter with books and instruments. What use will they be to you now?"

"They'll keep me company," I say without knowing how true this will be in the years to come. "My father loved music."

"Your father was a very good man," Mutti says, laying a steadying hand on my lap. "May God rest his soul." She makes the sign of the cross and Uncle Franz sucks in the air through his teeth.

"A few things are about to change around here," he warns. His big fleshy cheeks have turned red. "There will be no more talk of God, for one."

Mutti gasps. This is her house, but without her husband she has as little say about any of this as I do.

"No more God, or Jesus, or the Bible—"

"Franz," my uncle Pepi interjects, "you don't think this is being too harsh?"

"The world is harsh! You want to bring up an orphan to believe that some invisible God will rescue her or do you want her to rescue herself? This child must work."

"But her father—" Aunt Anni begins.

Uncle Franz gives his wife a withering look.

"She works like the rest of us," he says darkly. "From now on she comes straight home from school to cook and clean. And if I catch her walking home with friends—"

"But I always walk with my friends!" I protest.

Uncle Franz glares. "You try it now and it will be the stick."

Mutti lets out a stifled cry and I look around the table to see who will come to my rescue. But no one meets Uncle Franz's gaze. His word is law in our house.

When my mother died I had been too young to understand what it would mean for me. But at nine years old I am big enough to imagine what life with Uncle Franz as my guardian will be like. That night I pray silently to God and ask Him to let me join my father. So it feels like a betrayal of the very worst kind when I wake the next morning in the same world I am so desperate to escape.

"Where is she?" I hear my uncle thunder from the bottom of the stairs, but his knees are bad and he is too heavy to come up and tear me out of bed himself.

"Gusti," Anni pleads from my bedside, "you have to go to school."

"I can't," I weep. I feel sick. And tired.

"Please." I can hear the nervousness in her voice. "I'll make you some breakfast. You'll feel better."

Uncle Franz starts shouting again. "If you don't get down here I'll come up and drag you out by your hair."

I sob. "I want to go to his apartment."

"Later," Anni promises.

But I don't believe her. "When?"

"As soon as you're back from school."

"But Uncle Franz said I have to come home."

"Then after you come home. Please." She pulls down my covers and I let her dress me. Uncle Franz is still waiting at the bottom of the stairs, glowering, as Anni and I make our way past.

"Do not give her any breakfast," he says.

Anni stares at him. "Her father just—" The slap he gives her is so swift I don't even see his hand move.

"I hate you!" I shout.

He lunges toward me and I run into the kitchen, where Mutti is stuffing food into my bag.

"That child is not to have anything!" he shouts, lumbering after me.

"Franz," Mutti says softly, "the child is still grieving. You of all people should understand this."

Whether he does or not, I don't know. I run the entire distance to school, afraid he might decide to drive his horse and carriage alongside me to make sure I haven't been slipped something to eat. It's only after I reach the schoolhouse that I open my bag. Mutti has packed my favorite breakfast. Bread with cheese and fig jam.

I sit on the stoop and eat, too upset to pay attention to the kids passing by. Our schoolhouse is tucked into the side of a hill. It overlooks a small trickling stream that, in the warm weather, is surrounded by wildflowers, but the entire world seems joyless now. When the school bell starts to ring I remain where I am. Finally, a teacher comes outside to fetch me.

In class, I explain what's happened to my father, and the other students are extra kind for the rest of the day. Helga offers me the best snack in her lunch and Therese gives me her pencil box, telling me she has another one. I don't want to take it, but she insists, and I run home, hoping to show it to Mutti. But as I step inside the door Uncle Franz is in the parlor.

"You were walking with friends, weren't you?"

I glance at Mutti, seated across from him with her sewing. "No! I didn't stop once," I swear.

"Then why are you late?" he thunders.

Mutti puts down her sewing. "Franz, it takes twenty minutes to walk from the school."

But he grabs the switch he has waiting beside him and Mutti jumps up from her rocking chair.

"What are you doing?" she shrieks as he raises the branch. But Uncle Franz can't hear her. He's deaf with a rage only he can understand.

That evening Mutti creeps up the stairs and sits at the edge of my bed while I weep. "I'm sorry, *liebling*." She reaches out to caress my face, but I turn to the wall. "Let's pray—"

"To who? A God who doesn't listen? I don't want to pray now or ever again!"

Mutti weeps softly at the edge of my bed.

I run back from school the next afternoon, abandoning my friends and returning out of breath. It's the fastest I've ever come home. But Uncle Franz is waiting for me on the couch. There is no sign of Mutti.

To hear it from Uncle Franz, I am a liar, a thief, a good-for-nothing orphan taking up food and space in Mutti's house. So what's the point in coming home? If I'm going to be beaten for returning on time and telling the truth, why not just do whatever I please?

At first, I simply walk home with my friends. But Uncle Franz eventually catches wind of this and begins waiting for me in his carriage on the side of the road. Years later, I will be told of his mental illness, a sickness that would eventually lead to the loss of his position as a judge in Salzburg. But at nine, I know nothing about this. I only know the terror I feel the moment he jumps from his carriage and grabs my arm, sending my friends shrieking down the hill. Enough of them must tell their parents, because eventually they're forbidden to walk home with me. After this, I begin wandering the hills on my own, playing in the streams and gathering wild-flowers.

Since I no longer care what happens to me, I begin behaving the same way in school. If a teacher asks us to pray, I challenge her. If she asks us to make a reference to something in the Bible, I laugh. After all, God has abandoned me, so why shouldn't I abandon Him? At lunch, my classmates are afraid to be seen with me. They don't want to be known to the teachers as "Gusti's friend." So I bring my guitar and my music keeps me company. It also reminds me of my father.

Then a wonderful thing happens when I am twelve years old. A girl named Adele moves to our school and is brave enough to walk home with me. She has coppery hair and cornflower-blue eyes. In the summer we play in the streams until it grows dark and in the winter we pretend we're elves scampering through the woods, making snow angels and snowmen until we can't feel our fingers.

Some nights, when I want to avoid Uncle Franz for as long as I can, I walk back with Adele to her tiny cottage. I think she understands my situation because hers was not much better until recently, when her father went to sleep with a bottle in his hand and never woke up. Needing to feed and care for seven children, her mother arranged for them to leave their home in Semmering and take up this cottage in Kagran. And from here she works as a laundress, scrubbing and cleaning until her hands are raw and peeling from the detergents.

One evening, when I'm thirteen, I run to Adele's mother

in tears, convinced I am dying. There is blood between my thighs, and she is the one who explains to me that this is how it will be until I am too old to have children.

"Gusti, you're a woman now." She smiles, swatting a stray curl from her face. "You need to tell your foster mother to start buying you undergarments."

I am terribly embarrassed, but Adele's mother has no problem speaking about this. Not like Mutti, who simply hands me a cloth when my cycle begins again the next month. There are no explanations about why I am bleeding. Not even a talk about what it means.

But becoming a woman doesn't stop my uncle's beatings. He's a tyrant, threatening and belittling everyone in the house except Mutti. I hate the sound of his voice, the way he breathes through his nose whenever he's reading, and how he chews like a cow whenever he eats. If I believed in God I would be ashamed at the thoughts I have about what might happen to him. And the older I get, the worse the beatings become.

Then one day I am suddenly bigger than him. I snatch the stick from his hand and snap it in two. "You will never, ever hit me again!"

He rises from the chair and slaps my face, bloodying my lip. But at fifteen years old I am five foot eight and no one is going to hit me anymore. He raises his hand to slap me again and I charge, knocking him off balance. He crashes to the ground with such a noise that the rest of the house comes running.

Anni gives a muffled cry and Mutti's eyes go big and round. But I stand my ground and wait for Uncle Franz to make the next move.

"You will never, ever get another *Krone* from me as long as I live!" he shouts. Anni rushes to his side to help him and he pushes her away.

That night, I tell Mutti about my plans. It's becoming harder for her to make her way up the rickety stairs to my room. But I think she is afraid for me.

"I'm graduating in two months," I remind her. "I want to go to the State Teachers' College."

She massages her hands, which are bent in painful angles now. "Gusti, I don't know where the money will come from."

"I'll earn it," I say.

"How?"

"Adele's mother has a house in Semmering." Mutti recognizes the name. It's a famous resort town. "I'll take a job there for the summer," I tell her.

But there's worry in her eyes. "Your uncle will never allow it," she warns.

I take her crooked hands in mine. "Then he doesn't have to know."

CHAPTER SIX
MARIA

Salzburg, Austria
1926

WHEN I AM FINISHED telling the Reverend Mother about my past she sits in silence for several moments, and I get the impression that she is sorry for me. Of course, I understand now what else she must have been thinking. That it was my fear of men as much as my love of God that sent me to her nunnery after I earned my teaching degree. At the time, however, I only recognized her pity.

"You understand that this Captain is not like your uncle or any of the other men you have come across in your life," she says at last. But tears are welling up in my eyes faster than I can blink them away. "Maria, this is a wonderful opportunity," she continues. "Not just for you, but for those children, who have been without guidance for who knows how long. Nanny after nanny—"

My head snaps up. "They've had multiple nannies?"

"Oh, yes. The Captain says they've been through twenty-six."

What sort of place is she sending me to?

"There are seven children," she explains. "You are only to instruct one of them, but I suspect it will be a somewhat"— she waves her free hand, searching for the word—"noisy household. When he asked if I had anyone who might be able to handle such a situation, I immediately thought of you."

I sit straighter in my chair. A sea captain and seven wild hellions. I can do this. I will.

The Reverend Mother gives my hand a little squeeze. "You are the only one for this job, Maria. I know it."

Bidding farewell to my little class of first graders is heart-breaking. They don't understand why I'm being called away any more than I do, but the main mistress of novices, Frau Rafaela, hurries me on before I can change my mind. She takes me to the candidates' room, which is filled with ward-robes and wooden chests. The last time I was here was two years ago. I was nineteen years old and newly converted.

"All right, my dear." Frau Rafaela opens one of the ward-robes and peers inside. "You'll need something to wear to meet Captain von Trapp."

I don't see why meeting some ancient sea captain war-rants changing out of my black skirts and veil, but I wait in silence as she begins to rummage. There's no chance she'll find my old clothes in there. They must have been given to the poor the week I entered the convent. Or thrown away. But eventually Frau Rafaela pulls out something from the back of the wardrobe and beams. "I've found something."

It's a blue twill dress with a wide lace collar. I put it on and

Frau Rafaela hands me a floppy hat. When the ensemble is complete, she gives a wistful sigh.

"So fashionable."

I catch a glimpse of myself in the mirror and have to keep from laughing. I do look fashionable! For 1915, the year Frau Rafaela last saw the world outside the convent. "You don't think it's a little big?" I venture. The novice who had owned this dress had obviously been quite a bit heavier than me, and without a belt the dress bears a strong resemblance to a sack.

"Big? It's perfection! Now," she says, radiating excitement, "a pair of shoes."

She picks out what my aunt would have called clodhoppers and claps her hands together at the picture I make. With my floppy hat and my oversized dress, I'm pretty sure I look ridiculous. Not that it matters.

"Come. It's time to bid your farewells."

I blink back tears and Frau Rafaela offers me her wrinkled hand.

"You are only on loan," she reminds me. "You'll be back before you even know it."

I nod and follow obediently as she leads me through the abbey. The other postulants have obviously heard what's happening. They're gathered in my room, and one look at their solemn faces and I begin to cry. The women huddle around me, telling me how wonderful it's going to be. But all I can think about are my first graders and how they're going to feel as though I'm abandoning them.

We cry together and I tell them that the Reverend Mother has made me promise to return every week on my day off. "I'm only on loan," I repeat what Frau Rafaela has said, but it doesn't make any of us feel better.

When the room clears out I stand at the window and look down at the Salzach River, winding its way through the valley. "I'm going to miss this view so much."

Frau Rafaela hands me a scrap of paper with directions to the Captain's home. "You'll be back in six days. Sundays are to be your day off."

I nod. I lived for nineteen years out there. I can do it for another ten months. "It's God's will," I whisper. I repeat this as I gather my things: a leather satchel with two changes of underclothes, my Bible, my guitar. Then I take a last look at the long white room that's been my home these past two years. *It's only temporary.*

Frau Rafaela follows me out as far as the gates, waving goodbye like a kindly old mother, and I'm reminded of the last time I saw Mutti. But this isn't Mutti's house. I will always be welcome in Nonnberg Abbey. Always.

As I pass from the cool interior of the abbey into the blinding autumn sun, I catch an inscription on one of the old gravestones that reads "God's will hath no why," and I repeat those words in my head. It's not for me to question this. I must follow and trust He will lead me to the path I am meant to travel. And today that path is down a hundred and forty-four stone steps descending from the abbey into the city of Salzburg.

I make my way down the mountain slowly, and when I reach the station I find the bus marked Aigen. It's the most fashionable district in the city of Salzburg.

"*Zwanzig Groschen,*" the driver chirps.

I have exactly this much in coins from Frau Rafaela.

It feels strange to be on a bus again, and stranger still to be wearing someone else's clothes. But if I look as ridiculous as

I feel, the driver doesn't say anything. I take the seat closest to the front, because even though I am miserable, I still want to see everything. Then the bus lurches forward and is off.

We roll down the Residenzplantz toward the river, then cross the rickety Karolinenbrücke to the green fields that lay beyond. I know every trail in this corner of Austria. The paths winding through these meadows were my salvation when I didn't want to be at home with Uncle Franz. Then in college I traded fields for mountains and explored every alpine pass and river valley I could find.

I think of those days as the bus rolls toward Aigen. I'd grown increasingly panicked as college drew to a close. Most of the girls planned to move back with their parents after graduation. Others were getting married. I'd been the only student without a place to go. Then one Sunday morning I elbowed my way to the front of the largest Jesuit church in Vienna, believing that Bach's *St. Matthew Passion* was about to be performed. Instead, a fiery priest by the name of Father Kronseder took the pulpit, and by the time I realized what was happening, there were too many people to make my escape.

For two hours I was forced to listen to nonsense about God. But toward the end the priest began to talk about signs. How divine communication doesn't happen with a fanfare of trumpets or singing angels. How it happens in the form of coincidences, synchronicities, that book you find at exactly the right time with exactly the answer you've been searching for. Now, this made sense. I'd experienced these kinds of communications before. And suddenly I found myself sitting in this priest's office discussing the possibility of God.

That's when I knew. All those years I'd been wrong. After

tittering with my friends in the halls and mocking the devout, there *was* a God, and God was calling to me now.

"Fräulein." Someone is calling me, and I realize that the bus is no longer moving. "Fräulein, I believe this is your stop."

"Aigen—yes!" I grab my guitar case and leather satchel and find myself standing near a small cluster of village shops. Beyond the shops are wide, open fields. I open the scrap of paper in my hand and read the address. The Villa Trapp.

An old man smoking a pipe looks over at me. "Lost?"

My father used to smoke a pipe, and I inhale the rich scent of the tobacco. "I'm looking for the Villa Trapp," I say.

The man leads me down the street and uses his pipe to point to a park surrounded by a high iron gate.

"A sea captain lives in there?"

The man cracks a smile. "He is not just a Captain, Fräulein. He is also a Baron."

I inhale. So while this captain goes off plundering on the high seas, his poor, sickly daughter lies abandoned on this estate, purchased, no doubt, with his ill-gotten gains. I understand now why the Reverend Mother needed me. And no amount of cursing or shouting will deter me from teaching this child. I know what to expect and he can try his worst.

I thank the old man and make my way toward the iron gate. Chestnut trees in the distance obscure whatever lies beyond the long gravel drive, and when I finally reach the clearing I stand in amazement. It's beautiful, a sweeping yellow mansion nestled in the heart of a thick copse of trees.

Several steps lead up to a heavy oak door, and I shift my guitar case to my other hand so that I can grasp the brass knocker. When the door sweeps open, I instinctively step back. The man in front of me isn't old. He's young, with a thick head of blond hair and vibrant blue eyes. He's dressed in the most expensive suit I've ever seen, with polished black shoes and immaculate white gloves. I'm in shock, and drop into my deepest curtsy at once.

"A pleasure to meet you, Captain."

The man's mouth twists wryly. "Save your curtsy, Fräulein. I'm only the butler."

I have no idea what this means. We don't have butlers where I'm from any more than we have villas. But I extend my hand and shake his warmly. "Well, I'm Maria," I say.

The man glances over his shoulder. "Hans." I have the impression that shaking his hand is the wrong thing to do, but he only clears his throat. "If you will come with me now, the Captain has been waiting and will see you shortly."

I follow Hans into a large foyer with such lofty ceilings that I can't think how anyone could possibly clean them. I'm about to remark on this when Hans suddenly retreats. I glance around, expecting to see that the Captain has arrived, but I'm the only person in the room. I listen as the butler's footsteps fade away, and it strikes me as strange that for such an enormous house, there's not a sound anywhere. The children must all be out.

I lower my belongings to the floor and, with nothing else to do, make a short tour of the room, wondering what sort of sea captain collects oil paintings. I'm marveling over this when a deep voice makes me turn.

"Fräulein Kutschera?"

While Hans had been beautifully dressed, this man is

taller and dressed even more elegantly. He has dark hair and an oiled mustache, and I guess him to be in his forties. Many years later, people will say that he looks like Clark Gable. At the time, however, I simply think that being handsome must be a requirement for becoming a butler.

"Yes." I smile, hoping I don't look as nervous as I feel. "And please, just Maria."

"Well, Maria, I see you've acquainted yourself with the paintings. What do you think?"

I make an unattractive noise in my throat. "I'm afraid I don't find fruit a very interesting subject."

"Ah. A shame. My grandfather painted these."

I look at the name scrawled across the bottom of the painting and the realization dawns on me about who he must be. "You—"

The warmth of his smile reaches his eyes. "Captain Georg von Trapp."

He's not like any sea captain that I've ever seen, and when I hold out my hand, I swallow my mortification. "A pleasure to meet you, Captain."

"I see you've come prepared." He's looking down at my old, beat-up satchel and guitar case. In such beautiful sur- roundings, they surely stick out as sorely as I do.

"Yes. I hope your children like music," I say.

"We are a very musical family." The Captain straightens, and I can see that he takes a great deal of pride in this. "All of my children play an instrument, and your pupil, Mitzi, plays the violin."

"That's wonderful!"

"Yes. There used to be . . . a great deal of music in this house." His voice trails away, and I can see that the memory of this is painful. He seems to shake himself free of its grip and clears his throat. "Would you like to meet the children?"

"They're here?" I blurt out. The house is silent.

"Certainly." He reaches into the breast pocket of his smart navy suit and takes out a shiny brass whistle. Then he plays a series of notes and the most extraordinary thing I've ever witnessed occurs. A procession of young children begins to make their way silently down the polished wooden stairs, led by a solemn young girl in her teens. At the bottom of the stairs they organize themselves into a neat line, from tallest to shortest, then bow in unison.

"*Grüss Gott,* Fräulein Maria."

The four girls and two boys are dressed in matching navy-and-white sailor's suits. I push back my hat to get a better look at this incredible sight, and the brown monstrosity flutters to the ground. The youngest child, with a head full of golden curls and bright eyes, rushes forward to get it and everyone laughs.

"Thank you, Martina," her father says. Then the little girl hurries to get back into line.

I feel that there's something I'm supposed to say. "Well . . . the whistle was very unexpected." I immediately regret being so honest, but the Captain smiles.

"I determined it was easier than constantly shouting up three stories." He fixes his gaze on the tallest child, a boy with auburn hair. "If you will introduce yourselves."

The children call out their ages and names, and from oldest to youngest there's Rupert (sixteen), Agathe (fourteen), Werner (twelve), Hedwig (nine), Johanna (seven), and little Martina (five).

"Very pleased to meet you," I say. But I'm confused. There are only six children. "And my pupil?"

"Upstairs," the Captain says quietly. He slips the whistle into his pocket. "We discourage her from coming down."

"I was told she is recovering from scarlet fever," I say softly, in case the little girl can hear us.

"Yes. But now she has influenza, and she doesn't seem to be able to shake it." He nods at the children, and this is evidently their sign to leave because they begin marching obediently up the stairs. They step in unison so that six pairs of feet don't create a cacophony that echoes through the house. And it's only when they've disappeared that the Captain picks up my guitar and satchel.

"Maria is on the third floor," he says, beginning the climb. "We call her Mitzi. She is thirteen and desperately wishes to return to school, but the walk is four miles down a road no car can possibly traverse, and walking is simply not a possibility right now for her."

We reach her bedroom and I stop to admire how beautiful it is. A wide balcony overlooking a meadow fills the entire room with light. Several pieces of antique furniture are positioned throughout, but the most eye-catching is a large wooden bed piled high with pillows. In the middle of the bed lies a very pale girl. Her face is yellow and her eyes look sunken, as if she hasn't had proper nutrition or sleep in some time.

The Captain crosses the room to sit at her side. "Mitzi." He puts down my belongings to take her hand in his, and I wonder if this is what most fathers do with their children. I can't remember my father ever holding me by the hand. "I want you to meet Fräulein Maria," he says. "She's come from the abbey to be your teacher."

The girl smiles up at me. "Pleased to meet you." Her eyes fall to the long case on the carpet. "Is that a cello?"

The Captain shakes his head. "A guitar. It belongs to Fräulein Maria."

"Oh, will you play it for me?" Mitzi sits up straighter in her bed, but the act brings on a violent coughing fit. Her father hurries to get water from her bedside table, and it's then that I notice that all of the books piled next to the water pitcher have something to do with math.

"You must lie back," the Captain says.

I can see how much this disappoints the girl. She's thirteen, after all. She should be out hiking the Untersberg and exploring Salzburg, not confined to her bed.

"Perhaps I can play for you tomorrow," I say, and this seems to brighten her.

"That would be wonderful."

The Captain studies me for a moment, and I wonder if I've overstepped my bounds. "Shall I show you to your room?"

I smile at Mitzi as we leave, thinking of how incredibly lonely and bored she must be with nothing but math books for company. Then I follow the Captain down the stairs. He stands back to allow me to pass, and when I enter the room that's to be mine over the next ten months, I simply stand beneath the chandelier and stare. From the large white bed covered in silk to the heavy antique furniture arranged tastefully throughout the room, it's fancier than any bedroom I've ever imagined.

The Captain places my belongings on a small brocade bench, then fixes me in his gaze. "Mitzi's last nanny only stayed with us for two months. I hope we will have the pleasure of your company for longer."

"Yes. Ten months," I say firmly.

"Right." He clears his throat. "Since their mother died four years ago they've had very little stability. Thankfully, the *Hausdame* has always remained." I'm not familiar with this term, and my ignorance must show because he adds, "The Baroness Matilda. She runs the house while I'm away."

Later, I discover that only a member of the nobility is fit to be a *Hausdame* for a baron. Her job is to instill manners and see that the traditions of the nobility are carried on by the younger generation. In Baroness Matilda's case, she was there to oversee a staff of more than twenty people as well.

"I'm sure you will get on well with the Baroness," the Captain says. "She was happy to hear that a postulant would be taking over Mitzi's studies."

I'm wondering why when the Captain suddenly gives a little bow and moves to the doorway. At the threshold, he pauses and says, "The dinner bell will ring shortly."

I walk to the bay window and look out. Meadows stretch from the back of the house to the base of the Untersberg, bright green and thick with marigolds and asters. I can recognize all the mountains in the distance, from the Hagengebirge to the Staufen, and the sight of them brings me some comfort. Somewhere out there, at the eastern foot of the Festenburg, the other postulants are setting up the evening meal. Ingrid is probably whistling in the kitchen while Gisela tests the soup and insists it needs more *salz*.

Tears prick the back of my eyes. But before I can start to cry, I cross the room and begin arranging my few things. My nightdress and coat look lonely in the giant wardrobe all by themselves. Even my extra pair of old boots looks sad to be there. I've never had so much space to myself. I place my

Bible and the Rule of Saint Benedict on my nightstand, then sit at the edge of my bed and wonder what I'm doing here. Tonight, there will be singing in the abbey, and tomorrow morning when the Gregorian chanting begins, I won't be there.

Just as I'm beginning to feel really sorry for myself, a bell starts to ring and there's the sound of many feet echoing on the stairs. There's whispering outside my door.

"Do you think she heard the bell?"

"I don't know. Should we knock?"

I open the door and two children jump back. I easily recognize Agathe, who is fourteen and the eldest of the girls. But I'm not sure about the younger one. "Agathe and Hedwig?" I venture.

The youngest giggles. "Agathe and Johanna," she corrects sweetly. "Hedwig is nine and I'm only seven. Did you know that it's suppertime?"

"Oh, is that what that bell is?" I play along.

"Yes." She slips her little hand in mine as if it's the most natural thing in the world. I can't remember a time when Mutti held my hand. Or anyone except the Reverend Mother, for that matter. "It rings three times a day," she says as we descend. "Cook rings it. Do you have a cook where you live?"

"Where I live, we all take turns being cook."

Johanna stares up at me with big, dark eyes. "You get to chop things and use a knife?" she exclaims.

"Every week. And sometimes"—I wink at her—"we even make stew."

She squeals and hurries down several stairs to tell Hedwig that the new nanny is a real live maker of stews. And there is no stopping the excitement after this. Hedwig, who is nine, wants to know if I've ever made pudding, while Agathe watches me curiously, then whispers, "Do you really cook?"

"Oh, definitely. In the abbey there's no one to do these things for us."

She looks at me as if I might be an actual saint and I laugh. None of these children has ever cooked a meal!

We reach the dining room and I'm pleased to see it's not as large as I feared. In spite of the elaborate chandelier hanging overhead, the room feels cozy. The Captain is already seated at the head of a long table set for ten. At the other end is a formidable-looking woman who must be the Baroness. She appears to be in her fifties, with white hair swept high into a bun. She doesn't smile as I enter the room or make any attempt to greet me.

The children rush to their seats at once, but I hesitate until the Baroness nods at the empty chair to her left. I take my seat and realize that Mitzi is sitting across from me. Like her siblings, she is dressed for dinner, and I wonder about the wisdom of such a sickly child being asked to put on heavy taffeta and lace. But then what do I know? I'm still wearing Frau Rafaela's oversized gown from the convent.

There's a great deal of noise as chairs scrape over the wooden floor. Then silence falls as the soup is being served and Rupert exclaims, "So what is it tonight?" At sixteen, he's the eldest, and I realize with a start that he's only six years younger than me.

"Oh, I hope it's pudding," Johanna shouts next to me.

The Baroness exhales slowly. "It's most certainly not pudding."

Hans arrives and, as if on cue, lifts the metal lid on a

steaming pork roast. There are no roasts of any kind at the convent, but all around the table are disappointed groans.

"Again?" Hedwig whines. She turns to me and explains in her most earnest nine-year-old voice, "Every time a new nanny arrives it's pork roast and potatoes. Pork roast and potatoes."

"We're tired of pork roasts," Johanna complains.

"Well, perhaps this will be the last pork we see for ten months," I say brightly.

"I doubt it," someone grumbles from farther down the table and the Captain scowls.

"Enough." He sounds less angry than tired, like a man who simply doesn't have it in him to fight. "If you wish, Fräulein Maria, you may say a prayer. Though it's not our custom."

"Oh, certainly." I'm sure it wasn't anything special. You would think I'm reciting the alphabet in Greek by the way the children look at me. At the end of it, the Captain smiles briefly and says, "Wonderful," then quietly turns to his food.

As Hans serves each of us in turn, there's silence. Of course, I am used to silence. In Nonnberg, we are allowed to speak for only an hour a day. But here it's unnerving. When I was a child, we always had lively discussions around the dinner table, even when Uncle Franz was present.

I listen to the sounds of forks clinking against china, then the sound of the wind rustling the autumn leaves outside. And just when I feel I can't bear the silence any longer, the Captain clears his throat and makes an announcement.

"Children, I am afraid I have business in Belgium to attend to tomorrow. I may be gone for some time."

I expect there to be protests, but the children merely pause for a moment to look up at their father, then return sadly to their plates. I glance at the Baroness to see what she makes of this, but her face is unreadable.

"Well, Belgium is lovely," I say, hoping to start up some conversation. "Will you be going to Brussels?"

The Captain frowns. "Antwerp," he replies, and it's clear by the way he returns to his dinner that he doesn't anticipate any more discussion.

"Ah, I've never been to Antwerp," I continue. At the other end of the table, Rupert and Agathe watch me intently. "You said you'll be gone for some time?" I ask. "What precisely does that mean?"

The Captain's eyes widen, and it occurs to me that he's probably unaccustomed to being questioned. But it doesn't matter. These are his children. They should know how long their only parent will be gone. "Perhaps seven weeks."

I feel a small hand reach for mine under the table. Johanna, one of the youngest, has tears in her eyes.

CHAPTER SEVEN

"I DON'T UNDERSTAND IT. HE has seven children who need a father. What could he be doing in Belgium for such a long time? Did you see that little girl's face? She was crushed, and he hardly even noticed!"

The Baroness watches me from her throne, which I suppose is actually a high velvet chair, but it looks to me like a throne, and the rest of her room looks like a chamber inside a fairy-tale palace. Every piece of fabric in trimmed in lace, from her long white curtains to her frilly bed, and the oversized vanity in the corner of the room has more bottles than most apothecaries I've seen. "If you'd care to have a seat, Fräulein, I'll try to explain."

I take the velvet bench across from her and wait. Outside, the sun has already set, and in the dim light of the room the Baroness's cream taffeta gown gleams like moonlight.

"The Captain must seem quiet and aloof to you, but he

was not always this way." She rings a little bell and a maid appears with a tray of tea. With one hand behind her back, she fills our cups, then offers us sugar and milk and retreats. *What a strange place,* I think, *where people come and go without saying a word. I might as well be in Nonnberg.*

"Long before the Captain met his wife," she explains, "he was a sailor. He joined the navy at sixteen and by eighteen was already decorated for his role in the Boxer Rebellion."

And I had mistaken him for a butler. I try not to dwell on this mortifying blunder and take a sip of my tea instead.

"The Captain understood from a very young age that technology would be the key to Austria's future, and when the opportunity arose to work on a new type of underwater craft, he leaped at it," the Baroness continues. "At that time, submarines were completely new. I've heard the Baron tell stories of how the periscopes couldn't turn and gas fumes would fill the entire boat until the men would be choking nearly to death. He was incredibly brave. So they gave him the command of his own submarine.

"This was how he met Fräulein Agathe. She was there at his submarine's christening. Her grandfather was Robert Whitehead, the inventor of the torpedo. Images of their wedding were carried in all the papers. They should have had a wonderful life." The Baroness pauses to sip her tea and her eyes grow distant.

"The war?" I ask.

She nods. "They had two small children by then. She stayed with her mother, and by the time he returned he'd earned every possible medal, including the Military Order of Maria Theresa."

Even I know what this means. The Maria Theresa cross is

the highest award an Austrian officer can receive. It's only given for a truly unbelievable act of bravery.

"And this is why he was given his baronetcy," the Baroness explains. "He returned home a hero and then had two more children. After that, the war ended."

And Austria was defeated. The Treaty of Versailles made sure that Austria would remain landlocked, without a navy or access to the Adriatic Sea. I lower my teacup. "And his career?"

"Finished. There had been talk of making him lord admiral. Then suddenly, there was nothing. Not a single ship left in the imperial navy."

So everything the Captain had ever known was taken away. "What did he do?"

"Some men might have fallen into drink. But he began writing about submarines, and when he wasn't writing he helped his wife raise their children. They taught them music, art, literature. . . ."

I can't imagine Uncle Franz and Anni working together this way.

The Baroness's eyes darken. "Then the fever came."

I hold my breath, willing the story to end differently, though I know it can't. I'd had scarlet fever as a child and remembered the delirium.

"Fräulein Agathe was gone within weeks. Little Mitzi was struck next, but it was God's will that she survive. As for the Captain . . . It had been a terrible blow to lose his career, but his wife . . ." She shakes her head, and her large pearl earrings glow dully in the low light. "After her death, he moved his family to this estate."

"This isn't where they used to live?" I exclaim.

"Oh, no. He came here to escape the memories. But he never stays long. Seeing his children without their mother is too much."

"So he hires governesses instead."

"An entire staff," she says proudly. "A governess for each child."

"But why would each child need their own governess?"

"Well, you can't have the older children with the younger ones."

"Why not?"

The Baroness places her teacup on the table. "Because that's how the aristocracy wants it." She rises.

I stand as well, placing my teacup on the table. "So each governess just takes a child and goes about their own business?"

For the first time, the Baroness laughs. "If their business is fighting with the other governesses, then yes. The Captain grew so upset over the bickering that he fired them all last month. Fourteen of them. I was trying to manage seven children on my own before you came."

I can see the weariness in her face. She's not old, like the Reverend Mother, but I suspect her size makes it difficult to hurry up and down three flights of stairs after so many children.

"Starting tomorrow, you will be in charge of both Mitzi's and Johanna's education," she says, walking me to the door.

"Johanna?" I think of the pretty child with pale skin and black curls. No one could be a clearer picture of health.

"The girl is too young to make the long walk to school."

I think she's joking at first, but when her face remains serious I point out, "But it's only two miles. And isn't Johanna seven years old?"

"Perhaps you're forgetting how small your legs were at seven." The Baroness smiles.

No. At seven, I was hiking across Kagran with heavy pails of water from the wells. But I don't say anything.

"Martina, of course, will remain at home as well. At her age, I doubt she requires much teaching. You will also see that the remaining four children are ready for school each morning and that they go to their separate rooms to finish their schoolwork in the evenings. When you're not teaching, it would be of great help if you could also take on some sewing and tidying."

"I assume the Captain told you that I'm only being loaned from the convent?" I ask, hesitating at the door.

"Oh, yes. Until August."

I wonder if anyone has also told her that I'm not being paid. That the abbey has sent me here to teach, not to clean rooms or darn socks. I step into the hall and ask my last question. "So why does the Captain only need help for ten months? What does he think will change? Martina will still be too young for school."

The Baroness's eyes go wide. "You haven't heard? The Captain is engaged to the Princess Yvonne. They are hoping to be married this summer."

My heart does a somersault in my chest. Then there will be no chance of needing me for longer! His wife will hire new governesses, women she'll approve of and will be here to oversee. A feeling of euphoria sweeps over me.

The next morning I'm awake with the light. For several

moments I panic, trying to remember where I am, then I catch sight of the heavy chandelier above my bed and my shoulders relax. The villa seems quiet. I put on my dress and begin my morning prayers, adding to the usual list of people I ask God to protect a new set of names, most of them children. When I'm finished, I stand at the window and look out.

The trees look to be wrapped in red and gold, and a wide, beautiful lawn stretches impossibly far toward the foot of the mountain. Such a wonderful place for children to grow up. Perhaps later we'll go for a hike or play volleyball in the garden.

I hear a bell ring downstairs and think that this must be the breakfast bell, but when I reach the dining hall, only the Baroness is at the table.

"Am I early?" I ask.

"Not at all. I take my breakfast at sunrise. That bell was for the children, instructing them to get dressed. They'll be down shortly."

I cross the room and notice that the Captain's place is not set.

"He left early this morning," the Baroness explains.

"Without saying goodbye to the children?"

Hans appears with another servant and meets my gaze briefly, and I can see the agreement in his eyes as he pours my tea. But the Baroness just sighs. "He feels it's better that way. However, he left something for you." There's a mischievous look on her face, and she nods toward a heavy box that's been left on my dining-room chair.

I have no idea what it might be. It's too heavy to be a Bible, too light to be a cross for my room. I lift the lid and stare.

"Some suitable clothes," the Baroness says, and I suspect she's had something to do with this.

"You mean, no one likes this?" I tease, holding up the edge of my brown dress. I see Hans stifling a laugh.

"Burlap is perfectly fine in the kitchen. For the rest of the house, these will do."

I return to my room with the heavy package as quickly as I can, and discover that there's an entire wardrobe inside. Five dirndl skirts in different colors, three beautiful embroidered vests, six white blouses, and a soft boxy coat in wool tweed. I choose the red skirt and a black vest embroidered with poppies, then finish the outfit with a thin white belt I find tucked between the blouses. I'm late for breakfast, but the children are amazed at my transformation.

"What happened to your dress?" Johanna asks.

"Oh, do you miss it? I can go and change."

There's a firm chorus of "No"s and Rupert can barely contain his laughter. "It did look a bit like a potato sack, Fräulein."

"But one you wore very well," Agathe pipes in.

Everyone begins laughing again and the Baroness clears her throat. "Enough. Let Fräulein Maria eat."

The children seem freer without the Captain, as if a storm cloud has passed and they can laugh again. Then the house descends into chaos as breakfast ends and four children search for shoes, hats, bookbags, and coats. The Baroness retreats to her room upstairs, leaving me to fix the problems of Agathe's missing leather glove, Rupert's misplaced bookbag, and Johanna's tears over the unfairness of everyone going to school except her.

"Next year it will be your turn," I promise, guiding her out of the way to a bench near the door. "And not everyone is going," I remind her, retrieving Agathe's leather glove from the inside of a boot. "Mitzi will be here."

"But Mitzi has to stay in bed," she wails, fat tears rolling into her long black curls.

"Martina will be here, too."

"Martina is a baby! I never get to do anything fun." She crosses her arms over her chest and I laugh, opening the door. "You wait here, and I bet we can find something fun for you today as soon as I get back."

I'm wrong. When I return from walking the children to school, the Baroness is waiting with Martina and Johanna in the hall. The three of them are arranged on the padded bench, and I wonder how long the children have been asked to wait for me this way, in total silence. All three rise as soon as they see me, and the Baroness says, "Come. There's quite a bit to do, Fräulein."

I suppress my irritation that I should be expected to do anything but teach, and I try to remember that I am doing this for the Captain. His wife may have died four years ago, but for him and the children it might as well have been yesterday. I peel off my gloves and put away my boots, then follow the Baroness across the manor to the nursery.

It's a large, bright room with windows overlooking the sunny meadows outside. There are mechanical horses and rockers, but nothing I can see for older children.

The Baroness explains, "This room is for the younger children. Martina and Johanna will spend their day here. You may teach them in this room once you return from taking the older children to school. At midday, while Martina and

Johanna are napping, you will return to the school and escort
the older children home for lunch. They will stay until two, at
which point you will need to walk them to school again.
When you return, you may go upstairs to teach Mitzi while I
care for Martina and Johanna in here."

So there will be three trips to the school and three back.
Twelve miles a day will take up a great deal of time. Plus
teaching. I nod. "And their schoolbooks?"

The Baroness walks me to a large white desk and indicates
the bookcase next to it. "You'll find everything you need in
here. While Johanna is working and Martina is playing, there
is a basket of mending on that shelf. The children's gloves are
in terrible shape."

"So why not use mittens? They're cheap. If they're lost or
damaged, you can simply get new ones."

"My dear, he may ask that we call him Captain, but Georg
von Trapp is a Baron and his children must look the part."

I wait until she leaves to look down at Johanna. "Sounds
like we have our orders." I wink. "Shall we get to work?"

"How about we play first?" Johanna begs.

I turn to Martina, trying to include her. "I don't know.
What do you think?"

But Martina hides behind her sister. She's the shyest of all
the children, and also the most solemn. She was just one
when her mother died, and since then has only known a series of governesses. Of all the children, she will benefit the
most from the Baron's marriage. When the Princess Yvonne
arrives, she will have someone to stay with her and finally
some stability. I think back to my own childhood with Mutti.
As terrible as it was to live with Uncle Franz, at least I always
knew I had her and Anni.

The little girl whispers something in her sister's ear, and Johanna says, "Martina wants you to know she doesn't want to play games. She wishes to color by herself instead."

The request tugs at my heart, but it will be some time before the child trusts me. "All right." I nod, and she runs off to hide inside a little white tent. "How about you and I play backgammon?"

We haven't played for very long before the Baroness is back, watching us from the doorway. Martina, in her white sailor's uniform and blue bow, is nowhere to be seen, while Johanna and I are sprawled out on the rug, cheering after every roll of the dice. Her bow is on the floor and her own pristine sailor suit is now a wrinkled mess.

The Baroness clears her throat and Johanna immediately scrambles to a sitting position. "It is almost eleven," she says.

"Is it?" I rise. I have no way of telling the time. "Then I suppose I should get to work with Mitzi."

"May I suggest you begin by reading the paper?"

"Of course."

I pick up the newspaper on Mitzi's nightstand and make a big show of opening it. The headlines are all predictable. Tension in the north. Economy worsening. Something about Hitler publicly agreeing to respect the law and seek political power only through the nation's democratic process. The Baroness leaves and I hand Mitzi the paper.

"Do you normally read this?" I ask.

"Every morning," she says. "Right now all the papers are talking about Hitler. Have you heard of him?"

"Oh, yes." He's the leader of the National Socialist German

Workers' Party, or Nazis for short. They're a group of disaffected citizens, still angry about losing the war and determined to see Germany rise again. They call for ludicrous things like conquering Eastern Europe and ridding Germany of its "Jewish government." Last year, Hitler and his band of misfits staged a coup to overthrow the German government. Predictably, it ended with his arrest. But the judge had sympathized with his cause, and instead of deporting him back to Austria, he allowed Hitler to carry out a token sentence in Germany. Nine months later, Hitler emerged from prison as both a martyr and an author. The book he'd written while in jail, *Mein Kampf,* is apparently a bestseller now in Germany, even with its passages about the "Aryan" race being superior to all others.

"I just can't understand it," Mitzi says.

"None of us can," I confide. "Best to simply ignore news like this." I take back the paper and fold it in half, returning it to her nightstand. "How about something a little more cheerful," I suggest.

Mitzi's face brightens. "Math?"

I laugh, because that wasn't what I was thinking. "All right."

We start with math, then German, and by the time we've done twenty minutes of French it's already noon and I must leave to retrieve the other children. Lunch is chaos with the cook coming out from the kitchen to see what all the fuss is about. Hedwig, who is nine, cannot stand sausage, and nothing on earth will compel her to eat it. Werner, who is twelve and should certainly know better, joins in the refusal and won't eat either. Within minutes it's a full-scale mutiny and the cook is telling everyone it's either sausage or porridge.

Hedwig accepts porridge while everyone else is suddenly fine with meat.

The afternoon is not much more successful. Upstairs in her room with nothing to do but read, Mitzi has turned herself into a dedicated student. But this is the extent of her life—books. We sit together while she scribbles away at her poetry and solves algebraic equations, and as the hours drag on the silence becomes oppressive. In Nonnberg there was always the sound of singing, or church bells, or mass. But this slow drip of time while this poor girl solves equation after equation is just intolerable.

"I know!" I exclaim, causing Mitzi to jump in her bed. "Why don't I go and fetch a game?"

She wrinkles her freckled nose. "A game?"

"Sure. Like chess or checkers," I say from her bedside. There's no use in looking over her last few math problems. They'll all be correct.

But Mitzi doesn't look convinced. "I . . . I think I'd rather just do some more math."

"Mitzi, endless work isn't good for you."

The girl looks shocked. "But I can't do anything else."

"I know you can't go outside, but what about inside? Wasn't there anything you liked to do before this?"

"I did love to play the piano. But I'm not allowed to get up to practice anymore."

"Well, what about the violin? I saw a violin downstairs in the study."

A shadow crosses her face. "That was Mutti's. She used to play with my father. But he put his away four years ago." Tears gather and I hesitate.

"I think your mother would love to know someone is carrying on her passion for music."

Mitzi wipes away the tears with the back of her hand and her shoulders sag. "I don't think the Baroness will agree."

"Well, how about I ask her after dinner? If she says yes, we can start tomorrow."

But that yes begins to seem unlikely as the children gather in the hall after school and prepare to take off their coats and gloves.

"Wait!" I cry, and everyone freezes. "Before we get down to your homework, who would like to go outside and play?"

A chorus of happy voices is raised before the Baroness asks, "I'm afraid what Fräulein Maria *means* to say is, who would like to take a brief walk outside?"

All around me hands are still raised, and I take a deep breath. "All right, a walk."

The Baroness nods approvingly and everyone makes for the door.

"Are we all going together?" Rupert asks.

"What do you mean?" I open the door and the youngest children run past me into the garden. It's a beautiful fall day, crisp with a cloudless blue sky.

"I'm wondering if the older ones will be walking with the younger ones?" he asks, uncertain if he should follow.

I turn to stare at him. At sixteen, he's already taller than I am, with a crop of strawberry blond hair and light eyes. There's a steadiness to Rupert, and I suspect he'll make a fine doctor or engineer. "Of course we're walking together." I hesitate at his surprise. "Don't you go for walks with one another?"

"No."

I look at Agathe, who is hovering near the door as well. She has darker coloring than her brother and is just as striking. "We take our walks in separate groups," she explains. "The eldest and the youngest."

So the children do their work separately, walk separately, play separately. I'm surprised they even eat in the same room. "Well, for as long as I'm here, we all walk together."

The six of them hurry out into the garden, and everyone has something different they want to show me. Werner, who is twelve, with broad shoulders and giant hands, guides me down the gravel path, naming the trees and autumn flowers that we pass. He's a little botanist, with a name for almost everything.

"But no one knows what that is," he says, pointing to a cluster of yellow and white flowers.

I squat down and smile. "Glacier buttercups," I tell him. "We have them in the fell-fields around Tyrol. But I've seen them around the Kitzsteinhorn glacier as well."

Werner studies me with openmouthed fascination. "How do you know this?"

I stand and Johanna slips her hand into mine, pulling me toward a courtyard in the center of the garden. "Oh, I did a great deal of hiking when I was your age. I was part of the Austrian Catholic Youth Movement. We'd travel throughout the Alps collecting folk songs and writing them down for future generations."

Agathe gives a little gasp. "Do you know any of them still?"

"Dozens. We would sing them at night while camping and I would play the guitar."

The children exchange glances.

"Oh, please, will you play some for us?" Agathe asks.

I laugh. "Of course."

The gravel path curves through the garden and ends at the verge of the meadow. This is where the children should be out running free, playing volleyball or tag. Instead, they're walking primly over the stones, quietly discussing the changing leaves. Johanna points out different clusters of wildflowers in between the beds of blush-pink roses, and Werner shows me the tall, showy flowers of a purple monkshood. But when we reach the verge of the meadow, everyone stops.

"This is where we always turn around," Rupert says.

That evening, I seek out the Baroness. She's not in her room, surrounded by ruffles and lace. She's not in the kitchen either. Instead, I find her by the fire in the Captain's library, sewing a dirndl. On her lap is a small dog I've never seen before, with curly white fur and expressive black eyes. His ears perk up as I approach, and the Baroness smiles.

"Fräulein Maria. Care to join me in some sewing?"

"Oh, no. No thank you, Baroness."

She indicates the leather couch across from her and I take a seat, wondering where to start. "Do you know why I work for the Captain, Fräulein?"

The question has never occurred to me.

"As a boy, the Captain was raised in a household that was probably very similar to your own."

I want to ask if he, too, slept in the attic, but I let her continue.

"However, as the Captain's fortunes grew, he married the daughter of a countess. When Fräulein Agathe was alive, she would tell the story of how the emperor used to visit her home. Fräulein Agathe understood the kind of expectations that would be placed on their children. Manners, education, dress . . ."

"But they're not living at court," I point out. "So why not let them be children?"

"Well, of course they're children." She looks affronted.

"I've never seen a quieter group walking past a meadow. They should have been climbing trees or playing tag."

"And ruin their clothes?" The Baroness is aghast. Even the dog struggles to a sitting position to stare at me.

"We could always get them some *Wetterfleck*," I suggest.

She makes a face. "*Wetterfleck?*"

"You know, short capes for playing. Then they won't have to carry around those ridiculous umbrellas. And if they get dirty . . ."

"Fräulein, an umbrella is a sign of good taste."

What a curse to be an aristocrat. "But who are they impressing in the garden?"

"Anyone in the village who might pass by! Imagine if someone comes and the Captain's children are dressed in waterflick."

"*Wetterfleck*," I correct.

She stands and puts down her sewing. "I am afraid the Captain would never approve."

She moves toward the door and I rise. "Then what about a violin teacher for Mitzi?"

The Baroness sighs. "Fine. Yes."

When Mitzi hears the news, she is almost in tears. "How did you do it? How did you convince her to say yes?"

I tidy up the papers around her bed and laugh. "By asking her for something that gave her heartburn first."

Mitzi is delighted. She pushes aside the pillows and asks to hear the story. When I'm finished, she pouts. "Well, I thought buying *Wetterflecks* was a wonderful idea. Even if I couldn't have used one."

"Of course you would have! Do you think you'll be sitting up here forever?"

Mitzi's face brightens and I can see her warming to the idea of being outside and playing for the first time in months. "So what will you do now?" she asks in a conspiratorial whisper.

"Well, it won't start raining for another few weeks. Until then, perhaps all we need are some playclothes."

"But what will the Baroness say? And where will you find them?"

I take the chair next to her bed to have a think when a movement in the center of the room catches my eye. The doors to the balcony have been left slightly open and the sheer curtains are dancing in the breeze. Mitzi's room has been decorated for airiness and light. But whoever decorated my room decided on curtains of heavy damask. I watch the curtains move and twist in the breeze, then a wild idea comes to me.

CHAPTER EIGHT

FRAN

Manhattan, New York
1959

"So it's true? The scene with the curtains is true?" Fran is aware that she's talking far too loudly in the dining room of the St. Regis, but she honestly can't help herself. She had assumed the scene where Maria had turned her curtains into playclothes for the children was an invention of the script-writers.

"Oh, it was real." Maria looks pleased with herself. "And a few weeks later the children all had matching outfits in yellow and green damask."

Fran has completely forgotten about her food. "And the Baroness? What did she say?"

"Nothing." Maria gives a little shrug. "It was already done."

"She didn't threaten to fire you?"

Maria chuckles. "The moment she saw them, she was shocked into silence. By the time she recovered, the only thing she could think to tell me was that she hoped the Captain had a strong sense of humor."

Fran sits back and smiles. "I wish I could see a picture of the Baroness. She sounds formidable."

"She was certainly set in her ways." Maria sighs, and Fran can see that her thoughts are somewhere else. "So what is to be done about the play?"

Fran has been waiting for this. "Well, I don't feel as if I've heard anything that's terribly different from what's written in the script."

Maria stiffens. "Because I haven't told you yet about Georg, or Father Wasner, or what happened to us when the Nazis came to power. And I can tell you, none of that is in the script."

Fran clears her throat. It's twelve o'clock, and Mr. Hammerstein probably has a pile of papers ripped from his yellow legal pad on her desk, waiting to be typed. "You're here for a week, is that right?"

Maria dabs her lips with a napkin. "Until Sunday."

"What if we meet here tomorrow at the same time and you finish telling me what concerns you? Or we could try somewhere new."

"We can meet wherever you like. The St. Regis. Central Park. Alfredo's Italian restaurant. What concerns me is the script, and almost all of it is *bockmist*, Miss Connelly."

Fran isn't sure what *bockmist* means, but it probably isn't German for wonderful. "Please," she reminds Maria, "it's just Fran."

"Well, Fran, the beginning of the script may be fine, but I can tell you that the rest bears only the remotest resemblance to my life."

"I'm going to read your autobiography tonight," Fran promises. She motions for the waiter and quietly tells him to place the bill on Hammerstein's tab. Then she rises. "We all want this to be something you're proud of." She leads the way across the lobby and back out into the sun. "Why don't we meet in the park tomorrow?" No point in wasting such glorious weather.

Maria gives a pointed glance at Fran's heels. "For sitting?"

Fran smiles. "Walking. I'll bring a change of shoes. We can start at the Bethesda Fountain."

At the office, everyone is getting ready for lunch.

"She returns!" Peter exclaims, grabbing his jacket off the rack while Fran takes hers off. "Well? What was she like?"

"Maria?" Fran settles behind her desk and takes a moment to think. "Like that stern grandmother you're slightly afraid of."

Peter laughs and the sound fills the office. "Really?" He looks like he wants to hear more, but Jack's face is stone.

"Don't tell any of this to Hammerstein right now. He's on a roll."

Fran looks at the closed door. "Writing?" she asks eagerly.

Peter snaps his briefcase shut. "Rodgers was in here earlier. Pretty sure there's going to be a new song."

"Shall we bring you back lunch?" Jack asks, buttoning his suit jacket.

"I had lunch with Maria, but thank you."

Jack hesitates. "She didn't mention wanting to put a stop to the play?" he asks, lowering his voice.

Fran glances at the closed door. "She's upset. But the rights don't belong to her."

"She could still be bad press," Jack warns. His father is a congressman. Bad press is even worse than bad policy.

"I'm meeting her again tomorrow morning," Fran says.

"I doubt Hammerstein wants this to drag on," he warns. "Tell her whatever she wants to hear, then he can keep her away from the premiere, let the reviews roll in, and that will be that." When he sees the look on Fran's face, he leans across the desk and briefly kisses her cheek. "It's the kindest thing to do. You sure you don't want anything?"

She shakes her head, and when the office clears out, she starts on the pile of yellow papers neatly arranged in the corner of her desk. Most are letters to various journalists, reminding them about the premiere in six weeks. Another batch of the same letters will go out in three weeks, then three days before opening night. It takes over an hour to type up the reminders, and Fran is finishing the last one when a door creaks.

"Miss Connelly!" Hammerstein looks as surprised as he sounds. "You must let me know if I've given you so much work that you have to skip lunch."

Fran laughs. "I'm not being as industrious as it looks. I just returned from the meeting with Mrs. von Trapp."

Hammerstein's face grows serious. "The author." He nods, as if he's steeling himself for some very bad news. "What did she say?"

"Well, the script doesn't seem to deviate much from the beginning of her life. She told me about her whistling in the nunnery and the curtains."

"Ah, yes." Hammerstein breaks into a smile, and Fran suspects that he admires Maria's impudence.

"However, she's asked that I see her tomorrow so she can finish her story. And I'm guessing this is the point where there will be some . . . deviation."

Hammerstein shoves his hands deep into his pockets.

"When Lindsey and Crouse wrote this script, they based it on the German film because it had been so successful. Perhaps I should've had a hand in the script," he says defeatedly. "Let me know what she tells you."

Hammerstein looks tired, pale even, and suddenly it occurs to Fran to ask, "Is everything all right?"

The front door to the office swings open and Hammerstein's assistants come piling in, all big energy and noisy feet.

"Just a little stomach pain," he says quietly. "Nothing that won't right itself," he adds with a smile. Then he grabs his jacket and is gone.

As soon as the door clicks shut, the assistants crowd around Fran's desk.

"Is he leaving?" Peter asks. "Did he just say he's sick?"

"Stomach pain," Fran whispers.

The office goes quiet, then Jack says, "He'll be fine. Look at him. He's built like a tank."

A few of the other guys agree. Nothing has ever stopped Hammerstein, and in six weeks he'll be sitting at the opening of his forty-second show. Everyone has stomach pains now and again. Most of the assistants disappear into their offices, but Peter lingers next to Fran's wooden desk.

"He's been working on a new song," Peter says. "He gave it to us yesterday. Did Jack tell you what it's called?"

Fran shakes her head.

" 'So Long, Farewell.' "

Fran can feel the color drain from her face. Perhaps she's overreacting, but the title feels ominous, and she can tell that Peter senses it, too. "Hammerstein hasn't been himself, has he?"

"No." Peter slips his hands into his pockets. "And he's not working like he used to. He said there's still another song he wants to write, but it's not coming to him. So he's waiting."

Fran turns toward him. "For what?"

"I don't know. But he's never waited this late to finish lyrics. And now he's going home."

"Maybe he's just getting older," Fran says hopefully. "He has to be almost sixty-five."

Peter shrugs out of his jacket and drapes it on the rack. "I guess he has to slow down at some point."

"Hey." Fran thinks of something more cheerful. "Don't you have tickets for the *Yves Montand Show* tonight?"

Peter pauses on the way to his office and the corners of his mouth turn down. "Nah. Eva has rehearsals."

"I thought she was finished?"

"Ah, you know. Broadway . . ."

But Fran is certain Eva told her that rehearsals were finished when she passed her in the lobby last night.

"Anyway, I gave the tickets to Freddy. He and Sue really wanted them."

Fran makes a mental note to ask Eva about this the next time she sees her, then continues with her work. At five o'clock the grandfather clock in the hall begins to strike and there's a mad rush to the rack for jackets and hats, then a wait for a cab under the neon lights.

"So how did it really go this morning?" Jack asks.

"I'm not sure." A cab pulls over and they get inside.

"West Fifty-Fourth Street," Jack tells the driver, then turns to Fran. "You don't think she'll make trouble, do you?"

"She's upset, and I can't tell if she has reason to be yet. I'm reading her autobiography tonight, then we're meeting in the park tomorrow morning. So no need to pick me up."

Jack glances at Fran. "You're really into this."

Fran isn't sure what that's supposed to mean. "Hammerstein asked me to interview her. He wants me to take notes."

"I wouldn't put too much effort into this, Fran. You know he's just going to throw them away."

"Why would you say that?"

Jack looks surprised. "Because he doesn't actually want to know what Maria thinks. It's like asking your constituents how they feel about some new building project." He gives a hollow laugh. "It's going to happen anyway."

Lately, Jack's cynicism has begun to annoy her. "Hammerstein wouldn't waste my time like that. He'll read the notes."

Jack gives her a long look. "Fran, Hammerstein may write about happiness and kittens, but this is business. You don't think he's the most successful lyricist on Broadway because he changes his scripts every time there's a complaint?"

"And how many of his plays are based on someone's autobiography?" she challenges.

Jack slides his arm around her shoulders. "Look, I'm just saying I wouldn't waste too much time."

Fran leaves the cab feeling upset, and when Jack reminds her of their date tomorrow—"Keens, six o'clock"—she has half a mind to cancel. She walks through the lobby and tries to remember all the reasons she fell in love with him. How patient he was when he taught her to drive, how encouraging he used to be about her writing. She's still reminding herself of the things she loves about him when an "Oh, hello" in front of her makes her stop.

"Eva." Fran is shocked. Her friend is dressed for the eve-

ning in pink satin, with matching pink pumps and a sparkling handbag. "Peter said you had rehearsals."

Eva giggles. "Change of plan."

"But the tickets—"

A gloved hand waves away the question. "Do you see that
out there?"

Fran turns. A car is waiting, long and sleek and red. Fran
doesn't know much about cars, but she thinks it might be a
Ferrari.

"That's Mack Russell," Eva confides.

Fran wonders if she's supposed to recognize the name, but
before she can say anything, Eva gives her shoulder a friendly
squeeze and walks out. She watches through the lobby's double doors as a tall man with broad shoulders and too wide of
a grin holds the car door open. But it's not until they're gone
that Fran feels she can move again.

Upstairs, she sits at her desk and tries to make sense of
what just transpired. She's not sure why she's shocked. Eva
had never shown more than a slight interest in Peter. But
knowing what Eva is doing without his knowledge is so upsetting that she can't focus on her writing.

Fran is still thinking about it the next morning as she puts on
her sneakers and walks over to Central Park. When she
reaches the Bethesda Fountain, however, all thoughts of Eva
and Peter vanish.

Maria is already there, surrounded by more than a dozen
women. They've obviously recognized her from her bright
green dirndl and giant crucifix. One has a baby buggy with
her, and Maria is holding up a laughing toddler. After work-

ing for several years near Broadway, Fran has gotten to know actresses who are like alcoholics, who can't put down the act, and she wonders if perhaps Maria is one of these.

She approaches the scene slowly, listening from the back as the women tell stories about seeing the von Trapps for the first time. Fran remembers her parents talking about them, and seems to recall hearing them sing over the radio at Christmas when she was very young. But these women all seem to have heard her in person, and Maria is beaming. She bounces the little girl on her knee for some time, only giving the baby back when she catches sight of Fran.

"Excuse me," she announces. "I have a meeting with Oscar Hammerstein's office."

Fran takes a step back as everyone turns to look at Hammerstein's office, giving the women a little smile. But as the crowd disperses, Maria's smile falters.

"Do you know what I did in my hotel room last night?"

Fran shakes her head, trying to clear it.

"I reread the script that Mary Martin was kind enough to share with me. And it made me more upset than ever. They've changed everything!" she exclaims. "Who is Max? There was never any Max. And where is Father Wasner?" She starts walking, but this time Fran is prepared to keep up. "And that scene in the churchyard where everyone is hiding? Total fabrication!" Maria continues. "There were *years* between that Salzburg Festival and the Nazi Party coming for us!"

Fran waits for Maria to finish. "It sounds like a great deal of your story has been changed. But you were telling me yesterday about the playclothes," she reminds her.

"Oh, yes." Maria finally smiles. "The clothes . . ."

CHAPTER NINE

MARIA

Salzburg, Austria
1926

I WAIT FOR THE CHAOS of four children returning from school to die down before making the announcement. "Today we're going outside to play!"

I pause, expecting exclamations of joy. Instead, there's silence and confusion.

"What do you mean, *play*?" Johanna asks.

"Oh, I don't know," I say, refastening my braids. "Perhaps we'll go for a hike. Or maybe we'll play chase or volleyball in the garden."

A few of the children dare to look excited, but Agathe draws her brows together. "I don't think the Baroness will approve," she warns.

"Unfortunately," I say, with far more empathy in my voice than I feel, "the Baroness is upstairs recovering from a cold."

Agathe's eyes brighten. "But if she should see stains on our clothes—"

I laugh. "Come. Mitzi and I have a surprise for you in the nursery."

There's a stampede up the wooden stairs, then shouts of disbelief when they see what Mitzi and I have accomplished.

"Are these your curtains?" Rupert exclaims. The Captain's eldest is a keen observer.

"They were. And now they're your playclothes."

You've never seen such excitement. Trousers and shirts for the boys, dirndls for the girls. Even Mitzi gets dressed and comes outside with us to watch a game of volleyball on the lawn. There is a good chance the Baroness might hear the laughter and come to investigate. But what can she do? Send me back to the nunnery? I actually feel a small thrill at the thought. Let the Captain send me back! The children will have experienced some fun for once and I'll get to go home.

But the Baroness doesn't make an appearance, and it's the finest afternoon we've spent together since my arrival. Seven of us play volleyball until the sun goes down and the cook takes up her residence at the top step of the mansion, violently ringing a handbell to call us in for dinner.

Without the Baroness to preside over the dining room, we chat throughout the meal. I ask each of the children to tell me something they're thankful for this day. The youngest ones say their playclothes, Werner says the volleyball and net that I purchased, then it's Martina's turn and the table goes quiet. The child has spent four of her five years on this earth without a mother, and I know what it is to not even remember the woman who was supposed to love and protect you.

"I'm not grateful for anything," Martina says.

There's a chorus of exclamations, but I hold up my hand. "That's perfectly fine. Perhaps she'll find something to be thankful for tomorrow." I give her knee a little squeeze under the table and I can see that this isn't the response she was expecting. Then I change the subject. "Now why don't we have a little music?" I suggest.

Werner looks around, wondering if maybe I've brought a gramophone with me as well.

"Who has a utensil they're not using?" I ask, picking up my dessert fork. There are giggles around the table, then everyone picks up their fork, even Martina. I strike the edge of my glass and a high, clear sound rings out. Everyone tries it.

"It's beautiful!" Hedwig exclaims.

I use Martina's glass and mine to play the nursery rhyme "Alle meine Entchen."

"How did you do that?" Johanna asks.

"Try it out. In fact, everyone must try it! And use the glass of the person next to you." Agathe and Rupert glance nervously toward the kitchen, and I assure them that it's fine. "It won't hurt the glass." I laugh. "Go on!"

High, sweet music echoes throughout the dining room, like crystal rain droplets bouncing along the roof.

"Now, let's tune our instruments!" I say. I take the water decanter and fill up my glass. "Almost to the top," I tell them, then we play our song again.

"The extra water lowers the pitch," Rupert realizes.

"Can we do this every night?" Johanna exclaims. Even Martina is smiling a little, striking both her glass and mine.

Hans pokes his head into the room to see what's happening, then grins. "You're lucky the Baroness is upstairs recovering."

"Oh, yes." I put on my most pious face. "Godspeed her healing."

But I should have known better than to ask God for speed (healing alone would have been enough), because our happy mealtimes come to an end two days later.

"Why is everyone so fidgety?" the Baroness snaps after she returns to her place at the head of the table.

Seven faces turn toward me, and I can feel my cheeks flush. "While you were recovering," I admit, "I'm afraid we made it something of a habit to talk about our day over dinner."

The Baroness makes a harrumphing noise in her throat. "Mealtime is for eating, not talking," she overrules, and silence falls over the room again.

"But what if . . ." I interrupt the silence, ". . . the children could each speak about something they're grateful to God for each day?"

I see the Baroness briefly touch the cross at her neck. "Well, I suppose there would be nothing wrong with that."

I sit straighter, feeling triumphant.

"However, there is a matter of some missing curtains that I would also like to discuss," she says. "Perhaps *after* dinner."

It's the longest meal I've ever eaten. I can barely concentrate on what the children are thankful for I'm so nervous, and as I look around the room at each of their sweet faces—Rupert with his grown-up haircut and steady gaze, Agathe with her pretty round face and chestnut-colored plaits, Werner with his ruddy cheeks and freckled nose—I realize how much I want them to be happy. It wouldn't be right to take away the playclothes we made. If you can't run outside and play as a child, then when?

I'm preparing to launch my defense in the library when the Baroness collapses into the nearest chair and sighs.

"Your curtains, Fräulein? What next? Turning the rug into winter coats?"

"I just wanted to give them the opportunity to have fun!"

"They have fun."

"*Real* fun." I remain standing. "Like all the other children in Austria do."

"They're not like all the other children, Fräulein. They are the sons and daughters of a Baron."

I shift from one foot to the other, searching for the politest way to say this. "With the greatest respect, Baroness, I believe those days are over."

Her eyes snap to attention. "We don't know that," she says, and maybe she's right. It's only been eight years since an emperor ruled over Austria, and though we are a republic now, there's no telling when the archduke might return from his exile to reclaim his throne. "And if the archduke should return, how will these children conduct themselves at court? What do you propose? That they run wild through the Hofburg?"

"No. I would propose that they become the rare breed of children fortunate enough to experience the refined world of the palace and the wilds of their own backyard." I straighten, ready for more fight, but her recent bout of the flu has drained the Baroness's energy and she doesn't have it in her.

"Just go," she says.

"But—"

"Leave." She waves me away with a gloved hand. "And try not to cause further disruptions. There is a reason for all of these rules, Fräulein, even if you cannot understand them."

I make my way toward the door and hear the scampering of feet outside. Naughty children! "Does this mean they can keep the playclothes?" I ask.

The Baroness glowers at me. "As long as I never have to see them looking like ruffians and they are properly dressed for dinner."

"Oh, yes. Of course." I open the door.

"And their nails will be clean. Always," she calls after me.

"Of course, Baroness!" I hurry upstairs to the nursery.

Seven nervous faces look at me.

I smile back at them. "Who wants to go for a hike tomorrow?"

After so many glorious days of sun it was bound to happen. I wake up on the seventeenth of November and hear the familiar patter of rain against the glass. At first, it's only a shower. But as the days march toward December, it begins to come down in sheets, making the walk to and from school unbearable. In German, we call this *Schnürlregen,* a rain so hard you can't even see through the drops.

"If they had *Wetterflecks* none of this would be a problem," I grumble. Our five umbrellas have to fight for space on the tiny country roads, then there's the mess they create in the hall for the maids. But I've probably pushed my luck as far as it will go with the Baroness.

The next week, when the rains are really terrible, I gather everyone together in the nursery and the children help me with darning their socks. It's supposed to be done while they're at school, but I've decided that teaching Martina and Mitzi is more important than patching up holes.

"Wouldn't it be nice if we had some music," Rupert suggests, tired of the constant drum of the rain.

There's a chorus of *"Ja"s* from around the rug.

"But how will we bring the glasses up here?" Johanna asks.

Agathe laughs. "We don't need glasses. Fräulein Maria has a guitar!"

My heart beats faster. There have been so many moments when I've wanted to reach for my guitar but was too nervous. What would the Baroness think? How would the Baron react? I study the hope in Agathe's face. "You want me to play?"

The agreement is near unanimous. Only Martina refrains from nodding, concentrating instead on mending her socks.

"All right, the guitar it is." I go to fetch my instrument, and when I return, there's a circle of eager faces waiting for me. It almost feels like my classroom at the abbey. I seat myself in the middle of the group, open the case, and take out my guitar. I haven't held it in weeks, and it feels wonderful to brush my fingers over the polished wood. "All right, how about a folk song?"

Rupert wrinkles his nose. "What's a folk song?"

"You know. 'In Stiller Nacht,' 'In Einem Kuhlen Grunde.'" There's no recognition on their faces and my fingers drop from the guitar. "Well, haven't you learned any folk songs?"

The children shake their heads.

"What about at school? Something simple like . . ." I begin to sing "Die Hoch Alma," but the children's faces remain blank. I put down the guitar. "No one can sing this?"

"We can if you teach us!" Mitzi says. She'll be the star of every classroom when she returns to school, so eager to learn whatever is on offer.

"Do all of you wish to learn?"

"Oh, yes!" Johanna exclaims.

I look at Martina. "What about you?" I ask softly.

Her dark eyes fix on mine for a moment, then glance away. "I don't care."

"Well, perhaps you can pick our very first song. What do you say?"

This time, she holds my gaze. "Me?"

"Why not?" I list for her a few of the songs I learned when I was traveling with the Austrian Catholic Youth Movement. Then I tell the children how we would walk in groups of four or five and return to our campsite at dusk. There, about thirty of us would sing the night away—ballads, church music, anything. Those weekends filled with hiking and song were the best times of my life.

Martina offers quietly, " 'Es wollt ein Jägerlein jagen,' I guess."

It's a beautiful song, and because most of the children can already read music, it doesn't take long to teach them the rhythm. At first, they have trouble harmonizing together. Then I split them into groups and have each group sing different lines, adding one line at a time until they are all singing the final verse. The sound they make together is surprisingly good. Rupert is a natural bass vocalist, Agathe a stunning soprano, Werner a truly perfect tenor, and Hedwig a born alto. They ask to sing it again and again, because none of us can believe how beautiful it sounds.

And so begins a new rainy-day tradition. When it's too wet for hiking and too icy for volleyball, we sit around on the rug in the nursery and sing. Two days before Advent, I ask if they would like to begin learning songs for Christmas. The vote is unanimous.

"Perhaps when Father returns home," Agathe says, "we can surprise him with a concert!"

The suggestion takes me by surprise. "Do you think he would like that?" I ask cautiously. Because the Baroness has implied that the Captain is a man with little time or affection for frivolity.

"Oh, yes!" Agathe replies. "We've never sung together before, but we used to play our instruments together after dinner. It was with Mama, when she was here."

Martina glances up from her dolls. She was too young to remember, of course, but I recognize the hunger in her eyes.

I'm shocked. "So what instruments would everyone play?" And why haven't they been playing them?

"Well, Rupert plays the piano and accordion," Agathe says.

"And I play the recorder!" Johanna pipes up.

"And now I can play the violin," Mitzi adds.

"That's lovely," a voice says from the doorway. Everyone freezes as the Baroness steps inside. She rarely comes to the nursery, although I know she must hear our singing. "And how are we doing on our sewing?"

"We're not sewing." Johanna laughs brightly. "We're singing."

"Yes, I can hear that. And I was not asking you, Johanna." The Baroness presses her lips into a very thin line. "Fräulein Maria, where are the socks?"

"Well, we haven't finished this week's batch," I admit. "But—"

The Baroness crooks a finger at me. "If you will," she says, and suddenly I recall the last time I was taken from a group of children. *If she forces me to leave, I will go back to my sweet six-year-olds in the abbey,* I think as I rise. *I don't even want to be here. Let her send me back to the nunnery.* Then I imagine the look on the Reverend Mother's face and my chest tightens. If I'm not seen as fit to be a tutor, perhaps she'll think I'm not fit to teach at Nonnberg. Or, worse, to take my vows.

In the hall, the Baroness's voice is stern. "What are these children learning in there?"

"Songs for Christmas," I tell her.

"And what about the socks?"

I want to laugh. Who cares about socks? They'll get done. But I school my features and tell her earnestly, " 'A time to weep, and a time to laugh; a time to mourn, and a time to dance . . . He hath made everything beautiful in His time.' I promise you, Baroness, I will get to them. And I will not ask the children to help."

This settles her a little. "The children do sound beautiful together."

My eyes brighten. "Don't they?"

"Yes. It's actually rather extraordinary."

"Perhaps we can—"

"No." The Baroness is firm.

"But I haven't even—"

"*Whatever* the question is, Fräulein Maria, the answer is already no."

CHAPTER TEN

HE RETURNS WITHOUT WARNING. One moment I am singing a *Weihnachtslied* with the children in the nursery, the next I whirl around and the Baron is standing there, immobilized. By shock or by awe? I wonder. His dark hair is swept back from his face, his broad shoulders squared. He's dressed casually in a blue tweed suit and cap, and it occurs to me just then what a handsome man he is.

"*Papa!*" Johanna exclaims. "This was supposed to be a surprise!"

The children rush toward him, an excited mob of tears and greetings, talking at the same time about what they've been doing in the weeks since he's been gone.

"All right, all right." He smiles. "One voice at a time." He clears the way and singles out Martina, who is standing at the edge of the group in silence.

"Tell me about what you've been doing," he says.

She tells him about our lessons together, and several times he looks over at me as I'm tidying the room, but I can't gauge his expression. Then the rest of the children take turns telling him about their school lessons, our singing, the Christmas presents they want, and how hard they've been working to decorate the house. I'm proud to say that it looks like a winter wonderland now, with gingerbread houses lining the mantel-pieces and vases filled with holly berries and spruce. There has never been this many decorations in their house, but this is what Anni and I used to do each Christmas back in Kagran.

When the dinner bell rings and the children dash down-stairs, the Captain stays behind. "You've taught them to sing."

"Oh. Yes. Well, it's just a few Christmas songs. But they've been getting all their work done," I assure him. "And all of them have been diligently darning their socks." Too late, I recall the Baroness's edict against this.

He watches me strangely.

"I didn't realize you were back," I admit. *Otherwise, I would have made sure they were seen to be studying.*

"I only returned this morning. I've been inspecting the grounds and meeting with various members of my staff." He takes the pipe from his mouth and steadies me with his gaze. "My meeting with the Baroness was particularly interesting."

I feel my face grow hot.

"You know, it usually takes our nannies several months to irritate her. But you seem to have accomplished it in only eight weeks."

I try to suppress the rising anger in my chest. "Because the Baroness is completely unreasonable!" I burst out.

His dark eyes widen. "She is following my orders."

"Then it's your orders that are unreasonable. Four children are racing around every morning searching for gloves and boots and hats. The last thing they want to remember are umbrellas, which only bend this way and that in the wind. They have to walk single file to school or else they'll be ankle-deep in mud. Yet all that's required are some sturdy *Wetterfleck*. And their gloves," I continue. "Those fancy leather things with all that fur trim and stitching—is it any wonder the Baroness gets cross when they lose them, which they absolutely will, as they're children. When all that's needed are some simple woolen mittens."

There seems to be amusement in the Captain's eyes. "Are you finished?"

"No," I say at the same time that I realize what's truly bothering me. "It's all very well for you to go off on your trips and leave these children to fend for themselves, but I can tell you that your presence is very much needed. By all of them."

The amusement in his eyes is replaced by concern. Even his voice sobers. "Then it will come as good news that I plan to be away much less frequently now."

"Oh." I'm so surprised by this that I can't think of anything else to say.

"Shall we go down and join everyone for dinner?" he suggests. "Or is there anything else?"

"No. Nothing else."

He replaces his pipe between his teeth and gestures for me to exit first. At the bottom of the stairs, we come to the painting of the table with its assortment of fruit and the Captain smirks. "Still not an admirer?"

"Not in the least," I say brutally.

"But the rest of my furnishings have been growing on you."

I turn to stare at him before we enter the dining room, wondering what he means.

"I've been told you liked my curtains so much you turned them into daywear." He leans forward and whispers, "I'm rather partial to the ones in my library, however. Perhaps you could see fit to leave those alone."

I'm mute with embarrassment for most of the meal, trying to remember how the curtains in the library look and wondering whether he was being sarcastic or serious. Then I hear him say something that catches my attention.

"I feel the time has come to host our Christmas party once again."

A cheer goes up in the dining room.

"When will it be?" Rupert asks.

"How about in two weeks?" he suggests, and I wonder about this change of heart. He seems happier, lighter even. It must be the joy he feels about getting married soon.

"Do you think we can sing for it?" Agathe asks. "Fräulein Maria has been teaching us Christmas songs. It would be wonderful."

"I don't see why not. That is, if Fräulein Maria approves of it."

Nine expectant faces turn toward me, and my heart warms. Nothing could make me happier. "Of course."

Excited chatter fills the room, with everyone suggesting different songs.

"Then it's decided," the Captain says. "A Christmas party in two weeks, and a concert by the von Trapp family, led by the illustrious Maria Kutschera."

"We will have to finish decorating," Johanna says.

"The house isn't finished?" The Captain is surprised.

Johanna laughs. "Not hardly! Fräulein Maria found the perfect place in the garden to pick holly berries, and our mantels need more spruce."

"And on that note," I speak up, "it's a week into Advent and I notice that your house has no Advent wreath. With your permission, I would like to have the children make one."

The Captain actually looks pleased. "Well, I don't see any problem with that."

"Yes, well . . ." I gather my courage to say something difficult. "The problem is not with the Advent wreath, Captain. It's where to hang it. Traditionally, the wreath is placed in the family room. But there isn't a family room in this house."

The Captain blinks slowly at me. "There are ninety-three rooms in this villa, Fräulein."

"That may be, but not one of them is a family room."

He remains perfectly still while the younger children snicker. From the look on his face, I might as well have told him his house was a dung heap. I smile. "It's no matter, Captain. I'm sure we'll find some place to put it."

The next week is so busy that on Sunday morning I nearly forget that I must leave and return to the convent. That afternoon, I sit in the silence of Nonnberg's dining hall, and for the first time in two years I have the feeling that I would rather be somewhere else. Namely, with the children, singing and decorating and preparing for Christmas.

I listen as the church bells ring one o'clock and hope the Baroness has remembered to give Martina her glass of milk before her nap. I imagine Agathe is snuggled up by the fire with a book while Rupert is studying for his exams. I think of the other children scampering around the house and suddenly feel lost without them. And it disturbs me that when they greet me at the door in the evening, I feel as if I'm coming home.

"Fräulein, you have to come and see!" Johanna says, dragging me inside.

"What?" I ask, laughing as she pulls me along.

"It's a surprise!" Rupert grins. He and Johanna take me by the hands. "Close your eyes," he instructs. They lead me to the door of the nursery, then shout together, "Surprise!"

The Advent wreath we've been working on all week, with a candle for each Sunday leading up to Christmas, is hanging suspended from the ceiling.

The Captain is standing there, grinning. "Your family room," he says quietly.

I'm so happy for the children that I blink back tears. "And I have something for you all," I say hurriedly so that no one will see how much this has affected me. "From the abbey," I tell them. I take a red Advent candle from my bag and place it on a side table. "We can begin our Advent reading now, if you like."

Johanna runs to fetch the Baroness and I wait in tense silence, wondering what she will make of all this. I see her eyes widen as she enters, taking in the scene: the Captain and the children together, along with the wreath, and finally, my tall red candle.

"We're hoping to do an Advent reading," I say, and I'm shocked when she smiles.

"I can't think of anything nicer, Fräulein."

While Rupert brings a chair for the Baroness and Agathe turns off the lights, I take a deep breath, enjoying the scents of spruce and pine. Then when everyone is seated, Mitzi hands me a match and I light our new candle. The flame dances cheerfully in the dim light of the room.

"We will start with Isaiah," I tell them, then begin to read, starting with, "The people who walked in darkness." When I look up, I see that the Captain is watching me intently, and the strangest warmth comes over me.

The party is to be held on the twentieth of December, and the children ask if they can spend the time between now and then adding more decorations to the villa and practicing Christmas songs. They've learned "Silent Night," "The Holly and the Ivy," "Jesus Refulsit Omnium," and "Good King Wenceslas." We practice until the children begin rehearsing their individual parts in their sleep, then we turn our attention to the decorating.

"Wait until Papa sees this!" Mitzi says, and I have to admit, it's a sight to behold, all the banisters garlanded with greenery, and the doors adorned with wreaths of fir and pine cones. An hour before the party is set to begin, I trim the candles and replace the water in the pretty jars of holly that have sprung up around the house. I'm replacing the final vase in the library when the Baroness appears. She's wearing a new gown of taffeta and lace and holding a long box tied up with blue ribbon.

"For you." There's a funny look on her face. "From the Captain."

I wipe my hands on my apron and frown. "Why?"

"I suspect it's his way of thanking you for leading the children in song tonight."

I lift the lid off the box and hold my breath. It's a beaded chiffon gown. I look at the Baroness. "But I'm not this fancy."

She chuckles. "It's only for one night, Fräulein. Try it on."

I hurry upstairs to change, and when I meet the Baroness in the library again, she gives a little gasp. "My goodness, Maria, you look like a film star."

I laugh self-consciously, because no one has said anything like that to me before. She admires the dropped waist with its elaborate beadwork, then the tiered chiffon, falling in gauzy layers to my calves. "But we must do something with your hair."

"Oh, no. It's fine—"

"Nonsense." She seats herself on the chaise. "Come."

I sit in front of her like an obedient child while she unfastens my plaits and sweeps my hair up into a chignon. Then she reaches into her beaded clutch for hairpins. When I catch my reflection in the round mirror above the Captain's desk, I don't even recognize the woman staring back. What would the Reverend Mother think if she could see me? Or Sister Rafaela? Suddenly I feel nervous, that I'm pretending to be something I'm not. "Who do you think will be coming?" I ask.

"Oh, all the important families in Salzburg, I suspect." The Baroness snaps her clutch shut and stands. "None of them have been invited to this villa before. The Captain moved here after Frau Agathe passed to the Lord, and since then there haven't been any parties."

Which makes it even more important that the singing go well. It's no wonder he doesn't want me in a dirndl.

Outside the library, the maids are rushing from room to room, lighting the candles. When the guests begin to arrive, I hurry to the nursery.

"Fräulein!" Agathe exclaims. Then all of the children gather around me, exclaiming at my dress. "Look at the beadwork," Agathe says.

"You look wonderful!" Johanna gushes.

"And look at all of you!" The children are dressed in matching outfits of red velvet and white lace. With their shiny black shoes, they look like porcelain dolls. Even Rupert, at his age, is adorable. I walk to the corner of the nursery, where Martina is playing with a small gnome family that she's created from leaves and sticks. I squat down and ask softly, "Are you ready to sing?"

She shrugs. "Will Johanna be singing?"

"I don't know. Shall we ask her?" I turn to find Johanna. Her pink cheeks are a stark contrast with her pale skin and dark curls. Such a beautiful child.

"Of course I'm singing!"

I reach for Martina's hand and pull her close. "Shall we peek at all the guests arriving?"

There's a flicker of interest in her eyes. I lead her to the window and the other children crowd behind us, watching as the cars crunch down the long gravel drive. It's fascinating to see the occupants who emerge, the men in their top hats and the women in their furs. Jewels wink in the flickering light of the gas lamps lining the drive, and I catch one woman briefly adjusting her diamond tiara.

"My goodness. Such a parade," I say, when what I'm really thinking is, *I don't belong here.*

"That's enough staring," the Baroness says from behind,

and I flush, as if I've been caught doing something illicit. "Fräulein, the Captain has a few people he would like you to meet."

I glance down at Martina. "But I thought I'd be watching the children—"

"It's just a few introductions," she says, guiding me away. "I'll stay in the nursery until you return."

My heart races as I make my way down the stairs. Who could he possibly want me to meet? Perhaps there's a priest here, I think. Or an abbess. I'm searching the crowds for familiar black robes when someone calls my name.

"Maria?" The Captain is standing in the center of a small group, dressed in a black tuxedo with silk lapels and pants with satin stripes down the sides. I've seen few men who fill out a suit the way he does, with his wide shoulders and narrow waist. His eyes linger on mine for a moment, then travel down to my dress.

"You look . . . stunning." His voice is quiet, as if he's not sure he should be saying this to me.

I feel hot with pleasure, but of course that's just vanity, and I know I should banish the feeling. "Thank you, Captain."

He holds my gaze, as if there's something more he wants to say, then he seems to remember that he's among a crowd. "Maria, I'd like you to meet the Hofmanns," he says. "They're our neighbors, and were instrumental in helping me find the Baroness."

Herr Hofmann extends his hand first, then his wife. They both have such startlingly blue eyes that it would be easy to mistake them for brother and sister.

"Pleased to meet you," I say, feeling as if I should curtsy.

The Captain looks more cheerful than I've seen him look

since my arrival at the villa. "The Hofmanns have children the same age as Rupert and Agathe."

"How lovely."

He moves on to a second couple. "And these are the Strassers."

Both husband and wife extend their hands. They are younger than the Hofmanns, probably closer to the Captain's age. The woman's expression is guarded, and I'm sure she's wondering why she's being introduced to a governess. I wait for the explanation myself, but none is forthcoming.

"The Captain tells us that you come from the hills," she says, fingering the fat string of pearls around her neck. I have no pearls. Even the clip in my hair is borrowed from the Baroness. "Would that be Hallstatt or St. Gilgen?" she asks.

"Tyrol." I smile, refusing to feel any less for this. "And which palace do you come from?" I ask.

The woman laughs. "Oh, we don't have a palace." She glances at her husband. "But we have been shopping for a villa."

"Really? Is that like shopping for a dress?"

The Captain clears his throat. "If you're in the market," he intervenes, "I've heard the Grubers are selling theirs."

"Is that right?" The husband appears interested. But Frau Strasser is watching me.

"I should go," I say. "The children . . ."

There's something unreadable in the Captain's expression. But he nods politely. "Of course."

"A real pleasure to meet you," Herr Strasser says warmly. His wife gives me a tight smile.

It's only after I return to the nursery that I can breathe again. Why did I think, even for a moment, that this family was beginning to feel like my own? I could never be an aristocrat, and I could certainly never understand their petty concerns.

The children are playing cards and look up when they see me.

"So what did Papa want?" Johanna asks. She's the loudest of the bunch, and also the most forward.

"Well, he introduced me to some of your neighbors." I smile, trying to look pleased. "The Hofmanns and the Strassers, I believe." But I can see the question on Rupert's face, so I continue. "Perhaps he wants me to arrange an outing with you and their children."

"But their children go to boarding schools," Rupert says.

"Well." The Baroness rises from the couch. "I'm sure the Captain had his reasons," she says swiftly. She smiles at me, and the gesture seems warmer than usual.

Later that evening, the children perform as if they've been doing it for years, their young voices rising and falling for nearly twenty minutes. I join them in the soprano part of the songs. It feels wonderful to sing together, and we finish with an a cappella rendition of "Silent Night."

When the children take their bows, the applause sounds deafening, filling the parlor as husbands and wives exchange looks of delight. I can see they agree with me that the Captain's children possess truly beautiful voices, and in their matching velvet outfits they look like an old Christmas painting brought to life.

"That was wonderful," the Captain says earnestly. "The nuns were right, Maria. You have a gift."

Next to the Captain, Herr Strasser looks deeply confused.

"Did you say this woman is a nun?" he asks.

"Not yet," the Captain replies quietly.

"But I plan to take my vows in six months," I tell him.

Herr Strasser turns a questioning gaze in my direction. "And that's truly what you want? To become a *nun*?"

"Oh, yes," I say vehemently. "More than anything in this world."

A look passes between Herr Strasser and the Captain that I can't decipher. But later, when I step into the courtyard for fresh air, I realize that the Captain has followed me outside.

"It's warm in there, isn't it?" he asks, coming to stand beside me at the edge of the flagstones.

"I enjoy parties, but sometimes all that conversation and pretense . . . it can all be a bit overwhelming."

"Yes. Not everyone is as grounded as you." A silence falls between us before the Captain gathers his breath to continue. "So is it true? Do you really wish to become a nun?"

"Of course," I say. What's the matter with everyone? And then it finally occurs to me. He doesn't wish to look for another governess. "I am here on loan to you, Captain. And while I love your children fiercely"—and this is the truth— "nothing will stop me from taking my vows. So I suggest you start searching for my replacement."

There is hurt on his face, but what does he expect? Waiting for me in Nonnberg is a home that will never cast me out. The women there will be my family, with the Reverend Mother watching over us all. He nods silently and leaves, but I look up at the yellow moon and feel a sudden surge of hope. Only six more months. Anyone can survive six months.

CHAPTER ELEVEN

THE DAYS LEADING UP to Christmas are magical. At a dozen different tables in the Captain's workshop, the children spend their time making presents for one another. Johanna is using sticks and moss to build furniture for Martina's gnomes and Rupert is carving elaborate jewelry boxes for his sisters. Werner, who is twelve and can handle a knife almost as well as his brother, is making each of his siblings a race car. My present to each member of the family will be rosaries carved from the olive wood near Nonnberg. But the Captain's gifts are more elaborate. He leaves every morning and returns in the evenings with dozens of beautifully wrapped boxes.

On Holy Eve we melt the red candles into their holders and clamp them onto branches of a giant tree, which towers twenty feet high in the center of the family room. When we're finished, it's a sight to behold. The tree is decorated with balls of marzipan, candies, cookies, and puffy balls of meringue we call *Spanischer Wind*. A hundred and twenty candles flicker between the tinsel, gilding the tangerines and *Lebkuchen*.

In anticipation of the Holy Child's arrival with gifts and chocolates, the children have been singing "Morgen, Kinder, Wird's Was Geben" all day, and the youngest ones continue to hum it as we crunch our way over the snow toward the church. Holy Eve is always the most beautiful night of the year, and when I catch the Captain looking at me, I know it's because he can see how happy this evening makes me. The candles and the singing and the story of hope that Jesus's birth has brought to us all. He's still looking at me as we make our way home under the glow of the streetlamps. Finally, he asks if I've had a good night.

"There's something magical about Holy Eve," I tell him, looking up. A scattering of stars spreads across the cold sky, as clear and crisp as slivers of ice. "How did you celebrate when you were at sea?"

He looks terribly handsome in his red scarf and wool coat. I can see where Johanna gets her arresting features. "With letters," he says sadly. "War is mostly about stopping things. Holidays, lives . . ." He looks down, digging his hands deeper into his pockets, so I try to change the mood by thanking him for allowing me to be a part of his family over such a magical time.

"We didn't sing or buy presents when I was a little girl," I tell him. "All of this is new to me."

"Then what did you do?"

"Decorate the house with spruce." I shrug. "Then go to church, if my uncle let us."

The Captain looks sorrowful. "You had a hard life," he observes.

I bristle. I don't want him feeling pity for me. "It made me strong."

Johanna slips her hand into mine and my shoulders relax. When we return to the villa, the rooms smell like cinnamon.

"*Zimtsterne!*" the children exclaim, and the cook brings out warm plates of star-shaped cookies with frosting. We stand beneath the Advent wreath as it flickers with all four lighted candles, and I think how nothing could be more perfect.

The next morning I'm startled awake by the sound of feet pounding down the stairs, then laughter and whoops of joy. "Fräulein, Fräulein!" Johanna and Mitzi are pounding at my door. "You have to come see this!"

Of course I saw it last night, when I helped the Captain and the Baroness arrange the gifts under the tree, but now I act surprised at the dozens of packages that the Holy Child has managed to bring in the space of one night.

There is so much joy. Even Martina is laughing. There is an electric railroad for Werner, a baby doll and pram for Martina. There are musical instruments for each of the children, BB guns for the boys, even Victrolas for Agathe and Rupert. I lose track of the number of books I see, and there are skates for everyone. Rupert has been given a new pair of skis and Mitzi a larger violin. Hedwig has received the beautiful red sled she'd been longing for, and the Baroness Matilda has a new set of pearls.

The children promise to treasure the rosaries I've carved for them, and I promise to always keep with me the drawings they've made. Then someone hands me a small gift in a long wooden box that makes me nervous. I've already opened up presents from all the children.

"From Papa," Agathe says eagerly.

I glance at the Captain, who just smiles softly and nods. The box is carved with edelweiss and Agathe offers, "Werner made it."

"But not what's inside it!" Werner adds swiftly.

I open the lid. Inside, on a strip of light blue silk, is a pair of pearl earrings. My hands shake as I lift the two large drops, and the room goes silent in appreciation of their beauty. "They're magnificent," I gush, knowing that everyone is waiting for some response. "But where will I wear them?"

The Captain laughs. "How about right here?"

I clip them on and the children are all full of admiration.

"And lastly, a gift to each of you from Maria," the Captain says. He takes out seven identical parcels from under the tree, each wrapped with a giant red bow. I'm about to protest that I've never seen these gifts when I catch the Captain grinning. As the children tear into the packages, I gasp.

"*Wetterfleck!*" I cry. I glance at the Baroness to see what her reaction to this might be. To my surprise, she looks amused.

That evening, I find the Captain sitting on the floor of the library, reading to his children from the Bible. I seat myself on the small chair near the fire and think of all the times the Baroness chastised me for allowing the girls to sit cross-legged on the floor. So all of those restrictions hadn't come from the Captain. They were simply old-fashioned rules imposed by the Baroness.

The room is so warm and delightful that even after the

reading has ended and I have put the children to bed, I return to the library. The Captain is still there, reading by the fire.

"The earrings look beautiful on you," he says when I re-appear.

I'm sure that I'm blushing. "Thank you for them. They're the most useless, exquisite gift I've ever been given."

He laughs. "Well, the children have never been happier since you've been here. It's the first time we've felt like a family since Agathe died, and you are the reason."

But I know where this is headed and I'm not having it. Not even on Christmas. "I'm not staying, Captain."

He holds my gaze. "But we would have you forever, if you'd like."

No. There is no such thing as forever. Someday soon the children will grow up and not need a governess. But I don't say these things, because of course no one wishes to imagine a time when their children have all left.

"Maria, what I'm trying to say is," he continues, "*I* would have you forever." His dark eyes are full of meaning, but I'm too set on my path to understand what he's saying.

"Captain, I love your family dearly. But my resolve is firm—I return to Nonnberg in August."

There is hurt in his gaze, but I am genuinely relieved when he doesn't mention it again. We spend the rest of the children's holiday hiking the Untersberg and skating on the lake. When it's almost time for classes to start again, Mitzi and Johanna prepare to join them. Only Martina will remain behind with me. You see, I think, I was right to imagine a time when I wouldn't be needed. And soon the Captain will be married to his princess and she'll be the one to take on this role.

We're all so busy that I don't give another thought to the future until the very last day of the children's holiday. We are sitting at breakfast when the Captain looks up from his pile of mail to make an announcement.

"It seems that the Princess Yvonne is coming."

His face doesn't betray any emotion, and he doesn't seem to me like a man in love. But then I've never been in love, so what would I know?

"What interesting timing," the Baroness says, raising her brows. "It's been years since the two of you were first engaged. And now she's finally moving it along and deciding to meet the children. I wonder why."

The Captain averts his gaze. "Yes, well—"

"And what if we don't want to meet her?" Johanna exclaims.

Mitzi puts down her fork. "Are you still going to marry her?"

"That has always been the plan," the Captain says quietly.

"But what do we need her for?" Johanna pushes away a plate full of sausage. "We have Maria."

The Captain turns red and my heart begins to race, imagining this princess taking my place. But it *isn't* my place. My place is in Nonnberg.

"Well, I won't be coming out of my room," Martina threatens, putting down her fork with a terrible clank.

"Now, that's no way to treat a guest," I say, although a part of me—a very secret part—is glad no one wants this woman. "I am sure the princess is very kind."

"Yes." The Captain smiles briefly. "And when she comes next weekend, children, you are to call her Aunt Yvonne."

I catch the look that Agathe passes to Rupert, and a panic

wells up inside me. For several moments, I can't understand what I'm feeling. It must be my concern about returning to the convent. If the children don't take to the princess, they'll want me to stay longer, and how will I be able to tell them no?

For the next week I make Princess Yvonne the subject of all our conversations. When we sing, I tell them how much the princess will appreciate it. When we walk to and from school, I tell them it's possible that she will love walking with them, too. And when we sit in the library and read at night, I ask them which stories they think she'll read aloud to them.

Then suddenly it's Saturday morning and the princess's car pulls up the drive. Everyone crowds the large window upstairs and I hold my breath. The children are dressed in their blue-and-white sailor's outfits, with satin hair ribbons for the girls and caps for the boys. I'm wearing my favorite dirndl and the Captain's pearl earrings. This is it. This is the woman who will become their mother. For reasons I can't explain I feel nervous. Possibly even a little sick. But I have no right to this feeling. Certainly I've enjoyed the Captain's easy banter and many kindnesses to me. But that was only natural— a desire to know that I am doing my job well. And of course it's logical to feel nervous about meeting the woman who will become a mother to these children I've come to love so much.

Below, a man in a black suit and cap hurries from the driver's side to open the car door. And the woman who steps out takes my breath away.

"Look at her dress," Agathe whispers.

"And her earrings!" Hedwig comments, pressing closer to the glass.

You can see the diamonds sparkling even from up here. How does she plan to sit on the floor with the children in such a tight dress? And I certainly hope that in one of her giant trunks she's remembered to pack some sturdy boots.

I watch as she offers the Captain her gloved hand and he raises it to his lips. It's not rational that I should have such an instant dislike for her. Then suddenly she looks up and our eyes meet, and I feel certain she knows exactly what I'm thinking.

"All right," I say swiftly, moving everyone back from the window. "Are you ready?"

"What if we don't like her?" Johanna asks again.

I straighten the large blue bow in her hair and swallow my fear. I know what it is to have a new family member suddenly appear. I was just her age when my father came back. "She'll be lovely," I promise.

But Johanna's lip trembles. With her dark curls, she looks just like a little doll. "What if she's not?"

I squeeze her hand to stop her from crying. "I'll be right here."

"But now you're going to leave us!" Johanna exclaims.

"Not for another six months," I say. "That is a *long* time from now."

She buries her face in my skirt. "But I don't understand. Why can't you stay?"

"Yes, why can't you stay?" Hedwig asks.

All seven children are looking at me, and my eyes begin to burn. "Come." I blink quickly. "We don't want to keep the princess waiting."

We descend the stairs and there she is, dressed in a long

beaded gown as if she's going to the opera. Her gold hair is swept up into a fancy swirl at the top of her head, and her green eyes are ringed by dark lashes. She's beautiful in the way that women are in films.

The children line up in a perfect row, and the Captain says proudly, "My children. Rupert, Agathe, Mitzi, Werner, Hedwig, Johanna, and Martina."

"How do you do?" they say in unison, and the princess's hand hovers over her chest.

"Oh, those outfits." She pats her heart theatrically. "How charming."

The Captain turns to me and his eyes seem to linger on mine. "And this is our governess, Maria."

The princess's hand drops to her side. "So you're the woman I've heard so much about."

I don't know how to respond to this, but Agathe exclaims, "Fräulein Maria taught us how to play volleyball."

"And she takes us on hikes!" Johanna pipes up.

The princess looks at the Captain for confirmation.

"It's true. She's turned them into a pack of wild roughnecks." He's grinning when he says this, but the princess stiffens and I notice a small furrow appear between the Captain's brows. "Aunt Yvonne will be staying with us for the weekend," he continues. "I expect you will give her our warmest welcome." He tries for a smile, and I wonder if I'm the only one who sees that it doesn't reach his eyes.

"Shall we show her the grounds?" Johanna asks.

The princess looks alarmed. "You mean, walk outside?"

"Well, perhaps not in that dress," the Captain says. "But I'm sure you've brought something else."

"Yes," she says flatly. "I'll go and change."

It gives me a selfish thrill that I don't have to do any such thing, and we all wait in the library while the princess finds something more appropriate to wear. I wonder what it'll be.

"It's muddy outside. Do you think she owns rubber boots?" Rupert worries.

"She can't see our winter cherry blossom in those high heels," Hedwig says.

The Captain looks uncomfortable, so I quickly suggest, "Why don't we read?"

"*One Thousand and One Nights!*" Werner exclaims. We're almost at the end. It's been one of their favorites.

We begin to read, and toward the end of the last story the princess reappears. She's wearing a much more sensible outfit. A khaki blouse and pants, with black knee-high boots. A neat green scarf is tied around her hair, and there's a matching green belt at her waist. She's perfect. I stop reading as she perches on the edge of the settee.

"We're almost at the end," I tell her. "Would you like to finish?"

"Oh, no. I don't enjoy reading very much."

I shut the book and look at the Captain, hoping my eyes convey exactly what I'm thinking. With thousands of eligible women in Austria, he'll be scraping the bottom of the matrimonial barrel if he goes through with an engagement to this woman. "Another time then." When the children groan, I remind them, "We'll finish it later. You have a tour to give!"

Everyone becomes excited about this, even the princess. She is viewing her future estate, after all, with its sweeping gardens and beautiful orchards.

The princess is given the same tour that I was given three months ago, but while the children try to point out their favorite bushes and trees, she's more interested in the fields closest to the house. "Oh, wouldn't that area make the most wonderful conservatory?" she asks the Captain, adding on to property that isn't even hers yet. "There's just so much potential here. So much potential."

It's a long afternoon. The princess isn't curious at all about our hikes up the Untersberg and has no interest in volleyball, biking, or even gardening. On our return to the house, Agathe stops at the end of the gravel path and finally asks, "So what do you enjoy doing in your spare time?"

"Spare time?" The princess tilts her head and smiles. "My dear, there's no spare time when you're hosting parties."

But the Captain likes to sit in his library and read in the evenings. What will they do together? I wonder. How will they carry on?

When we return to the villa, the Baroness instructs the children to go to their rooms and rest. I'm preparing to join them when the princess stops me on the stairs.

"Maria, why don't you come up to my room," she suggests. "I would love to chat."

The Captain stops to look at us, and as his gaze meets mine, I'm struck once again by just how handsome he is. His dark hair falls in waves to the collar of his shirt, and he must be one of the most eligible bachelors in Austria, with a passion for music, reading, and the military. Yet soon he'll be marrying a woman who wants to spend her time decorating and entertaining. I narrow my eyes so he knows just how terrible this arrangement will be, and when I turn to make my way up the stairs, I can see the princess trying to decode the secret message between us.

I follow her down the hall, determined to make her understand what this family will need after I'm gone. I'm composing the list in my head when she stops in front of her room and turns.

"Remind me of how old you are again." The princess is smiling, but I sense danger in the question.

"I'll be twenty-two next week."

She nods thoughtfully as she opens her door. Inside, the room is filled with hatboxes and open trunks. A silk dressing gown is tossed carelessly across the settee and a pair of cream slippers lies next to the wardrobe. "Please, sit down." She perches on the edge of her bed and indicates the wingchair near the window. Then we stare at each other for several moments. I guess her age to be about twenty-five. "The children really like you, don't they?" she asks.

"I certainly hope so. They're wonderful children."

"There are just so many of them, aren't there?" She laughs.

"Seven," I say flatly.

"Yes, I can hardly keep them straight. Agathe and Rudolph—"

"Rupert," I correct.

She waves a manicured hand through the air. "I don't know how he does it. So many people in one house."

"I think it's lovely."

She stares at me as if I've just spoken some other language. "Well, I suppose the children needed some comforting after losing their mother. But it's time they begin acting civilized. Those little girls running through the gardens, telling me they dress in trousers when they're playing."

I can feel an intense burning beginning in my chest. "And what's wrong with trousers? I made them for the girls myself."

"My dear, little girls belong in dresses. No matter. Their new schools will sort them out."

I lean forward in my chair, and the scent of her perfume is overwhelming. "What do you mean?"

"Boarding schools," she says, as if it's obvious. "The Jesuit School for the boys and the Sacre Coeur for the girls. Oh, it won't happen immediately. First Georg has to *officially* announce our engagement. Then we'll be married in June, and after that we'll be off on our honeymoon."

The burning sensation turns into a fire. "Without the children?"

"Couples don't take children on their honeymoons, do they, darling?" She laughs again, because everything I say is just so amusing. "They can go off to their schools when we return." She reaches over for a long black box on her nightstand and snaps it open. Inside is a cigarette holder. "I'm guessing you don't smoke?"

"No."

"Shame." She twists a cigarette inside the holder and lights it. "No drinking either?"

I place my palms flat against my knees to keep myself from leaving. "I take my vows in August. Certainly no drinking."

"Well, you really are an enigma, aren't you, Maria?" She takes a deep drag of her cigarette and exhales. "Preparing to become a nun in just a few short months. Yet here you are, leading the Captain to believe that you're in love with him. And the problem is that now he's in love with you."

I'm so shocked that I rise in anger. "That isn't true!"

The princess doesn't move from the edge of the bed. "Oh,

yes, he believes he's in love with you. Georg has practically told me as much."

Thoughts—sudden and confused—begin coming too fast. Everything I had wanted to say to her is gone, replaced by fear. What would the abbey do if they came to hear of this? Who would they believe?

"Of course, this doesn't make any difference to me." She exhales. "All of Salzburg knows he's about to announce our marriage, so he will have to go through with it. But—"

"I must leave." I move toward the door and she hurries to block my exit.

"Where are you going?" There's panic in her eyes.

"To pack. If what you say is true, then I can't stay here a moment longer."

"You must!" Her breath is coming quickly. "If you leave, he'll think you're jealous," she warns. "It will only fan the flames."

"You said I led him to this when I've never done any such thing. Which means that merely my presence—"

"You *have* to stay!" she exclaims.

"No." I maneuver around her and open the door. I catch Johanna on the landing outside, her eyes big. "Aren't you supposed to be resting?" I demand.

She nods silently, then hurries back off to the nursery.

In my room, I can't pack fast enough. My hands are shaking. There can be no goodbyes. Everyone will want to know why I'm leaving. And then they'll try to persuade me to stay. For the next thirty minutes I force everything I own into the old bag that I came with. The jewelry box Rupert made me, all the drawings from the children, my sack dress from the abbey. I hesitate over the beautiful box with the pearl ear-rings. Soon the Captain will be giving gifts like this to the princess. The idea of it makes me feel sick, though I have no idea why.

I leave the earrings in the wardrobe. I'll have no use for them in Nonnberg. But then I imagine him finding them here when I leave and my heart aches. How could he be in love with me when he knows I'm to become a Bride of Christ? I imagine how disappointed my sisters would be to hear I wanted to marry after they'd welcomed me into their hearts and home. But then I also think of the way the Captain looked at me on the stairs and how he watches me in the li-brary when I'm reading to the children, and my chest hurts again.

I'm wiping away tears when there's a knock at the door. I ignore it, but the knock comes again and then the door opens.

"I have someone who wishes to speak with you," the prin-cess says swiftly.

I stiffen.

"My priest is coming," she says. "He happens to be in Salz-burg and I've gone to him before in times of great stress. I'm hoping he can counsel you now."

A priest. And he's coming to see me. I pat my cheeks dry and smooth my dirndl, then follow her down the stairs to the library. "The Captain—"

"Don't worry about Georg. I've told him I invited Father Huber as a matter of courtesy. Since I'm in the area."

When we reach the library the priest is already there, dressed in long robes and talking to the Captain. Both men pause as soon as we enter, but when the Captain searches my face I look away. He is above my class in every way, but when I imagine him taking my hands in his, heat warms my cheeks. How could I ever betray my sisters that way? To say nothing of the princess.

The small talk between the Captain and the priest seems to go on forever before Hans arrives with some urgent matter and takes the Captain away.

"If you will all excuse me," he says.

I wait until the doors swing shut before blurting out, "I'm sorry. I can't stay here."

"Please, just take a seat," the priest suggests.

All three of us sit in the Captain's favorite room. I can smell the tobacco he keeps in his top drawer for his pipe, and the sound of the fire snapping and crackling reminds me of evenings he and the children and I spent together in here that are now over.

"The princess tells me there seems to be a problem," the priest begins.

Outside, it's beginning to snow. It will be a cold walk to the bus stop and then on to Nonnberg, but I've certainly braved worse. "I'm afraid I cannot stay," I repent.

His old face is kindly. "And why is that?"

The princess explains the situation and Father Huber nods in understanding.

"It seems this family is in great need of your help, Fräulein Maria. And while it may be true that the Baron has developed warm feelings toward you, I suspect these flames can be extinguished by simply avoiding him."

"You wish for me to live here and *avoid* the Captain?" I ask, disbelieving.

"As much as possible." The old priest shrugs. "Yes. And

once it is clear to him that you do not return his feelings, the matter will be put to rest."

"Oh, no." I shake my head firmly. "No. I will leave."

"You can't leave!" the princess exclaims. "That would only increase his interest in you."

The priest is nodding in agreement.

"The wedding will happen in June," the princess says swiftly. "It's only a matter of avoiding him for a few short months."

"And then what?" I challenge. "I stay with the children while you leave on your honeymoon?"

"If you wish."

"And shall I prepare them for boarding school while you are away or will you be doing that yourself?"

The priest lowers his brows, unsure where this anger is coming from. "Fräulein—"

"Don't bother," I interrupt. "I will stay only because that is what's right for the children. But I will never be the one to tell them they're going to be sent away. *Never.*"

"Oh, Maria." The princess smiles sweetly at me, as if I'm the youngest, most foolish child in the world. "This is simply what noble families do."

I look at the priest. "It was a pleasure to meet you," I tell him. Then I turn my back on them both and hurry up the stairs. The Baroness stops me before I enter my room.

"Maria, what's the matter?"

I can't speak. I can't even see through the veil of my tears. She steers me by the shoulder to her room and shuts the door. When I'm finished telling her, the Baroness's face is stern.

MARIA
143

"Don't worry about how the Captain feels," the Baroness says. "Think about how you feel. What do *you* want?"

"I want the children to be happy!" I exclaim. "That woman will take all their happiness away."

"But what did you think would happen?" the Baroness asks. "You let the children run wild."

"I let them *live*!"

"And you didn't think there would be consequences? They are in for a very hard road with the princess," she predicts. "They'll be forced now to unlearn everything you've taught them."

No more cozy nights in the library, no more singing, no more hikes in the mountains. They won't even be together once they're shipped off to their schools. Even tiny Martina will be sent to the Sacre Coeur. When I think of how much kindness she needs, and how devastated she'll be to leave behind her little gnomes, my eyes well with tears all over again.

The Baroness thins her lips into a disapproving line. "There's nothing to be done," she says stoically. "This is how children have been raised for hundreds of years."

"That doesn't make it right," I whisper.

But her eyes say what she will not. That she had warned me.

CHAPTER TWELVE

W HEN THE PRINCESS RETURNS to her castle in Graz at
the end of January, an uneasy tension settles over the
house. We still sit together in the library at night, and the
children still ask me to teach them new songs when they
come home from school. But now, whenever the Captain
asks to join us, I'm forced to excuse myself.

"Don't you like it when Papa plays volleyball with us?"
Agathe asks one rainy evening several months after the visit.

I keep braiding her hair. "Of course I do."

"Then why do you always excuse yourself?"

I let the braid fall through my hands and she turns to face
me. I'm glad it's just the two of us in her pink and white room,
so there's no one else to see me blush. "You know I leave for
the convent in August," I tell her. "In a few months I won't be
the one playing with you anymore. I want you to become
used to playing with your father."

But Agathe is fourteen and can see through this. "No one will be playing anything if you leave. Aunt Yvonne will send us all to boarding schools."

I lower my voice. Outside her window the rain is falling, turning the grounds sodden. No volleyball tomorrow. "Does your father know?"

"Rupert asked him and he promised we're not going anywhere. But what if she changes his mind?"

This is my worry, too, but I don't let Agathe see this. "Your father was one of the first submarine captains in history. Do you really think he's so easily led?"

She doesn't answer. "I don't understand why you won't stay. Don't you like us?"

I swallow the rising pain in my throat. "Of course. More than you know, Agathe."

"Then why won't you stay?" Her dark eyes are wide and glassy with tears.

"Because your father is getting married and there can't be two young women in the house."

"Then he can marry *you* instead!"

My cheeks are on fire. I'm sure of it. "I think my sisters at Nonnberg would be very surprised to hear of me getting married." I smile uneasily and rise, refusing to examine the pain in my chest. Because if I think of myself actually marrying the Captain . . . I simply can't. My stomach tenses and I immediately push the thought away. "It will all work out," I promise. "You'll see."

And I believe this. Something has changed since the princess's visit. Over the ensuing months the Captain hasn't left on a single trip. Instead, he spends his time in his library, writing a book about his experiences in the navy. He also accompanies us on hikes when the weather is good, making a point of joining us once we've already left and it's too late for me to turn back. At the end of May I take the children up the Untersberg and am admiring the view when the Captain comes over to stand beside me.

"I'm going to miss these days," he says quietly.

I study his profile etched against the red glow of the setting sun—the curve of his forehead, the strong line of his nose, his chin. "And where do you think this is going?" I laugh uneasily. "The mountain will still be here."

"Yes. The mountain will be."

When I catch his meaning, I hurry to excuse myself. I must never allow myself to think about marriage. It would be a betrayal to the women who sent me here. But the thoughts creep up anyway. Silly things, like when I'm combing my hair, I wonder how it would be to share a bathroom with the Captain, his razors and brushes crowding the sink. Over lunch, I imagine the feeling of waiting for a husband to join me in the dining room. But this is not my destiny. I have given my promise to God.

That evening the Captain makes an announcement over dinner. "I shall be leaving for Graz tomorrow," he says, and the entire room falls silent.

I stare down at my plate of *rouladen* with gravy, but don't feel hungry. Not even for the dumpling or *blaukraut*.

"Are you going to see Aunt Yvonne?" Hedwig asks.

I glance up.

"Yes," the Captain says, briefly meeting my gaze.

I feel queasy. But this has always been the plan. The very first day I arrived at the villa, the Baroness told me that this marriage would take place. So why is the Baroness suddenly fidgeting with her napkin? And why do I feel as if I'm going to be sick?

No one speaks. For a moment, the children don't even move. Finally, I break the silence. "Well, why don't I teach you all a traditional wedding song after dinner," I suggest, trying to brighten the mood, but the words feel dry in my mouth. And no one is enthusiastic. Least of all me.

It is a long two weeks. Every car that rolls up the drive could be his, and I find myself lingering at the windows more than I ever have before. On the last Saturday in May, Johanna is the first to spot him coming up the drive. "Papa's back!" she cries out. "His car is here!"

All seven children hurry to the door to see him inside, but there's a strange look about him, and he doesn't seem like a man who's just made the happiest decision of his life. After hugging each of the children, he retreats to his library without a glance in my direction. He's silent at dinner, then again at breakfast the next day.

"What the matter with Papa?" Agathe asks while we're playing volleyball after school. "He hasn't seemed himself since he returned."

"Maybe he's not feeling well," Mitzi worries.

"Or maybe he doesn't love us anymore," Martina says.

"My goodness." What goes on in Martina's mind? "Of course he loves you!"

"Then why does he stay in his library all day now?" she asks, her voice nearly as small as she is.

I don't have an answer. He's hardly looked in my direction since coming back.

"Well, why don't we go and ask him?" Johanna suggests.

"Yes, we should ask him," Werner agrees.

And so the children rush inside like a pack of wolves while I return the volleyball to the hall cupboard and try not to worry. I make myself tea and am settling into a comfortable chair in the family room when the hallway becomes filled with the sound of stampeding feet. Johanna bursts through the door, followed by all the children, and suddenly they are talking at once.

I put down the tea and raise my hands. "One at a time!"

Werner inhales and then exhales a response. "It's because he's decided not to marry Aunt Yvonne after all!"

I gasp, unable to help myself.

"But that's not what Papa is sad about!" Johanna exclaims. "He's sad because he's not sure whether you truly like him."

I'm shocked. "Well, of course I *like* him." When have I ever . . . Then I think of all the times I've brushed him aside recently or excused myself from the room the moment he's entered, and my cheeks feel warm. I can't believe he called off the engagement. He's not marrying the princess after all. And the children won't be going away! I'm overwhelmed by the news, but I'm not quite sure why.

"So you like him?" Mitzi asks. "Do you really like him?"

"Of course, Mitzi. Your father is a wonderful man."

The whole pack of them goes running back to the library, then there's the strangest silence in the house. Suddenly, the Captain is standing in the doorway, staring at me. He crosses the room and takes my hand.

"You have no idea how happy you've just made me."

I rise from the chair. "What do you mean?" What *does* he mean?

"The children said you accepted my marriage proposal." There's so much joy in his face, and now the children are crowded around the family room door with so much joy on their faces that I burst into tears.

"Are you really going to be our mother?" Mitzi asks.

"We have a mother!" Johanna says, hugging me fiercely.

"That's wonderful news," Rupert says. "Truly. Congratulations."

"But the abbey—" I'm panicking.

The Captain takes both of my hands in his, and it feels as if my entire body is on fire. "Why don't you go and ask them," he says tenderly. He is standing so close that I can smell the scent of tobacco on his suit.

I can't breathe. There's too much happening. "I should do it now," I tell him, and hurry up the stairs to my room. I just need to be alone.

"Can I help you pack?" Mitzi asks, coming in and sitting next to me on the edge of my bed.

Her face is so bright with happiness that it crushes my heart. How can she understand that I've given my promise to God? That He'll never forgive me if I turn my back on Him in order to marry? Perhaps the Reverend Mother will come back here to explain. "Oh, there isn't much to pack," I say distractedly. "Just a shawl and a—"

Suddenly, she leans forward and wraps her arms around my neck. "Now you'll never ever leave us," she blurts out. Tears are streaming down her cheeks, and tears are on my cheeks, too. I love these children so much. And this home. But I've never truly dared to imagine loving the Captain. He's always belonged to the princess.

In the hall, the Baroness is waiting. Her look is stern, and from the velvet choker around her neck to her beaded dress, she's dressed entirely in black. She approaches me swiftly, then her face breaks into a smile. "I couldn't have imagined a better ending!" she exclaims, and I wonder what has brought her around to this. Perhaps she feels that anything is better than having to tolerate that princess.

"But the nuns won't allow—"

"Well, of course they will." She laughs. "It's an abbey, not a prison."

"But I gave God my word."

The Baroness smiles warmly, touching my shoulder. "I suspect He'll understand."

It's the longest trip to Nonnberg I ever make. I have no idea how many people I pass on the street. And no memory at all of taking the bus from Aigen to the center of Salzburg. I approach the familiar stone steps leading up to the abbey and it's as if there are two Marias inside of me. One desperate to return to Nonnberg where the world is predictable and safe. Then another Maria who isn't afraid to stumble into things she knows nothing about—marriage, nobility, motherhood. And then, of course, there's the matter of the Captain . . .

I begin the climb and recall the way his dark eyes searched mine on the mountaintop before he left for Graz. What did he tell the princess? Was she angry? The thought of him marrying her had made me sick with dread. But the thought of marrying him myself makes me feel—*what*?

I imagine the Captain clasping his hand over mine again and my heart races. There's desire there, but mostly there's fear. I don't know how to be a wife. Anni kept away from Franz at every opportunity. He was a monster. I don't know how women behave with men they might love. And what of my vows? What of the women who were going to become sisters to me? And my Reverend Mother?

I think of leaving another family and tears burn their way down my cheeks. When I reach the gates, Frau Rafaela sees my face and stops polishing the bars.

"Maria!" She drops her rag. "What's happened?" She takes me by the shoulders. "Why are you here?"

"I need to speak with the Reverend Mother," I say. "At once."

CHAPTER THIRTEEN

FRAN

September 1959

FRAN STOPS IN HER tracks, standing beneath a cherry tree in Central Park. She simply can't believe it. "So all of that was *real*? He changed his mind about marrying a princess?"

"Yes," Maria says. "He did. But why does the script call her a Baroness?"

Fran shakes her head. She doesn't know. She looks out over the reservoir toward the skyline and frowns. Wouldn't it have been more glamorous to call Yvonne a princess? Perhaps they're trying to protect her identity, she thinks, and offers this line of reasoning to Maria.

"Perhaps," Maria huffs, and they continue to walk.

"How much more time do you have in the city?" Fran asks. "Can we meet tomorrow?" Suddenly, it isn't enough that she read Maria's autobiography last night. She wants to hear all of it from Maria herself.

"Same time, same bench," Maria jokes. "Bring those sensible shoes again."

At the office, everyone is headed to lunch.

"You coming?" Jack asks.

It's Thursday, and the lunch counter at Woolworths will have the best baked ham and cheese anywhere in the city for sixty cents. Fran is starving, but there's a pile of work on her desk. She's about to refuse when the door to Hammerstein's office swings open.

"There she is," he says, his voice filling the room. "Author of 'This Little Town.' Very impressive, Miss Connelly."

"It came out?" Fran exclaims. How could she have forgotten to get a copy this morning?

Hammerstein returns to his office and emerges with *The New Yorker*, folded open to her story. He hands her the copy and she runs her hand across the page. It's real. She's been published.

"If I may ask, how old are you, Miss Connelly?"

She holds the magazine in her hands, breathless. "Twenty-four."

A smile creases Hammerstein's face. "You have a real future as a writer," he says. Then he notices that she's taken off her jacket. "Aren't you going to lunch?"

"I just returned from another meeting with Maria."

Hammerstein narrows his eyes. "Progress?"

Fran shakes her head. "But she leaves on Sunday, so there's time. Anyway, I have quite a few press releases—"

Hammerstein waves them away. "Go."

She's about to protest, but Hammerstein looks firm. And tired. Does he seem paler than usual? She offers the magazine back to him, but his smile only widens. "Keep it."

In the elevator, Peter is the first to reach out. "Let's have a look!" Of all the young people working now in Hammerstein's office, Fran is the first to be published. "We should hit the kiosk and get as many copies as we can!"

Peter hands Jack the magazine and Jack studies it carefully. "It's four pages," Jack says, and Fran can't make out the expression on his face. It certainly doesn't seem to be excitement. "I thought it was going to be three."

Fran's pretty sure she's glowing. So why doesn't it feel that Jack is just as happy? The other assistants congratulate her, and one of them asks if she might give him a few tips on approaching editors.

On the cab ride home that evening, Jack takes another look at the magazine, lingering on the byline. "Your publication made everyone pretty excited today."

"But not you." It's a statement, not a question.

"Well, of course I'm happy. I mean, obviously, I want to publish, too."

"And what do your writing ambitions have to do with my publication?" Fran asks. "This isn't a competition."

"No? Not even when Hammerstein singles you out to say that you're the one with a future in writing?"

Fran sits back against the leather seat of the cab, taking him in. "You are really unattractive right now." She's not lying. The sneer on his face is ugly.

"Is that right?"

The cab pulls up to the curb and Fran snatches back Hammerstein's copy of *The New Yorker*. "Yes. Don't bother picking me up tomorrow," she says. She slams the door and is thankful that Eva isn't in the lobby. Because she's in tears by the time she reaches her apartment.

"Honey, what is it?" her father asks when her voice catches on the line.

"My story was just published in *The New Yorker*," Fran chokes out, and there's whoops of joy as her father leaves to tell her sister. Then her mother is on the line.

"Well, that's wonderful. Really, just wonderful. And how is Jack?" Because this is actually what her mother wants to talk about.

"I frankly don't care how Jack is doing," Fran snaps.

There's a little gasp on the line. "Why would you say that, honey? Did you break up?"

"Maybe." Fran's throat is becoming thick again. "Is Dad there?"

Fran can hear the phone being passed. "Your daughter. She just broke up with Jack."

"Dad, he wasn't happy for me. The story came out today and even Hammerstein congratulated me. But not Jack." Fran begins to cry, realizing what this means.

"Do you want to come home?" her father asks quietly.

Fran wraps the phone cord around her fingers and thinks. "No."

"What will make you happy then?"

The answer comes before she even has to think about it. "Writing."

"Then you do more of that."

"Mom would die," Fran whispers into the phone.

"Mom will be *just fine*," he says loudly. "What about your book? Is it done?"

She looks across her bedroom to the stack of printed papers on her desk. Four hundred and fifty-six papers to be exact. "Yes."

"So what are you waiting for? You're a published author now."

The question lingers even after Fran has hung up the phone with her father. *What are you waiting for?* Her book has been finished for months. Has she been waiting to submit it to publishers until she heard back from *The New Yorker*? Or has part of her always suspected that if she were to have success at publishing before Jack, he'd resent it? She thinks of the way Peter's eyes lit up when Hammerstein mentioned her story, how genuinely pleased he was for her success, and suddenly she feels not just angry but disgusted with Jack.

She crosses the room and picks up her manuscript, feeling the weight of it in her hands. Then she sits down and begins her query letter, briefly describing what the book is about and ending by mentioning her publication in *The New Yorker*. The next morning she puts on her favorite tailored suit with kitten heels and a matching scarf, then hails a taxi. "The Villard Houses, at Madison and Fifty-First."

"Random House?" the man asks.

Fran glances down at her large handbag with the manuscript inside. "That's the place."

By the time the cab pulls into the gravel courtyard of the sprawling brownstone, Fran's pulse is racing. Is she being foolish? Maybe the book isn't ready. But then she hears her father's voice and she knows.

A secretary directs her to the north wing, where she finds another secretary tapping away at the same typewriter Fran uses in Hammerstein's office. "Who's your appointment with?" the woman asks without looking up.

"I don't have one. I've come to drop off a manuscript."

The older woman stops typing. "You a writer here?" She peers over her large glasses at Fran.

"No. But I'd like to be." She fishes in her handbag and lifts out her manuscript. "For Mrs. Ollander. One of your editors." Fran hands over her work, two years in the making, and the secretary leaves it on the corner of her desk. "I'll see that she gets it. Thank you, Miss—"

"Connelly."

"Connelly. If she likes it, you can be sure she'll be in touch."

Fran hesitates. "And if she doesn't, will I get it back?"

"Did you include your address?" She glances at the title page and sees that Fran has. "If it's not Mrs. Ollander's cup of tea—and I'm going to be frank, most things aren't—I'll send it back in the post."

"Thank you. I look forward to hearing, either way."

The secretary indulges Fran with a brief smile and then it's done. All those months of twisting herself into knots over whether she should change the title or do more research, and now it's out of her hands.

Outside, Fran looks across the courtyard to St. Patrick's Cathedral and offers up a little prayer. Then she changes into sneakers and practically runs toward Central Park.

CHAPTER FOURTEEN

OSCAR

Manhattan, New York
1959

I N HAMMERSTEIN'S PLAYS, BAD news is always delivered with fanfare. There's a pregnant pause, followed by a great dramatic reveal. But when the news comes for him, there's nothing remotely dramatic about it. Dr. Schwartz simply leans forward in his chair, and for several moments the creaking of metal is the only noise in the room. Then the doctor confirms what Oscar's been suspecting for several months.

"I'm sorry, Ock. But you have cancer."

For him the moment is more of an exhalation than an inhalation; a sudden release after months of wondering. But there has been no foreshadowing for his wife. No way of preparing for this devastating news. Dorothy collapses in Dr. Schwartz's office and Oscar is forced to comfort her as she cries, the patient caring for the woman who will soon be his nurse.

Later, when they're alone together in their apartment, Dorothy asks him if there were warning signs. "A few," he whispers. And when she screams in frustration, demanding to know why he never went to be checked, he shrugs helplessly. "I didn't have the time."

Now *not enough time* takes on a different meaning. An emergency surgery has been scheduled for next week to remove the tumor that's growing inside his stomach. What happens afterward is no longer up to him.

That same morning he goes to work despite Dorothy's protests. The musical isn't finished and there's at least one more song he needs to write. Since he's always done his best thinking while he walks, he makes for Central Park, where Fran is waiting on a park bench for Maria. He won't see the two of them meet or hear Maria question why the play shows her deeply in love with the Captain, when in reality that wasn't how she felt about marrying him at all. Anyway, he can't think about Maria right now. A song is missing. Something moving and heartfelt for when the family has to bid the only world they've known goodbye.

CHAPTER FIFTEEN

MARIA

Salzburg, Austria
1927

I CAN'T BREATHE. FRAU RAFAELA ushers me into the abbey and I walk through the grounds without actually seeing them. The broken statue of the Blessed Mother may or may not have been replaced, and there may or may not be new paving stones where the old ones had been cracked and chipped. But I can feel the eyes of the sisters watching us as we pass through the open galleries.

A year ago, everything made sense. But now I can't untangle my growing sense of panic from my feelings for the Captain. We climb the flight of stairs to the Reverend Mother's rooms and Frau Rafaela knocks. Then I hear a comforting voice call out to us from the other side. The room looks the same as it did eight months ago. Even the blanket on the back of the Reverend Mother's chair is folded in exactly the same way.

I don't even wait for Frau Rafaela to leave before blurting

out the story. By the time I'm finished, a crowd has gathered outside the Reverend Mother's door.

I stare at the Reverend Mother through a veil of tears, and inside, I feel as if everything is breaking. Yet her face remains calm.

"Ah, Maria. This is certainly a turn of events I didn't foresee." She smiles, and the panic rises inside of me.

"But I've given my word to God. Surely He has plans for me here."

The Reverend Mother leaves her chair and comes to stand in front of me. "Is it possible that God brought you to our abbey because He knew it would eventually lead you to the Baron and his children?"

I look up through my tears. Is it true? Was that God's will all along? "But what about the children here? And the abbey?"

"Well, it seems to me you have a choice to make. A new family with children who need a mother or your family here. In both cases, my dear, you will still be serving God. He doesn't disappear outside the walls of this convent."

I look around. Who is going to give me the answer? Where will it come from?

The Reverend Mother puts her hand on my shoulder. "I think you know what you've been called to do. Go, and have a beautiful life. We will always be here."

I begin to tremble. "But not as my family."

"We will always be your family, Maria."

The terror squeezing my chest feels tighter. And suddenly I'm reminded of a time when I was young and just as scared. I had begged my father to let me stay the night with him, and his voice had the same mix of certainty and regret as the Reverend Mother's. *Gusti, my apartment's not fit for a little girl.*

I stand, but my knees feel weak.

"Congratulations," one of the sisters says. And then everyone is saying it as the Reverend Mother leads me back toward the gates.

"Maria, are you happy?" she asks.

I stand on the threshold of the convent. "I'm frightened."

The Reverend Mother's eyes crinkle with kindness. "We're all frightened of change. Just tell me this. Can you love him?"

I think of how patient he's been—all the ways he's tried to ask me, again and again, if I would be his—and my heart begins to swell. I nod.

"Then I give you my blessing."

Frau Rafaela's eyes are filled with tears and so are mine. "You will make the most beautiful bride in Salzburg," she promises.

"But what if I can't do this?" I ask. "I don't know how to be a mother. Or a wife."

"It will be simple." The Reverend Mother reaches out and squeezes my hand. "Just follow God's lead."

But I'm confused by God. Why has He done this? Why has He taken my devotion to Him and given it away?

I hesitate at the gates, panicked to take a step beyond the abbey. But the Reverend Mother nods encouragingly, and all of the sisters who've crowded around her watch me with anticipation. Why are their faces so full of excitement? Didn't they want me here? I give a little wave and my throat tightens. Then I force myself to turn my back on them and take my first step away from the abbey and into my new life.

It's nearly evening by the time I'm on the bus, and I weep all the way back to the villa and the children. *My* children.

Seven of them. They will be mine now to shelter and protect. Mine to raise. And any bad behavior or annoying habits will be mine to correct.

The entire family is assembled on the steps of the villa, enjoying the evening air. I can see the children playing tag while the Captain is sitting on the first step, nervously smoking his pipe. He rises the moment he sees me. Then silence falls across the entire courtyard, and I begin to cry in earnest.

"What happened?" He holds out a hand toward me.

"The Reverend Mother said yes."

Suddenly, the Captain pulls me toward him and wraps me in his arms. No man has ever done this, not even my father. I stiffen, and he immediately seems to realize my discomfort. He pulls back and gently caresses my arm. "Maria," he says, and there is so much love, so much desire in that one word, that I reach out to him and take his hand.

The news of our engagement spreads faster than you could imagine possible. The entire household knows by dinnertime, and by dessert even the gardeners are coming in to congratulate me. When the children go upstairs for the evening, the Captain finds me in the library, cradling a mug of tea.

"Are you happy?" He sits on the chair across from me, so close that our knees are almost touching.

I look down into my steaming mug rather than into his eyes. "I thought the Reverend Mother would fight for me." My chin begins to tremble, and he places a steadying hand on my knee.

"Is it possible that's what she's doing?"

I glance up.

"Rupert wishes to become a doctor," he begins. "In a year, we'll say goodbye to him and he'll be off on his studies. And we'll say those goodbyes because we love him."

I put down the tea. "Why are you so patient with me?"

He doesn't have to reach for the answer. It just comes to him, as if he's known all along. "Because I'm in love with you, Maria."

I reach out and place my hand in his.

"But it may be a while before we can be married," he says. "There are rumors. I will leave next week for Italy and return at the end of November for our wedding."

I withdraw my hand. "In *six months*?" I don't understand. "But why?"

He looks at me tenderly. "It's what has to be done."

When I reach the children's school the next morning, Johanna's teacher hurries her inside the little schoolhouse, as if she doesn't want her student to hold my hand for a moment longer than she absolutely must. There are people who are giving me strange looks in the courtyard, but it's Hedwig's teacher who finally remarks, "So I suppose our schoolhouse should be expecting another von Trapp."

I think of Martina back home and nod eagerly. "Oh, yes. But not for another few months."

The old woman inhales and looks down at Hedwig. "And how do you feel about your governess becoming your mother now?"

Hedwig beams widely. "I'm the luckiest girl in Salzburg!"

Her teacher stares at me, then shuts the classroom door without another word.

When I return to the villa, I tell the Baroness what's happening. She sits me down at the long dining table and wears the same patient look the Captain wore last night.

"Imagine for a moment that you're the princess, Maria, and the wedding that you've been anticipating for several years is called off. Instead, the Baron suddenly plans to marry his governess. It's very embarrassing. And all of Salzburg is bound to find out. So what might you go on to tell all of your friends?"

I study the fancy table runner, with its blue and gold thread, trying to think about anything but this. "That I stole him away?"

The Baroness presses her lips together. "Yes." She sighs heavily. "How?"

My temperature rises. "I don't know. How can a woman steal a man away?"

She clasps and unclasps her hands.

"What is it? What is she accusing me of?" I exclaim.

The Baroness exhales. "I am guessing she has started a rumor that you are pregnant with his child."

I sit back against the chair and consider what she's telling me. Then I hold my stomach and laugh. "Pregnant!"

The Baroness's face remains serious.

"Well, no one could possibly believe that! We aren't married. What? Do people think we were secretly married and that our wedding will just be for show?"

She frowns. "Maria, you do understand how pregnancy works?"

My cheeks redden. "Of course. A married couple decides that they wish to have a baby."

I have never seen the Baroness's eyes so wide. "Maria, a baby can come without a couple being married."

Now I feel the color drain from my face.

"Dear God." She looks genuinely shocked. "Has no one explained this to you?"

And so I'm given a lesson on the making of babies, and when the Baroness is finished, I'm stunned into silence. "This is why the Captain is leaving," I whisper.

"Yes." The Baroness's face looks grave.

I think of what I told Hedwig's teacher and want to cry. "And the teachers—"

"Can very well mind their own business." The Baroness rises. "Anyway, it will all be clear enough in several months when it's obvious you're not with child."

"And until then?" I exclaim.

"Until then I suggest you become accustomed to some unpleasantry."

"But why would she do this?" I cry. "Why would the princess do this?"

The Baroness smiles. "Because she couldn't control you, Maria. So now she'll wage a different battle. Trying to control what others think about you."

When I go at lunch to collect the children from school, I pass the headmistress in the courtyard and she gives me a tight smile.

"I hear the Baron is leaving for Italy tomorrow."

I hope my cheeks are not on fire. "Yes, for six months," I say.

Behind her large glasses, she raises her sharp brows. "So will the wedding take place tonight?"

I stare at her. "Of course not. Why would it?"

Her eyes drift to my stomach, but I keep my gaze steady.

And when I don't say anything, she makes a dismissive noise in her throat. "Well, congratulations."

I want to say something biting in return, but what will it prove? So instead I blink back tears and collect the children, who are too full of the day's news to notice that I'm upset. In the villa I sit at the long table, and while everyone else eats the *belegte Brote,* I imagine the princess whispering to her friends, "Well, obviously, she's pregnant with his child!" She's probably spreading the word right now, whispering about "that postulant from Nonnberg" and what a conniving girl she is.

"Fräulein, aren't you hungry?" Agathe asks.

I shake my head.

Under the table the Baroness pats my knee. "Don't worry about the gossips, my dear. Just imagine the bitterness of the princess's disappointment when she discovers how wrong she's been."

I know she's trying to make light of it, but when the family assembles on the porch to bid the Captain farewell, a panic seizes my chest and makes it hard to breathe. Johanna notices it first.

"Fräulein, are you all right?"

The Captain moves through the crowd of children and stands in front of me, taking my hands in his. "Only six months."

I press my lips together and nod silently, so that my fear won't come tumbling out. The princess has done this. Forced him to leave until enough months have passed that the world will know I'm not with child.

"I'm sorry," he says quietly, and the children press closer

to me, as if they can sense how difficult these six months will be.

I take a shallow breath and gasp, "I'll miss you, Captain."

He leans forward and lightly kisses my lips, and the feeling is like nothing I've ever experienced. "You can't think of me as 'Captain' anymore, Maria. I'm just Georg now."

I can smell the pipe tobacco on his vest and the fresh scent of soap on his skin, and when he pulls away I have to resist the urge to reach out and pull him back.

I have never had a reason to write many letters, but the moment Georg is gone I hurry to the wooden desk in his library and begin. The children become prolific letter writers as well, and over the next six months Georg tells us about his goings-on in Italy, while we tell him about affairs inside of Villa Trapp. In July, we hike the Untersberg and celebrate Hedwig's tenth birthday at the top. I tell him about the cake we share on the mountainside, near thick bunches of wildflowers and magnificent views of the Hoher Göll, and he writes to me about the crowded markets of Florence, where he's managed to find Hedwig's favorite treats, jam-filled *pizzicati*, which he's sending in several tins.

In September we have Mitzi's birthday to celebrate, and I tell him how Werner is all but a man, going to his room to study now without having to be told. But Martina remains a challenge. She hides whenever it's time for dinner, forcing Agathe to launch a search party throughout the villa. I write to him about my suggestion of leaving Martina to her own devices, as going without dinner will surely cure her of this, but Agathe says she doesn't mind dragging Martina kicking and screaming back to the table.

Her tantrums are growing worse, and I wonder if it has to do with the new role I'll be taking on in the house. I know that the children refer to their beloved mother as Mama whenever they talk about her, so I asked Martina if there was something she'd like to call me.

"I'd prefer not to talk with you at all," she said. At six years old!

Johanna, naturally, came to the rescue, and suggested that the children call me Mother. But I wonder if Martina will ever be persuaded. It's such a terrible loss that she's experienced, and while so young.

In October there is the Feast of the Guardian Angels, and I tell Georg, whose knowledge of the church is somewhat lacking, how we laid out an extra plate at the table for each of our angels. *We are so fortunate to have these guardians to watch over us,* I write. And I tell him that I have taught the children the Angele Dei and have instructed them to pray it daily.

But I don't write to him of how the teachers have suddenly grown warm and affectionate. I smile at them, but I'll never forget how they treated me when they thought I was with child. Nor do I write about the strange loss I feel when the Baroness informs me that after the wedding, she should like to return to her sister in Vienna. "I miss her," she admits. "Oh, don't look so panicked. You have no need for me. Besides, you will be a Baroness then, with all the responsibility such a title conveys." But it's the responsibility I'm most fear-ful of—and the expectations.

However, I don't have time to fret over this. Because sud-denly it's the twenty-seventh of November and the entire villa is in a state. Johanna can't find her fur-lined gloves, Hed-wig's fancy patent leather shoes are missing, Werner hasn't given a thought to his hair, and Martina is once again in hid-ing.

I continue pinning up my hair and tell Agathe, "Ask Jo-hanna if she's looked for her gloves in the parlor, tell Hedwig her shoes are definitely in the hall, and instruct Werner to use Rupert's brush if he must, but he's not going looking like yesterday's breakfast!"

Agathe hesitates at the door. "And Martina?"

I glance at myself in the mirror. My two thick braids are wrapped around my head, creating a halo where my veil will rest. I should probably continue pinning my hair back in case the wind is strong, but Martina . . .

I rise from my dressing table. "I'll find her."

I look in all her favorite places: the cupboard under the stairs, the closet in the ground-floor hall, Rupert's tidy ward-robe. Then I hear a sniffling coming from Johanna's room and I open the door. The sisters are sitting together on the bed, holding a portrait of their mother and weeping. I freeze, and immediately Johanna stuffs the picture frame under her pillow.

"You don't have to hide it," I say at once.

Johanna wipes her tears with the back of her hand. "You saw?"

I nod. "It's a portrait of your mother." I sit on the edge of the bed next to Martina. Johanna hands me the frame. I wipe away the tears that have collected on the glass and stare at the image of Agathe von Trapp. She was beautiful. Much prettier than I am, with a softer mouth and kinder eyes. What sort of bargains must she have tried to make with God before her death? And why would He take the mother of seven children?

"She was very, very beautiful," I say.

Johanna nods and reaches for my hand.

"I don't remember her at all," Martina whispers.

My heart breaks, and an idea occurs to me. "Shall we bring her portrait to the wedding?"

Both children look up at me, wide-eyed.

"I would think she'd like to be part of this day, too," I tell them.

"Yes." Martina begins to cry again and I take her in my arms, and suddenly it doesn't matter that there are a hundred things to do, or that my hair isn't finished, or that Hedwig may never find her shoes. "I'm sorry I'm always hiding," she says.

I stroke her hair. "You can hide any time you like," I tell her.

"And you won't be angry?" She looks up at me with her pretty brown eyes.

"Never," I promise. "And when you're ready, we'll always be waiting."

We leave the villa more than twenty minutes late, but it doesn't matter. The children are dressed in their beautiful white coats and their patent leather shoes gleam against the snow. As we pile into multiple cars and drive toward the abbey, I think of Mutti waiting there for me, and Anni, and Uncle Franz. I imagine the displeasure on my uncle's face at the thought of me becoming a Baroness, and though I deeply disagree with the idea of nobility, the idea of him apoplectic with rage does make me smile.

"Are you excited?" Hedwig asks, smoothing her skirts. The bow in her hair needs straightening, but I can hardly move in my heavy white dress. I instruct Agathe to fix it, then take a deep breath.

"A little nervous," I admit. "I've never been a wife before. Or a mother."

"You'll be wonderful at both," Agathe promises. She's only fourteen, but the seriousness with which she says this makes me think of the Baroness.

The caravan stops outside of Nonnberg, and I look up at the eighth-century abbey that was to be my home and feel a tugging in my chest. But I'm getting a new home. A different one. With children who need me.

Outside, the air is bitterly cold, and I hurry the girls through the gates into the cloisters while the boys go on into the chapel. "Would anyone like to come while the sisters put on my veil?" I ask, and all five girls follow me up the stone stairs into the Reverend Mother's chambers. Frau Rafaela is waiting for me inside, and she crushes me in her embrace. I don't want to cry. I've told myself I won't. But when the sisters arrive and excitedly begin pinning my veil into place I can't help it.

Agathe passes me a tissue and Mitzi asks quietly, "Are you sad?"

"Oh, no. It's just—it's a very big moment," I gasp.

When Frau Rafaela hands me a mirror I stare at myself in the glass.

I'm beautiful. It's the first time in my life that I've ever thought of myself this way, but with the white veil falling over my hair and a crown of flowers framing my face, it feels as if I'm staring at someone else. The girl in the mirror looks like someone whose parents loved her dearly and gave her the best of everything that money could buy. Her father probably bought her a pony for her birthday, and her mother was certainly the kind who had fussed over her hair each morning. She went to a fancy school, then on to the university to study poetry. And now she's marrying a Baron.

"Are you ready?" Frau Rafaela asks.

I take a deep breath and the girl in the mirror becomes me again, masquerading as the future Baroness von Trapp. I hand back the mirror and nod. "Yes."

We walk in the solemn procession toward the chapel, where Martina stops at the entrance and gasps. "Look at all the flowers!"

"And the people," Agathe says.

Frau Rafaela motions for the children to go on, but I'm to be kept out of sight until the music begins to play. The room is bursting with faces I've never seen before. The women have come dressed in their best jewelry and furs, and their perfume hangs heavy in the air. Next to them, groups of men with expensive cuff links and silk lapels stand laughing with one another, turning the quiet chapel into an echo chamber. I search the faces for someone I know, and just as I begin to panic that no one in my family has remembered my wedding, I see them. Mutti and Anni, surrounded at the front of the chapel by all the women who were to become my beloved sisters at Nonnberg. It's with deep relief that I note that there is no sign of Uncle Franz, who must have decided to stay home for this occasion.

My new children make their way to the first pew, and I watch from the back of the chapel as Martina props up the photo of her mother in the empty space beside her. I think of Frau Agathe watching me from the confines of her frame, frozen in time, and my chest aches. Would she be proud of the way I'm caring for her children? Or would she worry that Martina doesn't eat, that Hedwig weeps in her bed late at night, and that Werner doesn't care as much for people as he does for animals? I begin to lose myself in these worries when the music starts and the guests begin rushing to find their seats.

A few more minutes pass, then Frau Rafaela gives my arm a little squeeze and beams up into my face. "It's time."

From the front of the chapel Georg turns to see me enter, and the intensity in his eyes is the same intensity he has that evening as the door to my new room clicks shut behind me.

"There's nothing I expect from you tonight," he says, but the desire in his eyes is unmistakable.

I place my hand on his chest and can feel his heart racing. "I want this," I tell him.

"Yes, but we can simply—"

I stop his words with a kiss, knowing that I can pull away at any time and he will honor my wishes. The Baroness has prepared me for what comes next, so there's no shock when he reaches for the buttons of my gown. He unfastens the top one, studies my reaction, then unfastens a second button and looks down at me again.

"I'm not going to run away." I laugh. His fingers begin moving quickly after this, making fast work of my gown as I strip off his shirt.

The experience of him as my husband is like nothing I could have prepared for. I put my head on his chest while he catches his breath and strokes the back of my neck.

"Just think of our honeymoon," he says breathlessly.

I pull away. "What do you mean?"

Georg frowns. "Well, our honeymoon—"

"We can't leave the children."

"But surely—"

I tug the covers up to my chest and hold them under my arms. "Did you know that Hedwig cries in her sleep? And that Martina isn't eating? We can't just leave them. Just go off—"

"All right," he says, but I don't hear him.

"And what if something happens to Mitzi?" I continue. "Sometimes at night I still hear her cough. And if Werner gets hurt with that carving knife of his? Something could happen to any of them if we leave."

"It's all right, Maria. No one is going anywhere."

But my eyes are filled with tears.

"And no one is leaving you either," he promises. He pulls me into the crook of his arm, where I lay my head on his shoulder and cry. "I promise," he repeats, "no more leaving."

CHAPTER SIXTEEN

MARIA

Salzburg, Austria
1934

I WAKE THE NEXT MORNING seized by the same panic that came over me on my first night in the villa and for several moments I have no idea where I am. The cranberry-colored walls are unfamiliar. So are the soft gray sheets and wooden bed. Then I turn and see Georg's naked back, heavily muscled from his years in the navy, and my heart stills.

"You can't be awake already?" he asks.

"Yes." I have the strangest feeling that I'm forgetting something. Then I glance at the clock on his nightstand and bolt upright. "The children will be downstairs in twenty minutes!"

He groans and turns over, reaching for me. "It's our first morning. Let the Baroness take care of them."

When I don't say anything, he scrambles to a sitting position. "There is no Baroness," he remembers.

I nod.

We are downstairs in fifteen minutes, sitting at opposite ends of what suddenly seems to be an extraordinarily long table. My place in the dining room has changed. I am seated in the Baroness's chair, a wife and Baroness myself. I stare across the room at Georg and begin to snicker.

He smiles. "What?"

"It's just . . . She was such a presence, wasn't she? It feels wrong to be sitting in her chair."

"You may have to start wearing corsets." He grins, and I like this new side of Georg. "She was all right in the end though, wasn't she? I believe she was happy for us." His eyes soften. He's about to say something more, but the sound of feet hurrying down the stairs cuts him off and suddenly the room is full of excited voices.

"So what are we doing today?" Rupert asks, wrapping his arms around his father's shoulders. There is so much affection between father and son.

"Yes, it's our first day together as a family," Johanna points out. "Should we play a game?"

"The sun is out," Werner says. "Let's hike the Unterberg."

"What? In our snowshoes?" Agathe asks.

"Oh, I like that idea," Georg admits. "What do you say, Frau von Trapp? In the mood for a game or for a little hike?"

It's a sign of how well my new family knows me that everyone exclaims, "The hike. She wants the hike!" And it's the most glorious trip we ever take up the mountain. We don't go all the way to the top, but on a ledge overlooking the snowy valley Georg slips his gloved hand in mine.

"It still doesn't seem real," he admits. In the bright winter's sun, his eyes are hazel, and I think of what a fool the princess was. "I'm glad we aren't leaving for a honeymoon," he admits. "I can't think of anything better than this."

But that evening, when the children are all in bed, I discover that there is something even more beautiful than the icy Salzach glittering beneath the winter sun. Our coming together had hurt last night. But this is different, more passionate, and Georg is not surprised in the least when I tell him one morning in June that I feel sick.

"It's like my stomach won't sit still," I complain, holding on to the bathroom sink.

But instead of the sympathy I'm expecting, Georg smiles. "It seems to me we've been working pretty hard toward this moment."

"What moment?" I cry, steadying myself in case I retch again. And then I know.

His smile widens.

But instead of feeling joy, a wave of terror sweeps over me. How could this be happening? I think of all the women I've known who've been called to God with children still in the nursery, and the fear of leaving a precious child alone is overwhelming. Even Agathe, with the very best doctors at her disposal, had left seven children behind.

Suddenly, Georg is crossing the bathroom and taking me in his arms. "Maria, it's going to be wonderful."

"But what if it isn't?" I'm weeping in earnest now. "Look what happened to Agathe. What if—"

He tightens his arms around me. "You're not going anywhere," he says.

"How do you know?"

"Because God didn't send you to us just to take you away."

He is right, and this thought comforts me throughout my pregnancy, through the birth of a beautiful little girl named Rosmarie, and then, three years later, through the birth of my sweet Eleonore, whom we all call Lorli, in 1934.

A family of eleven. Can you imagine? I find myself saying at least a dozen times a day, "Agathe, did you remember..." But she always remembers. She is a godsend. At twenty-one she is as old as I was when I arrived to tutor her younger sister. And now she has all but taken my place, looking after the little ones, taking care of the sewing, seeing that everyone is off to school. Although by now many of the children no longer require watching. Rupert is twenty-three and studying to become a doctor in Vienna. Mitzi is twenty (yes, that Mitzi, *my* Mitzi) and teaches in Nonnberg in the very same classroom where I used to teach. Werner is nineteen and working on a nearby farm, hoping to own a farm of his own one day. And Hedwig, who is perhaps the most help to me after Agathe, is already seventeen. But the rest of the children need looking after, as my own time is taken up with overseeing the villa.

It's a full day's work to make sure the house runs as smoothly as it did when Baroness Matilda was here. There are excursions to plan and gardeners to oversee and a household staff of more than twenty to manage. Some days, I don't see little Lorli or Rosmarie until the cook rings the bell for dinner and Agathe brings them down from the nursery. Then it's "Mama! Mama!" and neither of them wants to do anything except wrap her arms around my neck and bury her face in my hair. But after a day of ordering supplies for the villa and frittering away my time on other useless tasks, I'm usually hungry and irritable. "Sit still!" I tell them, and then their eyes fill with tears and it's Agathe who reminds me gently, "Mother, I think they simply want cuddles." And so one of the girls will always end up eating dinner on my lap.

It's a full life, a wonderful life, and no matter how busy any of us might be, everything comes to a stop after dinner. Some families use this time to play board games or cards. But the von Trapps sing. We've made our very own choir in four parts, with Agathe and Johanna as first sopranos, Martina and Mitzi as second sopranos, Hedwig and I as altos, and Werner as our tenor. When Rupert is home, he becomes our bass vocalist.

We sing the folk songs I learned while wandering through the Alps, and sometimes the more popular songs that Werner and Agathe like to play on the gramophone, like "Gitarren Spielt Auf." On Sundays, we sing Gregorian chants or chorales by Bach. Every day it's something different, and many times the neighbors will come for tea to hear our songs—often the Hofmanns or the Strassers. When the singing is finished, the men retire to talk about their time in the military, while I'm left with the women to chat about housekeeping and raising children. One evening, Georg comes to me in bed and asks whether I am happy.

"Do you ever regret not taking your vows?"

I turn and stare at him. How could he think that? "Never."

"Then why are you always so tense?"

I feel my cheeks warm. "Because I don't think I was cut out for this," I blurt. "All this house minding and talk about shopping and servants. I can't stand it."

"You mean with the Strassers today?"

"With anyone. I don't care about where I can buy the finest dirndl in Salzburg!"

He laughs.

"I'm serious, Georg. You get to talk about your time in the military. What you did during the war. What's happening in the world. The book you're writing. I have to talk about the best leather shops in Barcelona."

"So, what would you rather talk about?" he asks.

"Literature, music, singing . . ."

He nods but doesn't say anything. Because there's no forcing his friends' wives to care about these things. And so it continues, my repetitive days as a vapid hostess, until a single phone call changes our lives. I am upstairs when I hear the phone ringing, a high tinny sound that echoes throughout the house until I reach the library downstairs and pick up the receiver. The woman's voice on the other end sounds familiar, but at first I can't place it.

"Maria?" She can hear from my silence that I'm drawing a blank. "It's Auguste, the owner of Lammar Bank."

"Oh, good morning."

There's a moment of silence on the line. "Actually, not so good. Is Georg home?"

I fight a strange tightening in my chest. "He's in the garden."

"Would it be possible to speak with him?"

"Of course." I turn and find him hovering in the doorway, his eyes alert. "It's Auguste. From Lammar Bank."

Something tells me to remain in the room while he takes the call, and I can see from the way his back stiffens that the news isn't good. "Are you sure?" he keeps saying. "All of it? What do you mean 'All of it'?" When he replaces the receiver, his face is ashen.

"What happened?"

"It's gone," he says like a man in a daze.

"What do you mean? What's gone?"

He sinks into the chair behind his desk. "Our money. All of it. Just . . . gone."

The entire world seems to slow when tragedy strikes, as if life is trying to give you more time to process what's happening. More time to see the chain of unfortunate events that has led you to this moment, link by link. Our money had always been kept in the Bank of England. But we had vacationed with Auguste and her family last year, and when Georg heard that her bank was floundering, he offered to withdraw his money from England and place it with her.

"You would do that?" Auguste had asked at the time, touched by this show of faith.

"Of course."

Now the Lammars have lost everything. And so have we.

"You have to call Rupert," I say. "He needs to come home tonight."

Georg nods, not really listening. His entire life he has worked, from the time he was fourteen and sent off to the naval academy. It was his wife Agathe, with her jewels and estates, who changed his life. And since her death, he had guarded her fortune carefully, only placing it with Auguste because he believed it would help not only her family but Austria. For if Austria's banks failed, her military wouldn't be far behind. He was simply placing his financial faith in the country he'd spent his youth defending.

I watch him open a desk drawer and take out a pipe, but his hand is shaking. I've never seen him like this. I hurry over and strike the match, lighting the bowl. "The children have to be told," I say. Lorli is three and Rosmarie six. It won't matter to them. But the others will understand the gravity of this development. "Is there anything left?"

Georg meets my gaze, his voice a whisper. "A few hundred pounds in the Bank of England."

He inhales and exhales, blowing smoke through his nose like a dragon. There's no career left to him. When the Treaty of Versailles cut off Austria from the sea, his maritime career of twenty years was finished. Perhaps he can lecture. He is writing a second book on submarines. But that will never be steady income. And what other jobs are fit for a Baron?

"We only need enough to maintain the villa," I say. "We can take on boarders."

I see him clench the pipe between his teeth. "Never."

"Students from the Catholic University," I say. "Or nuns traveling from afar to the abbey. We could even apply to the archbishop to have our own chapel! Plenty of estates have one."

"And where would we put it?"

I think for a moment. "The reception room," I tell him.

Georg stares at me in disbelief. "You're indefatigable, aren't you?"

The children take the news better than could be imagined. For several moments there is silence in the library, with only the terrible, loud ticking of the clock echoing throughout the room. Then everyone begins asking questions at once. Mitzi wants to know if this means she'll have to stop going to school. It doesn't, but Rupert will now have to go to work to finish his medical degree. Lorli wants to know if we'll still have food to eat. Georg tells her that we will, but that the money will have to come from boarders.

"The rooms on the first floor will all have to be vacated," I say. "Our family will keep to the floors above."

"But what will we do for clothes?" Johanna asks. At sixteen, this is what's most important to her.

"We've lost our money, not our clothes," I say wryly. "We'll make do with what we have."

"So no more vacations?" Martina confirms.

Georg shakes his head. "Not for some time."

"But does no money mean no money *at all*?" Hedwig asks.

"None," I say quietly. "This morning, your father sold off his last remaining piece of land in Munich. All we have left now is this house."

The youngest children find this hilarious. "Our money is gone! Our money is gone!" Rosmarie begins dancing around the room, and Lorli takes up the chant.

"This isn't a game," Agathe snaps.

But I don't chastise them, and there's no need for the older children to be anxious, even though Johanna is blinking back tears. "We're not the only family to have this happen," I say, "and we won't be the last. God will provide. *Nec aspera terrent*," I tell them.

It's the von Trapp family motto, now mine as well, and it means Frightened by No Difficulties.

The news of our sudden misfortune travels even faster than the news of our marriage, and a small part of me is glad that my uncle is dead and cannot gloat over this. Instead, the

neighbors do it for him, stopping Georg on the street to remark on how thin he's getting.

"Times are hard," our neighbor Herr Weber commiser-
ates, building a protective wall around his finances in case we
should come knocking, "but we have extra potatoes and onions if you'd like. I can have my butler bring them over."

Our butler, Hans, and our laundress are the only staff
we've continued to employ, so the offer doesn't sting as much
as it might. But Georg is still enraged.

"Potatoes and onions!" he shouts when he finds me cleaning the kitchen. "The same man who ate white caviar at our
Christmas parties."

I continue wringing out the dishcloths and shrug. "Isn't it
nice to know who your real friends are?"

But a week before our first boarders arrive, Georg returns
in the darkest mood I've seen. I have to leave my dusting to
Agathe and join him in the library before he'll talk.

"Those Hofmanns!" he seethes. I've rarely seen him angry.
But his fists are clenched and the veins in his forearms are
bulging.

I sit across from his desk. "You mean Ingrid or Stefan?"

"The wife!"

He has never referred to Ingrid as "the wife" before and I
can't imagine what's happened.

"She stopped me in the street to tell me how happy she
was to see that we were all carrying on. As if what? We were
supposed to shrivel up and die? And then—" He takes hold
of his pipe. "Then she said she was impressed to see that our
children still managed to be well dressed."

Now it's my turn to look horrified. "What's the matter
with people?"

"I have half a mind—"

But I shake my head. "It doesn't matter, Georg."

"It does!" He bangs his fist on the desk.

"I promise you, it doesn't." And then I quote softly, "'And again I say to you, it is easier for a camel to go through the eye of a needle, than for a rich man to enter the kingdom of God.' Haven't you always wondered?" I ask.

"Wondered about *what*?" He stuffs his pipe full of tobacco.

"About whether you have what it takes to still have faith without your career, your wealth, and everything that once defined you? Anyone can be pleasant when life is going well. We only truly know who we are when life stops going according to our plans. You were a good, kind man when we had money, and it turns out that you are a good, kind man even without it. Don't let the Ingrids of the world take that from you."

He thinks on this for a moment, then sighs. "How do you keep so much faith, Maria?"

"Because I came from nothing and God provided. He will provide now, too."

The first indication that our faith has been rewarded comes in the form of a letter. The Bishop of Salzburg has granted our request, and it takes only a few days for us to transform our dining room into a chapel worthy of the name. The abbey gifts us a beautiful altar while the boys go about building wooden pews. Martina sets to work with Agathe on sewing an altar cloth, while Georg and Rupert turn our music room downstairs into a dining room. It's hardly the life the children have been accustomed to, but when our first boarders arrive and turn out to be a pair of gregarious theology students, we wonder if perhaps this is something just as good. And when word begins to spread that we are taking in boarders from the university, students begin lining up for places in our villa.

Soon our evenings are filled with the sound of a dozen voices discussing politics, music, science, and the arts. Johanna, who cooks as beautifully as she sings, oversees the menu each night, and while the boarders debate music and politics, the younger children bring in platters of bread, vegetables, and roasts. It's the kind of world I've been yearning for since arriving in Salzburg. And now we have it every night—a villa full of the intellectually curious.

In June, a professor by the name of Dillersberger arrives, and suddenly we have a priest for our chapel. In the mornings, before going to the university, he says Mass in our chapel, and we all crowd together in our beautiful little sanctuary to receive the Eucharist. And nothing can be sweeter than seeing our three-year-old pressing her chubby palms together, offering up her prayers of thanksgiving each morning.

"You're happier than I've seen you in a long time," Georg remarks one night, stroking my hair. "I'd hate to think we had to lose everything for you to be this happy."

"Because we've been set free. We don't have to worry over what the neighbors might think if the children are too loud or if they're dressed in your bedroom curtains. It simply doesn't matter anymore!"

Georg smirks. "It is freeing, isn't it?"

"And now you can write your book in peace."

"Yes. No one visits us anymore, do they?" There's a tinge

of sadness to his voice but also wonder that even the Strassers are too afraid to pay a call in case we should ask them for something.

But it doesn't matter. Our house is full, and the conversations last long into the night: through dinner, then dessert, and once the children are off to bed, over late mugs of chamomile tea near the fire. In early July of 1934, our talk once again turns to Hitler. Before, he had been an oddity, a nuisance. But suddenly he has risen to chancellor of Germany and has done the unthinkable. He's used the SS to murder his predecessor, Chancellor von Schleicher, as well as many opponents of the Nazi regime.

With the children in bed, Georg carries the day's papers across the squeaky floorboards of the library. Then ten of us sit in a half circle and listen while he reads from the *Neue freie Presse*.

" 'More than five hundred insurrectionists are thought to have been executed on the night of June thirtieth, as Hitler began his purge of the country's rebels.' "

"Is that what they're calling them?" Professor Dillersberger exclaims. "Rebels?"

"I'd think 'critics' would be more appropriate," I say.

" 'The purge began at midnight and among those killed are SA Chief of Staff Ernst Röhm and his most senior commanders.' "

The room falls silent.

"This is serious." Dillersberger is the first to speak. He runs a shaky hand through his mop of dark hair and suddenly seems much older than his thirty years.

"What is England's take on it?" another boarder asks, and Georg reaches for the *Daily Express*.

He shakes out the newspaper and reads the headline. "'Captain Rohm Executed. Arrested Storm Troop Commander Given Ten Minutes to Kill Himself—Shot When He Refuses.'"

"Hitler's become dangerous," I say, voicing my fear.

"He's always been dangerous," Georg says darkly. "But he couldn't have done this without the support of the army's commanders. He'll need them if he wants to reach the top."

I gasp. "By the top you mean president?"

Dillersberger nods grimly. "That's where this is leading. He wants the critics of the Nazi Party silenced, and somehow he's gotten the army's commanders to agree."

For a few days it's all anyone can talk about, then the world seems to settle and our concerns grow mundane again—the basket of chalk that Rosmarie has lost, the mutton we'll need to buy for tonight's dinner. Summer rolls into autumn and the chestnut trees burst orange and gold across the horizon. Then in the spring of 1935, Professor Dillersberger announces his departure from Villa Trapp. We are all terribly sad about this, particularly as we've grown accustomed to his morning Mass and Sunday sermons.

"But who will do our church now?" Lorli asks over dinner, her little voice rising above the din of the table conversation.

Dillersberger puts down his fork and smiles. "A wonderful man by the name of Father Wasner. You have nothing to worry about."

Georg has known Franz Wasner for years. And although we're both the same age—twenty-nine—Wasner has done more in his time than I have ever dreamed of. After getting his degree in theology, he was ordained and began serving as a priest in Tyrol. When this was not enough, he traveled to

Rome to study ecclesiastical law and graduated with a doctorate in canon law. Now he is an instructor of Gregorian chants at the most prestigious university in Salzburg.

That Wasner has agreed to say Mass at our villa on Saturdays is wonderful news, and I tell the children what an honor it will be to have him with us.

"But why not every day?" Lorli complains.

Dillersberger laughs. "I'm afraid he's a very busy man."

When Wasner comes the entire family stands in the drive to wait for his arrival. I have never met him, but he looks just the way Georg has described: tall, bespectacled, with unruly blond hair and earnest blue eyes. He is wearing the black clothes and white collar of a priest, and as he crunches up the drive I think of how familiar he seems with his cleft chin and boyish face.

"A pleasure to finally meet you, Frau von Trapp." He reaches out to take my hand, and when we shake, it suddenly comes to me. He looks like the American movie star Errol Flynn.

"Please, just Maria," I say.

"Have you come to teach us about God?" Lorli asks. With her braids wrapped in a halo around her head, she looks older than three.

Wasner laughs. "Well, yes. And I thought perhaps you might sing for me while I'm here. Is it true that your entire family sings?"

Lorli nods. "Oh, yes. Everyone loves it. Except Rosmarie. She sings because Mother makes her."

I flush, and Rosmarie does her best to avoid my gaze. "It would be our pleasure," I tell him.

He falls into step with Georg, and I go to Rosmarie. "Is it true?" I ask her as we enter the house. "Do you not like to sing?"

She scuffs the floor with her patent leather shoe. "It makes me nervous," she tells me in a small voice.

"You're six! What do you know about nerves?" I laugh, and the look in her brown eyes is one of deep betrayal. Of course, I think of my laughter now and it mortifies me. But I was twenty-nine and what did I know about anxiety? So we perform for Father Wasner. Agathe suggests the Gregorian chant "Tantum ergo sacramentum," and after we sing, our guest joins us for breakfast.

We wait to hear what he is going to say.

"Maria, your voice is lovely. And I don't think I've ever heard of an entire family that sings. You actually have a choir," he marvels. "How did this come about?"

Everyone begins talking at once, then Georg tells him about his first wife's love of music and her passion for violin. "Then Maria came into our lives and continued the tradition."

"It's extraordinary," Wasner says, looking around at us. "And who taught you this Gregorian chant?"

"Mother did," Johanna says proudly. "She's taught us all the songs from her time in the Catholic Youth Movement."

"Wonderful," he tells me, and just as my head is beginning to swell, he asks why I decided to change the harmony at the beginning of the song.

"I didn't."

"Then you've been singing it incorrectly."

Lorli snickers, possibly because I'm usually the one going

around telling the family that what they're doing is incorrect. Even Wasner smiles a little at the surprise that is evident on my face.

"If you would like," he offers, "I am happy to teach you the right way to sing it."

It is the start of something extraordinary. Now, instead of spending our Saturdays tidying up the villa and pruning in the garden, we gather in our music room downstairs and sing Gregorian chants with Father Wasner. By May, we have committed nearly every chant he knows to memory.

One Saturday he hurries in with his hair uncombed and a satchel full of papers. "You won't believe what I've found in the university's archives," he says, coming into our dining room and spreading the papers across the table. "This music hasn't been heard in hundreds of years!"

Eleven of us gather around the table and begin sifting through the piles like archaeologists searching for treasure.

"Look at this!" Johanna says, holding up a piece from the fifteenth century.

Lorli reaches for one of the papers and Georg gasps. "These aren't originals, are they?"

Father Wasner grins. "Copies. I spent the past three weeks on this."

By August, we are singing pieces that haven't been heard in Austria since Mozart was a child. We sing for ourselves, for our boarders, for visiting family. One weekend, Father Wasner brings his colleagues from the university to hear us sing what he's discovered in the archives, and the next weekend we find ourselves making a recording so that the professors can play it for their students.

And I suppose it would have gone on like this—our family performing simply for the joy of it—if not for the sudden appearance of someone famous on our doorstep. I'm helping the laundress hang out the clothes when Hedwig comes running, her braids swinging behind her.

"Mother, you're not going to believe this, but Lotte Lehmann is in our parlor."

I exchange a look with Petra, our young laundress, who immediately puts down the pegs. "*The* Lotte Lehmann?"

Hedwig nods eagerly. "The soprano!"

"Well, what is she doing here?" I wipe my hands on my apron and flatten my skirt.

"She wants to rent rooms in our villa during the Salzburg Festival!"

I hurry into the parlor with Petra on my heels to see if it's true. It is. Lotte Lehmann is there, dressed in a pink silk top and matching skirt. And she's just as beautiful in person, with the same porcelain skin and startlingly blue eyes as she had on the cover of *Time* magazine.

"You must be Frau von Trapp," she says, extending a gloved hand.

There's dirt under my fingernails and a stain on my sleeve. "Please, just Maria." I'm staring, but I can't help it. I've never met a famous person before. And then I remember—my children! "And this is Hedwig."

"Lovely to meet you." She smiles.

"And Lorli," I say, motioning for her to stop peering around the doorway and step into the parlor. "And this is Petra," I add, nudging Petra forward. She flushes red, and I'm sure our faces look similar.

"Well, I've heard this is the place to stay near Salzburg. Do you think you might have room for me here during the festival?"

"Oh, yes. Absolutely," I tell her. And soon neighbors who haven't visited us in a year are dropping by "just to see how you're all getting on."

But I stand on the doorstep and block their view inside. "Oh, it's been busy," I say as Ingrid Hofmann tries to peer over my shoulder. "Just trying to keep nine children well dressed."

If she understands the reference, it's not evident from her face. "I imagine a family of nine means there's always something to do. Still, it's a shame we haven't even had coffee recently."

I nod without saying anything, then we both look at each other until the silence becomes awkward.

"Well, if you'd ever like to come by for dinner . . ." she begins, and the invitation hangs in the air, waiting for me to catch it and reciprocate. I don't.

"That's very nice. Thank you."

The same scene is repeated the next day with the Strassers, only it's both of them who appear on our doorstep, dressed in their Sunday best, trying to catch a glimpse of our famous guest.

"You know, we can't turn them away forever," I tell Georg. "They've been your neighbors for ten years."

But he just puffs on his pipe and returns to his typewriter. His book is coming out next month, and this means preparing talks and giving radio interviews. "If they're still coming around after Frau Lehmann leaves, we'll invite them in."

Our entire family is entranced by Lotte. The way she walks, the way she dresses, the way she tells stories over dinner about her trips to America.

"But I hear I'm not the only one in this villa who sings," she says after dessert one evening. She is on her second helping, and I'm not surprised. Agathe has outdone herself, and the whole house smells of baked apples and cinnamon. "Is it true that this entire family sings?"

"Well, not Papa," Johanna says. "But the rest of us do. Especially Mother."

Everyone nods eagerly, including the six boarders, who have no choice but to listen to us practice.

"Well, when am I going to be invited to hear something?" Lotte asks.

We don't need any further encouragement. As soon as the plates are cleared, we assemble in the music room and our boarders seat themselves in wooden chairs.

I look around. "Where is Rosmarie?"

"She was here a moment ago," Agathe says.

"Rosmarie?" I call. She's not in the dining room. Or the kitchen.

"Try under her bed," Martina suggests dryly. "That's usually where I was before you'd come dragging me out."

Martina is thirteen. It's been years since we've had to go searching the house for her. But now it's Rosmarie. . . . I glance at Lotte, who is looking through one of our binders filled with Father Wasner's Gregorian chants. "I'm sorry," I tell her. "I'll be right back."

Upstairs, Rosmarie is exactly where Martina said she would be. Under the bed, crying.

"What's the matter with you?" I exclaim, holding up the

covers so I can see her. Her eyes are squeezed shut, and the two braids on either side of her face are sweeping the dust.

"Please don't make me go down there and sing. Please," she wails.

I grab her arm and slide her out. "Why not?"

"Because I hate it!" she cries.

I kneel on the wooden floor. "Ros, you have a beautiful voice."

"I don't care! I hate it."

My heart races. Downstairs, the world's most famous soprano is waiting. Her good opinion could keep boarders coming to us for months. Possibly years. "I don't ask you to do many things," I say sternly, "but this is important."

"It's *always* important!" She rubs at her eyes, turning the skin around them red, and now it's obvious that she's been crying.

"I want you to go down there and sing," I say sternly.

"And if I don't?" Her voice trembles.

She is only six and one of three sopranos. We don't really need her. Still . . . "We are a family," I say. "And families stand together." I reach for her hand.

When we return to the music room, I make a joke of it. "The escapee!" I say, and everyone laughs. I place Rosmarie next to me in case she tries to bolt. But once we start singing, even she doesn't wish to stop. We sing two of Father Wasner's latest discoveries, then "Jesu, meine Freude" by Bach. And when we're finished, the only sound is our own ragged breathing as we try to catch our breaths. Then suddenly our audience members are on their feet.

"Extraordinary!" Lotte begins clapping wildly. For us. "Just extraordinary!"

Around the table and chairs in our garden the next morning, Lotte can't stop talking about our performance. While Agathe and Mitzi bring out fresh lemonade, she tells us that there's nothing like our little singing group anywhere in Europe.

"No one would believe that an entire family has its own choir. You should be singing for the world."

I can see the color drain from Georg's face, because there could be no greater shame than a nobleman's family being seen to work. And at singing, no less. But Lotte is looking at him with such big, earnest eyes.

"Oh, yes," he says, laughing, as if this is a good joke.

"But I'm serious," she says. "They could tour Europe. Even America!"

Now Georg is beginning to look alarmed.

"You can't keep this hidden," she presses. "They should enter the folk singing competition tomorrow at the festival."

Georg takes the pipe from his mouth. "What? You mean to sing onstage?"

She laughs. "What do you think I do?" Then she turns to look at the rest of us, gathered in the sunshine around the picnic tables. "What do you think? Would you like to enter the competition?"

The cheer that goes up startles even me. I look at Georg.

CHAPTER SEVENTEEN

MARIA

Salzburg, Austria
1934

WELL, FRAN, I SUPPOSE you are waiting for the illustrious Max Detweiler to make his appearance, and for
us to plan a daring escape from the Nazis just as we are about
to give our performance. But these are your scriptwriters'
fanciful creations. We won't meet our smooth-talking manager, Fred Schang, until we reach America four years from
now. And on this beautiful day in September, Hitler is still
Germany's problem. A month ago, the Germans went and
elected him president, only to have him abolish the office and
declare himself Führer a few weeks later. But we are Austrian,
and if our westerly neighbors are misguided enough to elect
themselves a dictator, we don't wish it to be any concern of
ours.

Of course, I know now what a foolish attitude this is. But
on that crisp fall morning, my only concern is to find our
skirts and braid everyone's hair. The boys can easily sort

themselves out, but the girls need matching dirndls and starched white blouses. Plus, Rosmarie has gone missing again. This time, I send Agathe to find her.

"And make sure she's dressed," I say. "And braid her hair."

"What if she doesn't want to sing?"

I give Agathe a long look. Rosmarie is mine from birth. She was born for this. And if Lorli can manage to stand there and try her best at three, then Rosmarie can certainly do it at six. I tell this to Agathe, and she hurries down the hall to start the pleading.

Lotte, who is taking coffee in our dining room, finds all the commotion hilarious. But I have to bite my tongue when Lorli comes to me with ripped stockings and Martina can't find the right dirndl. "We are going with green today," I say, pausing outside Martina's room and forcing myself to breathe. "So find your green one, and Lorli—" I spin around. "Find some new stockings!"

Lorli stops in the hallway and begins to cry. "But I don't want new stockings."

"That doesn't matter!" I hiss. "You can't go like that!" I try to focus, but what I want to do is scream. At Martina, who should know we must color coordinate. At Agathe, who is still down the hall pleading with Rosmarie. At Lorli, for being too young to fetch the stockings herself. And at the boys, who are already dressed and gathered in Rupert's room, wasting their time listening as he recounts some foolish cricket match he played at his university. Shouldn't they be helping Martina find her skirt? Or dragging Rosmarie from her hiding place?

It's a miracle that we are ready by noon.

"We have to leave now if we're to be there on time," I say,

hurrying to tie a green ribbon in Hedwig's hair. "Where's Georg?" I shout. No doubt in the library, enjoying his pipe. "Has Father Wasner arrived? Is everyone ready?" A line of children stretches down the hall. I take a quick head count and down we go.

Lotte rises from her chair as soon as she sees us. And I suppose we do make an interesting sight, with all ten of us dressed in matching green lederhosen and dirndl. "My goodness." Her blue eyes are wide with some emotion I can't pin down. Disbelief? Admiration? "Your whole family!"

"Even Georg," I say, who arrives on cue with his pipe. "He can be our manager."

But he holds up his hands. "Oh, no."

Rupert slings his arm around his father's shoulders. At twenty-three, he is now a full head taller than Georg. "Ready?" he asks.

Georg surprises us all by nodding. "Oh, why not?"

Something in the way he says it must fire up even Rosmarie, because there's no whining or crying as we file out the door onto the drive. Two polished black Austro-Daimlers sit waiting for us in the bright sun. They are luxuries we could never afford to buy now, so Georg keeps them well maintained. Today, with the weather so beautiful, Hans has lowered the tops. The children split themselves into groups and pile inside, shouting that the leather is too hot.

"I'll see you there," Lotte says. Her chauffeur is waiting patiently beside her open door. "You are going to be brilliant."

The moment she says this, a rush of fear tenses my stomach. It's just a five-minute drive into Salzburg.

"Just remember the high C," Agathe tells Mitzi as we head toward the city.

"And don't take any big breaths," Hedwig reminds Werner. "You'll tighten your shoulders."

"Why are we going with an open top?" Johanna complains. "Look at my hair."

"Your hair is fine," I say quickly. "Everyone, whatever happens, we're not here to win. We're here because we wish to share our gifts with the world. There is no family in Austria like ours, and God has seen to it that we each have a part to play, from soprano"—I look at Rosmarie and smile—"to tenor."

Werner beams, and although he's nineteen, I can still see nervous excitement on his face. "I think we should call ourselves the Trapp Family Choir. It has a nice ring to it, doesn't it?"

So that's the name Father Wasner tells the director of festival when we enter the tent and are asked what we're called.

"And who might you be?" the man asks, tugging his mustache.

"Father Wasner is our conductor," I tell him.

The director scowls. "Can't say we've ever had a choir with a conductor," he says. Then he peers at me intently. "Are you professionals?"

Georg sputters at the idea. "Certainly not. We sing in our music room."

"Fine." The director hands each of us red and white pins for our shirts to show that we're entrants. "You'll be on at one. We have three acts to get to before yours." He grabs a clipboard and hurries from the tent. "Take a seat and wait."

It's the longest wait of my existence. We entertain ourselves with several games of charades until the barker finally calls for the Trapp Family Choir.

"Line up!" I cry. "Rupert, what are you doing with those

cards? Rosmarie, get your thumb out of your mouth. Wasner! Where is Father Wasner?"

"Here!" He comes around the corner of the tent, music in hand. "Everyone ready?"

Georg looks as if he might be having trouble breathing, and as we leave the tent I squeeze his hand. "It's going to be great."

The audience is bigger now than they have been for the previous acts. Perhaps it's the novelty of seeing a Baron's family taking the stage or maybe it's the time of day, but people fill the wooden chairs practically as far as the eye can see. As we take our positions I spot Lotte near the front, along with several of our neighbors. But as soon as we begin to sing, the entire audience fades from view. There could be three hundred people watching us or three. I'm so focused on the music that it no longer matters.

I can see from Father Wasner's face that we're hitting every note. All of us—even tiny Lorli. But when our song is finished, my heart begins beating so wildly in my chest that I can't hear anything else. For several terrible seconds I think the crowd is mute with disappointment. Then suddenly the entire audience is on its feet, giving us a standing ovation. The children look at one another in disbelief.

"Let's go," I say quickly. "Let's go." Our act is over and the judges are motioning us off the stage. We hurry away to shouts from the crowd.

"That was amazing!" someone says.

"Yes. Just unbelievable!"

"Frau von Trapp." A wiry man with a mustache and a gray fedora pushes through the crowd. "Frau von Trapp!" He reaches out and shakes my hand. "Franz Ackermann." He hands me a small paper card. "Next Saturday," he says. "At the station."

I glance at Georg. "What station?" Where does this man think we'll be going?

Ackermann laughs, as if I'm the first person to have ever asked him this. "The *radio* station on the Mönchsberg. See you at four o'clock." He winks and disappears into the crowd.

Georg stares at me, agape. "He didn't even ask!"

I raise my brows. "Guess that means that not many people turn him down."

But I can't think about a radio station right now. The judges have taken the stage and the crowd of several hundred people has gone silent. A man and a woman dressed in similar black suits are about to announce the prizes. Rosmarie slips her hand into mine and I can feel the nervous sweat between her fingers.

"And the third prize in the Salzburg Festival's Singers' Competition goes to . . ."

The blood is rushing so fast in my ears that I can't hear who they announce. I just know it isn't us, because a couple who did yodeling is smiling and moving toward the stage. My heart isn't racing nearly so fast when they announce the second prize, which goes to a man and his daughter who performed "Land der Berge, Land am Strome." And I'm completely calm as they prepare to announce first place because it certainly won't be us.

"And the first prize in this year's Singers' Competition goes to . . . the Trapp Family Choir!"

Suddenly, everyone is looking in our direction.

"It's us!" Johanna shouts, taking Agathe by the hand. "It's us!"

Georg is beaming so widely that tears are forming in his eyes. And this makes me happier than anything.

I don't even remember what we do onstage. Is there an acceptance speech? If so, who gives it? Because I know it isn't me. Instead, I am rooted to the center of the stage, looking out at the sea of smiling faces, in shock. And for the first time, I know what it is to feel wanted by so many.

At home, instead of basking in the moment of our very first singing triumph as a family, I immediately begin planning the next. "Saturday at four," I remind everyone gathered around the fireside with their mugs of cinnamon and cider.

"Perhaps we should talk about this," Georg says. The room is heavy with the sweet, pungent scent of his pipe, and from the open windows you can smell the seasons changing, the warm summer grass giving way to the fresh scents of fall.

"A *radio* invitation?" I laugh. "You said it yourself. No one turns that down! Rupert, what about school?" I worry.

"If the trains are running on time I can be here by noon."

I look around the library. "Everyone else?"

Rosmarie is picking at a loose thread in the carpet, but the others are all wide-eyed with wonder at their own accomplishment and obviously excited to repeat the experience.

"Then it's decided," I say.

Rosmarie looks up and her face is pale. In enough time, I reassure myself, she'll love the stage. I pick up the phone to confirm the booking.

And just like that, our entire lives change.

Although Georg has given more than a dozen radio interviews to promote his book, the rest of us have never been to a radio station, and the twenty-minute drive is full of excitement. I lean my head back in the sunshine and inhale. Autumn leaves and fresh pine.

"So who do you think will hear us?" Johanna asks. Since there's no need to wear matching dirndls or starched blouses, she's dressed in a gray skirt and embroidered top.

"Who knows?" I say eagerly, letting her mind wander. "The whole of Austria listens to this station."

"Germany, too," Werner puts in.

My stomach clenches. Then I remember the feeling I had when everyone rose to their feet at the festival and how our awful neighbors had watched as men like Franz Ackermann had surrounded us afterward, offering things like free tickets to Rome to sing at the Teatro dell'Opera. We're on the brink of something, I realize. I'm not sure what, but our trip up to the Mönchsberg radio station gives me the same feeling I used to have while standing on the edge of the diving board, waiting to jump.

The parking lot is filled when we arrive, and for a moment I wonder if they've all come for us. Then I realize with embarrassment that other singers are obviously recording here as well. We hurry out of the cars, and a receptionist leads us to a waiting room with long green couches and framed photos of all the famous singers who've come here before us.

"There's Lotte Lehmann!" Johanna exclaims.

It's true. She's on the wall, smiling next to a large microphone suspended from the ceiling. "Is that what we're going to do?" I ask.

"Probably, because there are so many of you," Georg says. "If it was just one or two, you'd be in the booth."

I try to steady my breathing. We'll be singing Bach's

"Hymn of Thanksgiving," and it's no different from all the other times we've performed it. But as I look around, I realize someone is missing. *Dear God.* "Where is Rosmarie?" I'm aware of my voice sounding more like a screech than a gasp, and before anyone can answer I'm out the door and halfway down the drive. Even from across the parking lot I can hear the sobbing.

"What are you doing here?" I shriek.

She's hunched down on the floor of the car, her face red and puffy from crying. "Please, I don't want to sing," she begs. "Don't make me sing."

"It's the same as what we did at the contest," I say.

"And I hated it!" she cries.

I hear heavy footsteps behind me and put my hands on my hips. "Get out!"

"Maria, you don't really need her, do you?" Georg asks. "She isn't first soprano."

I wheel around to face him. "She's part of this family, isn't she?" I demand. This delay might make us miss our slot!

"But she's six years old."

I open the door and pull her out. "What is wrong with you?"

She's crying so hard she's hiccupping now.

"We can't stand here all day," I warn. "So make your choice." I glare at her, silently promising future retribution should this continue, then I walk away. A few seconds later, there are hurried footsteps behind me.

"Wait! I'll come!"

I turn and smile, wiping the tears from her face. "Thank you." I stroke her hair. But she's shaking, and I can't understand it. "You're such a beautiful singer, Ros. You'll get used to this—and there's no crowd watching us today." I kiss the top of her head.

Georg holds his pipe and considers me for a moment, as if he's really seeing me for the first time. But I don't care. We're a family and we do this together.

Inside the radio station, Rosmarie runs to Agathe, who enfolds her in her arms like a tiny, wounded bird.

"She doesn't want to sing?" Father Wasner asks as I sit next to him.

"She'll get used to it."

But his eyes search mine. "She's quite young and we don't actually need her. She can—"

"It's fine," I repeat. Then a door opens and a toothsome young man, dressed in gray suspenders and a flat gray cap, bounces into the room.

"The von Trapps?"

We could hardly be anyone else. But we all stand and proceed to shake the disc jockey's hand. He's smaller than I imagined. And younger.

"Very nice to meet you all," he says. "*Very* nice. My assistant Anya will show you to the recording studio. Captain, if you will come with me."

Georg is taken to the booth, where he'll be interviewed about our singing family. The rest of us follow a red-haired woman into a small studio like the one in Lotte Lehmann's photo. She explains what a green light means and how we'll hear Georg's interview in our headphones.

"You'll start to sing as soon as you hear Karl say 'And now the Trapp Family Choir!' "

Father Wasner arranges us around the microphone while Anya fits headphones onto the children.

"I don't like these!" Lorli complains, and everyone laughs, because it looks as though her three-year-old head is being crushed by a pair of giant boulders.

"It's only for while we're singing. Put them on," I say tersely. I want this to go well. I *need* this to go well, for reasons even I'm not entirely sure of.

It takes a few minutes to become accustomed to wearing something over our ears, but we can hear the disc jockey talking to Georg.

"So, welcome back to the studio, Captain von Trapp. A few months ago you were here to give an interview for your autobiography, *Memories of an Austrian U-Boat Commander*. But today you've come for a very different reason. We hear that your extraordinary family sings together under the name the Trapp Family Choir. Is that right?"

"That's right."

"All *eleven* of you?"

He laughs. "Well, ten. I don't sing."

"And is it true that you even have a conductor?"

"Yes. A family friend by the name of Father Franz Wasner."

"Well, let's hear them, shall we? Bach's 'Hymn of Thanksgiving' by the Trapp Family Choir!"

The phone doesn't stop ringing. The first calls come from Georg's friends, then Anni, then our neighbors, and finally, someone completely unexpected. When I hear Georg go quiet on the line, I know it's something unusual.

We sit in the library, sipping our mugs of tea, and wait for him to speak.

"All right then. Saturday at six." He puts down the receiver and stares blankly ahead. "That was Chancellor Kurt von Schuschnigg."

Rupert lowers his mug. Because you have to understand, the chancellor of Austria is the same as your president or England's prime minister.

"He heard us on the radio and wants the Trapp Family Choir to perform at a reception he'll be hosting in the Chancellery. He's sending three private cars from Vienna to collect us."

Who can describe the excitement over that next week? We starch our blouses and air out our best dirndls and Father Wasner comes to us each evening to rehearse.

"But what about my homework?" Rosmarie complains, obviously searching for an excuse.

"We'll worry about it next week," I tell her, gathering her socks and best patent leather shoes and shoving them into the suitcase.

"Just be thankful," Mitzi says from the doorway. "At least all you're missing is homework."

At twenty, Mitzi thinks she is old enough to be serious about a local boy named Alfons. They've been twice to the movies and on several picnics. But if her two older siblings can find time for singing, then so can she.

"Oh, I'm sure there will be plenty of eligible young men at the Chancellery," Johanna teases.

The girls giggle and I turn to reprimand them. "Have you both packed? Is everyone ready?"

We arrive at von Schuschnigg's palatial residence in a caravan of black cars, then take several moments to stand in the grand courtyard and stare. Down the street rises the impressive winter palace of the Hapsburgs. I'd learned in school about the twenty-seven hundred rooms inside. But I'd learned almost nothing about the Chancellery, with its white and gold facade silhouetted against a purple sky.

"Look at this place," Mitzi says in awe.

"Nervous?" Agathe asks.

"Are you joking?" Mitzi is the first to go inside, followed by Georg and Father Wasner.

It's as beautiful from the inside as it looks from the outside, with high arched ceilings and chandeliers. A man in a tuxedo takes our coats and I catch a glimpse of myself in the hallway mirror. I look older than my twenty-nine years, in a formal dirndl and the diamond earrings that had once belonged to Georg's first wife. I hadn't wanted to wear them, but Georg insisted. "It's the *chancellor*," he pointed out. But how would the children feel to see me wearing something that had once belonged to their mother? "I'll need to ask Agathe first," I said.

But Agathe just smiled. "Oh, it's only a pair of earrings. Wear them."

Now I look at myself and hardly recognize the little girl who used to hide in the attic, too afraid to go downstairs in case Uncle Franz was at home. What would that little girl think if I could tell her that someday she would be standing in the Chancellery, preparing to sing alongside her giant family?

"You look beautiful, Mama." Rosmarie comes up and takes my hand. "But everyone's leaving without us!"

In the sea of tuxedos and glittery black gowns, it's easy to spot our family. The boys may be in black suits, but the girls turn heads in their long green skirts and billowy white blouses. I tighten my grip on Rosmarie's hand and hurry after the others, catching whispers as we pass. "Are those the von Trapps?" "Those have to be the von Trapps!"

When we enter the ballroom, Rosmarie and I both gasp.

In all my life, I have never seen anything so magnificent. Garlands of red and white flowers hang from the ceiling and are draped across the windows, perfuming the air and making the ballroom feel like a summer garden, even in October. From a polished wooden stage, the Viennese Philharmonic Orchestra is playing "An der schönen blauen Donau," the most joyful waltz ever written. And in the center of the room people are laughing and dancing, their crystal champagne glasses catching the light of a dozen chandeliers.

A man introduces himself as an aide to the chancellor, then guides us toward the stage and explains what will happen. When the orchestra begins to play "Wiener Blut," we are to take our places to the left of the stage. Once the orchestra makes its exit, the stage is ours. Father Wasner will stand on the same wooden podium currently being used by the conductor of the Philharmonic. Then, once we're ready, we may begin.

"I've never met anyone more passionate about music than the chancellor," the aide says. He's a cheerful-looking man, with a thin mustache and round glasses. His resemblance to the chancellor is so striking that I wonder if they're related. "When he heard your family on the radio," he continues, "he didn't stop talking about it for days." His eyes come to rest on Father Wasner and he grins. "And you must be the conductor."

Father Wasner smiles. His blond hair is slicked back and

his eyes seem brighter in the candlelight. "We are humbled by your invitation."

"Oh, no." The aide is shaking his head. "The honor is ours. We've all heard about your discovery of new music in your university's archives. And the chancellor has told all of his guests about the Trapp Family Choir. Everyone is looking forward to this."

Perhaps this is the reason that our performance feels different from any we've ever given before. We've never had such an expectant crowd waiting to hear us. The entire audience falls silent. While the orchestra had been playing, people had been drinking and chatting merrily. Even at the festival people had come and gone, tending to crying infants or simply just moving on. But now everyone in the room is turned toward us, and for the next forty minutes we are given their undivided attention. When we finish, the entire room erupts into thunderous applause. Even the members of the Philharmonic Orchestra are clapping.

"Stop grabbing my skirt!" I whisper to Rosmarie.

"But I feel like I'm going to faint."

"Then wait until we're off this stage," I tell her, irritated by her theatrics.

The clapping seems to go on forever, and the feeling is like floating. The chancellor's wife appears and asks if we would like to meet a few people. I look down at Rosmarie.

"Go take Lorli to the gardens," I suggest.

The chancellor, meanwhile, whisks Georg and Father Wasner away to another corner of the room.

By ten o'clock I want to collapse. I've met politicians, musicians, bankers, and all of their bejeweled wives who want to know if it's true that I was going to become a nun eight years ago. I've answered so many questions that my mind is numb. And I've completely lost track of the children. . . .

I see Rosmarie and Lorli chasing each other in the gardens. And Mitzi is sitting with three girls her own age, the four of them laughing and glancing across the room at a group of teenage boys. Then I spot Johanna, alone with a young man near the table for desserts. I watch for several moments as their heads come close together and they laugh. Then I'm crossing the room to see what this is about. At fifteen, I would have gone red with embarrassment if I'd been caught alone with a boy. But Johanna just smiles.

"Mother, I would like you to meet Ernst Winter. His father is Karl Winter, the vice mayor of Vienna."

Ernst flashes me a wide smile, and immediately I'm suspicious. He's dressed in an expensive suit, with polished loafers and a fancy watch. His blue eyes look steady enough, but I don't like how his shoulder brushes against Johanna's. Or the easy way he's been laughing with her. "Your family has unbelievable talent, Frau von Trapp. It was the highlight of the evening, listening to you."

I smile briefly. "Thank you, Ernst. Johanna," I add sternly, "I think it's time."

"Just a few more minutes?" she asks, glancing at the vice mayor's son. "He's telling me about the history of the piece we just performed. Did you know that Bach would sign all of his music 'I.N.J.'? It's Latin for—"

"In Nomine Jesu," I reply.

"Yes." Johanna nods eagerly. "Bach was deeply pious. Like you."

I stare at the young man next to Johanna. "Five more minutes. But that is it."

When I turn to leave them, the chancellor is standing be-hind me with Father Wasner and Georg. All three of them are smiling.

"What?" I ask, immediately suspicious, and the chancel-lor laughs.

"Frau von Trapp, I believe I have convinced both your husband and your conductor that it would be a crime to hide away a family like yours. The entire world should know of your talents."

I glance at Georg.

"The chancellor believes we should go on tour," he says, smiling as if he can't believe it himself.

"But where would we go? How would we—"

"Oh, just leave that up to me." The chancellor adjusts the round glasses on his nose and smiles.

We don't leave the Chancellery until eleven o'clock, but only Lorli falls asleep in the car. Everyone else is too full of stories about the night. When we've returned to the villa the next day, our phone won't stop ringing. Rupert is forced to take up residence in the library, jotting down every invitation that comes in. An offer to perform in Munich. Free train tickets to Paris. A chance to perform at the great Staatsoper Berlin. We all listen and clap with each offer that comes in, laughing as we imagine ourselves boarding a train to perform at the Vienna State Opera.

"It all seems a little much," Georg worries, perched on the edge of the couch.

"But it's a great opportunity to see the rest of Europe," Werner says.

"And we would all be together," Agathe points out.

"Oh, please can we do them all," Mitzi begs. "Please." After being bedridden for much of her childhood, I can sense her longing to go out and explore.

"What do you think, Ros?" Georg asks tenderly.

Our daughter climbs into his lap, then glances at me. "Whatever everyone else wants," she says.

"No, no. What do *you* want?" he repeats, tapping her little nose.

"I want to be with you," she whispers, snuggling into his chest.

"And Lorli," Georg asks, ever the diplomat. "What would my smallest princess like?"

"Strudel," she announces, and everyone laughs.

"I think we should do it," Rupert says, surprising everyone.

Georg frowns. "What about your studies?"

"We could conduct the tours during my school breaks. Like Werner said, it would be a great way to see the world. And he can go back to farming when we return."

Georg strikes a match and lights the bowl of his pipe, and for a moment his face is obscured by wisps of smoke. He sits back and thinks while the scent of his tobacco fills the library. When his silence continues, Rupert persists.

"So is it settled then? Shall we accept the offers?" he asks.

Georg sighs. "Why don't we start off with just one or two."

CHAPTER EIGHTEEN

FRAN

Manhattan, New York
1959

I'T'S ONLY WHEN MARIA stops speaking and primly folds her hands in her lap that Fran realizes she's been holding her breath. So this was it. This was the start of the Trapp Family Singers.

"And the Nazis at the Salzburg Music Festival—"

"Never happened," Maria says harshly, rising from the park bench. Around them, men are shrugging into their jackets and women are buttoning their sweaters as the wind picks up.

"Mr. Hammerstein is going to want my notes by Monday," Fran says, also rising from the bench. "I wouldn't wish to impose on your weekend, but I don't suppose you're free tomorrow?"

"If you don't mind me bringing Lorli. She's driving down from Connecticut to see me tonight."

"That would be wonderful!" Fran exclaims. Little Lorli, who must be almost thirty by now. "Connecticut," she repeats, surprised. For some reason, she imagined that all of the children would have settled close to Maria, in Vermont.

"Yes. It's not so far away." But Maria's voice catches when she says this. "She's married with five daughters. Can you believe? I have twenty-nine grandchildren now."

"It must be wonderful to have so much family." Fran herself has no one in the city, and even though she loves her job at Rodgers & Hammerstein, there are times when she catches herself thinking of home.

They begin to walk, and she's reminded of something Hammerstein said when he'd heard that Maria was in New York. "I realize it's still a month away," Fran tells her, "but let me know how many tickets you'll want for the premiere. You can take up an entire row—even two—if you'd like."

But Maria's smile falters. "I doubt that will be necessary."

"Oh, it's no trouble. It's your story, after all. We—"

"One ticket."

Fran stares at her to see if she means it.

After work that evening, over hamburgers at the Moondance Diner, Fran repeats the story for the table. Jack is there, and while they drove to the diner together, an obvious separation exists between them. His arm isn't slung casually around her shoulders, and the big smile he normally reserves for her is now flashing at the waitress. Then a memory resurfaces of him playing the piano with Hammerstein in the Hamptons. Maybe Eva had been right.

For once, she's glad Eva isn't here, even though Friday-night dinners have become a tradition. Instead, Peter is on his own, seated between two men who work for Dick Rodgers. The three of them are absorbed in her tale, trying to figure out what it means.

"I don't think it's exactly a mystery," Jack says, plunking down his empty beer glass. "Her children are still upset about seeing the German film."

"Which was the basis for this script," Fran points out heatedly. "And no wonder. The last half of this show is nothing like her life."

But Jack isn't bothered by it.

Peter puts down his napkin and frowns. "So is she angry?"

"I can't tell," Fran admits. She leans back against the booth. "But she knows it's unlikely Hammerstein will meet with her and that I'm simply typing up notes for him."

"Oh, Fran." Jack says her name as if the effort is exhausting. When did he become so condescending? "I really wouldn't put too much effort into that."

Fran is about to respond, but Peter beats her to it. "Why not?"

Jack laughs. "Because he'll take one glance at them and then toss them out. You really think he's going to change the show?"

"Why not? He changed the lyrics in 'My Favorite Things' after you made that suggestion," Peter argues.

Fran looks at Jack. "What suggestion?"

He doesn't answer.

"Jack thought 'pink satin sashes' should be changed to 'blue,'" Peter explains. "For the longer vowel. And Hammerstein took his advice."

Fran is staring at Jack so hard it's a wonder he doesn't melt into the plastic booth. Then suddenly he gets to his feet.

"You know, who even cares what happens to this play? The whole thing will probably run for twelve nights and never be heard of again." He grabs his leather jacket and meets Fran's eyes. "Go ahead and waste your time."

Everyone in the booth goes silent with shock. Then after Jack is gone, Fran says quietly, "*I* made that suggestion about the color."

There's an intake of breaths around the table, and one of the men who works for Dick Rodgers tells her it was smart. "But why would Jack do that?"

"Yeah," chimes in another guy. "What's the matter with him?"

Peter looks at Fran and shakes his head. "I'm sorry. I didn't mean to cause an argument."

The waitress makes a cheerful reappearance with their desserts, but Fran isn't in any mood for eating. The *New Yorker* article has been nothing but a curse. First her mom, now Jack.

"You know, I'm actually not that hungry. I'm sorry." Fran grabs her handbag and gets up to leave.

"Wait." Peter rises as well.

"Hey, what about dessert?" one of the guys shouts after them.

"You have it," Peter calls over his shoulder.

Outside the diner, Peter exhales. He looks as worn out as Fran probably does, and she wonders if it has to do with Eva. They stand together beneath the neon lights and quietly take in the rush of Manhattan's evening traffic. Perhaps her article is less of a curse and more like the sign over the diner, a garish illumination of everything that hasn't been right in her life.

"Not been a great week, has it?" Peter shoves his hands into the pockets of his sports coat.

"I can't believe he did that. Took my idea and passed it off as his."

Peter shakes his head and a loose curl falls into his eyes. He quickly brushes it away. "Jealousy does funny things to people," he says quietly. They begin to walk toward the station. Peter lives only two blocks from Fran, but they've never ridden the subway together.

"Where's Eva?"

"Probably with her new guy," Peter says, turning away from her.

"Oh, Peter. I'm really sorry."

He shrugs. "She told me last week. I was pretty cut up about it at first. But, you know, I'm not sure I'm all that upset about it anymore."

"Still, four years—"

"It's a long time, isn't it?" His hazel eyes focus on hers. "You all right?"

Fran blinks back tears. "I just . . . I feel like my ambition is a curse."

"What?" Peter stops walking. "Franny, you should never say that."

"It's true. My mother thinks I'm wasting my time with writing. And now my writing has come between me and Jack—"

"Jack came between you and Jack," he says firmly. "Not the writing." They've reached the station, but Peter pauses at the top of the stairs, causing a line of people to grow behind them. "You have a gift, Fran. The curse would be if you abandoned it."

Fran thinks about Peter's words the next morning as she makes her way back to Maria's favorite bench in Central Park. She hasn't heard from Jack since he stormed out of the diner last night, but she'll have to face him at work on Monday. And what then? At first, Fran had been hurt. Now she simply feels angry.

She sits on the bench and looks out at the cherry trees. In April, pink blossoms will fill the skyline. But in mid-October the trees are burnished gold. She wants to focus on the task at hand. Finish the interview with Maria, then pass on her notes. But she can't stop thinking about Jack's duplicity or the way Peter had said to her that the real curse would be if she never wrote at all.

Fran is still thinking about Peter when a familiar voice makes her look up. Maria is there in her green dirndl and next to her is a striking young woman. Lorli. Her daughter is dressed almost exactly as she is, in a voluminous green skirt and crisp white blouse. Both women smile, and Fran sees they even share the same rosy cheeks.

"You must be Eleonore." Fran extends her hand, and the young woman shakes it warmly.

"Oh, goodness, just Lorli," she says. "Mother has told me so much about you."

Fran steals a glance at Maria to try to guess what might have been said.

"Only kind things." Maria laughs. "I try never to dwell on the negative."

Lorli's raised brow tells Fran that the truth is somewhat different, but Fran appreciates the remark anyway. She scoots over in order to make room on the bench, but Maria shakes her head and Lorli tells her, "My mother is hoping to make the ten o'clock service at the cathedral."

"Oh, of course." Fran rises. "We can chat as we walk. You leave tomorrow, right?"

Maria sighs. "Yes. Lorli will be here a few more days, taking care of family business. But I need to get back to the lodge."

"My brother is there right now," Lorli explains.

"But he's only twenty," Maria interjects, "and it's a big responsibility."

Fran can see that Lorli is biting her tongue. Maybe Maria doesn't like being away from home. Or it could be that she prefers being in control. Whatever the case, it seems impossible to believe that she has a boy of her own who's now twenty years old.

"So my mother tells me that this show is a lot like the German film," Lorli says. She has no trace of Maria's German accent, but she is blunt like her mother, and for this, Fran is actually grateful.

"Yes," Fran admits while they walk. "Right now, the play and the film are not very different."

"But you will change that," Maria says forcefully, and both women look at her.

Fran inhales. "I'm hoping that Mr. Hammerstein will make some changes, yes. But from a writer's perspective, I can tell you that there are elements of the play that he may not want to alter."

Maria's voice grows thin. "Such as?"

Fran steels herself for their outrage. She has no idea how Lorli will react to the news that her father will be portrayed as a hard-nosed disciplinarian once again. But she imagines it won't be with indifference. This is her father's legacy, after all. "Well, I'm guessing that Mr. Hammerstein will choose to keep your husband's character somewhat rigid. But perhaps it helps to remember that in the end, it's just a character."

"Except that everyone will believe it," Lorli says, incredulous. "How is this happening *again*?"

Because the writers were lazy and didn't want to change what had obviously worked so well in Germany, Fran thinks. But to Lorli she says, "This is why I'm taking notes."

Maria begins zipping her crucifix back and forth along its chain. "I promised Georg. I went to his grave and promised him."

Fran swallows. "There are things to be hopeful about," she points out. "This isn't just a play. It's a musical, and Mr. Hammerstein is writing the songs. That will make this very different from the film."

But Lorli isn't buying it. "How?"

Fran can feel herself grasping. "Well, songs add new dimensions to the characters. And I wouldn't think of this as anyone's life story. I would think of it as being *based* on your life story. Loosely."

"And when people come running up to us in the streets with the assumption that all of it is true?" Lorli challenges.

"Then perhaps you will tell them to visit the lodge for the real story."

The walk to the cathedral is mostly silent. No one is happy, least of all Fran, who should never have been given this job. Because Maria is right. Everyone will believe what they see on the stage. And why should they think anything different?

How many of them will bother to visit the lodge in Vermont or read a copy of Maria's autobiography?

While Maria enters the cathedral, Fran waits on a bench with Lorli, and Fran thinks they probably look like sisters. They both have the same light eyes and dark hair. It's Lorli who breaks the silence.

"My brothers and sisters won't be happy to see our father portrayed as a humorless disciplinarian again while my mother comes across as a saint."

Fran nods, understanding. "I'm sure it wasn't easy when the film was released. From what your mother has said, she seems to feel a great deal of guilt."

Lorli seems surprised. "About the film?"

"Yes, and now the musical."

"What you just said to my mother about using the show to lure people to the lodge—none of her children care about that. She might be blinded by the publicity, but what matters most to us is our father and our loving memory of him."

"In the end, the audience will see him just as valiant and lovable as he was in life," Fran promises, her voice steady.

"His children owe that to him. My mother—" But Lorli cuts herself off, not sure if she should go on. Then she draws an unsteady breath. "I'm the one child who consistently visits her," she confides.

"But there are ten children."

"Nine," Lorli corrects quietly. "Martina died in childbirth seven years ago."

Martina, who had been so difficult for Maria when she was young. It seems impossible to think of her as old enough to have children of her own. "I'm so sorry."

Lorli nods, and Fran can see how painful this is for her.

"No one but Johannes is even interested in the lodge," she reveals. "We all just want to move on."

Suddenly, Fran feels overwhelmed. What has happened to this family? And why did Hammerstein think she was up to this task?

"You bought into Germany's film version of our lives, didn't you? The happy story about all the children who loved to sing."

Fran's embarrassed to admit that she did. And she can't understand how a woman who married a man for his children no longer retains their affection. "Was there an argument?" she asks.

Lorli laughs. "Just pick a topic and I can tell you what the arguments were about. Religion? None of us were religious enough. Bible every night and Mass every Sunday wasn't adequate. It needed to be about sacrifice. The way Jesus sacrificed for us. So some weeks we went without meat. Other weeks without milk. Or the radio. Or TV."

"Was she always this way?"

Lorli glances toward the cathedral. "She almost became a nun. She's passionate about whatever she does," she explains. "When we could pay the mortgage on the lodge by giving fifteen concerts a month, she used to book thirty. And if one newspaper ran an interview about our family, she wanted another ten. It exhausted us. Because we weren't like her. We needed rest sometimes. And to do other things."

"And she never stopped?"

Lorli shakes her head. "Not even when Rosmarie went missing."

Fran leans forward, the noise of the traffic forgotten. "When was this?"

"Just after my father died. Rosmarie was eighteen and didn't want to sing anymore, but my mother wouldn't hear of it. And without our father, who could my sister appeal to?"

Fran's heart aches for the little girl who once hid in the family car rather than sing on the radio.

"She was gone for three days," Lorli remembers. "The entire city came out to try to find her. When they did, she was wandering barefoot across an empty field. She couldn't even remember her name."

No wonder Maria always lingered on Rosmarie's story. It wasn't disapproval. It was guilt.

"My mother sent her to an institution where they tried to help her. And everyone thought the electroshock therapy had worked because she returned to singing the next month."

Fran can feel her heart actually drop in her chest. "And her stage fright?"

"It turned out they hadn't cured her of that. She had a second breakdown seven years ago and never sang with us again." Fran is shocked to learn this, but Lorli just sighs. "My mother is terrible at facing painful truths, but when Father died, we all felt that a chapter of our lives had closed. It was only my mother who disagreed."

So without Georg—the source of reason and calm—to hold it together, everything began to fall apart.

Lorli glances at the cathedral, obviously wondering how much time she has left. She must decide it's enough, because she continues, "You should understand, my mother grew up very lonely, and her greatest fear has always been that she'll be left on her own. She didn't intend to hurt Ros, she just couldn't understand. And now her misunderstandings and anxieties and fears have driven everyone away."

Which is why she asked for only one ticket to the premiere, Fran thinks. "So did everyone want to quit after your father died?"

"Not immediately. But after Rosmarie had her break-down, Johanna asked to get married. Of course, my mother's answer was no. But Johanna was already twenty-nine and her boyfriend had been proposing to her for more than ten years. She'd met him at the Chancellery—"

Fran gives a little gasp. "Ernst? The vice mayor of Vienna's son?"

Lorli looks shocked. "My mother told you about him?"

"She mentioned he was there."

Lorli gives a little sniff. "Did she mention that when Ernst finally got tired of waiting, he told my mother himself that they'd be getting married with or without her blessing? Well, you can imagine how she took that."

But Fran didn't understand. "Didn't she want Johanna to get married?"

"And lose one of her lead sopranos?" Lorli smiles ruefully. "She tried locking Johanna in her room," she confides. "But my sister escaped through her window and eloped."

Locking a daughter in her room at the age of twenty-nine! What could Maria have been thinking? Fran tries to imagine how Maria would have felt without Georg, her entire world spiraling out of control. For twenty years she'd been the en-gine that drove the train, then suddenly the cars were detach-ing. And what was left? For all of her drive and ambition, she'd come to New York alone, with only Lorli willing to visit.

"I shouldn't have painted my mother in such a dark light," Lorli worries, twisting her hands in her lap. "We would never have survived without her ambition, and that isn't an exaggeration. Our family repeatedly turned down performance requests from the Nazi Party. And the third time we refused, the request came from Hitler himself."

Fran doesn't think she remembers anything about that in Maria's book.

"If my mother hadn't encouraged us to sing and go on tour, we would never have had a way out of Austria. And eventually, they would have sent us to one of the camps over our family's criticism of the Nazi Party. If that had happened, we would have died there." Lorli's eyes grow dark. "Without a doubt. So she saved us. And every one of her kids is grateful to her for that. Who could imagine we would all end up here?" She smiles. "In America."

"And with a Broadway musical," Fran points out.

But Lorli doesn't seem impressed by this. "My mother is stubborn," she warns. "If you can't convince her to fall in love with your play, she might make things difficult."

Lorli's remark has the desired effect on Fran. She smooths the fabric of her skirt with her palms. "Do you think your mother would talk about it to the press?"

"I'm sure she would."

This is what Fran has feared. She can see Maria making her way out of the cathedral, stopping to socialize with people in the narthex. Lorli follows her gaze.

"I apologize if what I've said about my mother is upsetting."

"No." Fran shakes her head. "It's just the truth, and families are complicated. Everyone comes away from their childhood with wounds, some deeper than others."

Lorli seems to connect with this. "Yes." She tugs her dirndl over her knees and thinks. "When we reached America, I was sent to boarding school. I cried bitterly when everyone left me to go on tour. I didn't understand the language or the customs—I didn't even know when they'd be coming back. It was traumatic," she admits. "I wanted to be on tour with everyone else. But if you had asked Rosmarie, she'd have traded places with me in an instant."

So even Lorli had suffered. How old could she have been when they left her? Seven? "And then your family toured all across America," Fran recalls.

"Yes. The touring was hard on them. Months and months on an old bus with no heat, traveling through snowstorms from motel to motel. When my mother became pregnant with Johannes, she let out her dirndl and didn't tell anyone, because a pregnant woman on tour . . . But none of it started off this way. In the beginning," Lorli remembers, "back in Aigen, it was actually magical."

Maria returns, gushing about the cathedral and interrupting their moment. "Have you been inside?" she asks.

Fran smiles warmly. "Oh, many times." Most days she passes it on the way to lunch. "It's one of the most beautiful buildings in Manhattan."

Maria looks between Fran and her daughter, trying to guess at the conversation, so Fran fills her in.

"Your daughter was just telling me how life was on tour. How magical it was when it first began."

Maria glances down at Lorli and seems surprised. "It *was* magical, wasn't it?"

CHAPTER NINETEEN

MARIA

Salzburg, Austria
1937

THE MORNING THE OFFERS start coming in, news begins to spread that the von Trapp family is going on tour. And when the day arrives, nearly all of Aigen turns up at the railway station to see us off. There are friends and neighbors crowded together, stretching beyond the platform. The sight brings tears to Georg's eyes, and mine as well, because even if some of these people have been awful, many others have been very, very good to us, especially after Georg realized that his fortune was gone.

As the train begins to pull away from the station, the children hang out the windows and wave, calling out promises to be back soon and to write. I watch our beloved Aigen fade from view, replaced by deep scarlet and purple fields of chard, then turn to my notebook and start to plan. It's the middle of November, and Father Wasner must be back in time for Christmas services. There are five countries on our tour,

eighteen concerts to give, and everyone has their own check-
lists of places they wish to see. Most of all, I want to tour the
Vatican, Georg wants to see the Colosseum, Mitzi and Johanna both wish to stand outside of Buckingham Palace, and
Rupert wants to climb the Eiffel Tower.

Over the next six weeks we do all of these things and
more. We have concerts in Paris, Rome, Brussels, London,
and The Hague. And each concert is more successful than
the last. But only because we continuously learn from our
mistakes. In London we discover that no one is particularly
interested in madrigals, while in Brussels we find completely
by accident that audiences love to see me play my guitar and
the children play their recorders. The constant program
changes keep Father Wasner continuously busy, rewriting
the music and making new books for each of us to use onstage. Georg, meanwhile, is in charge of our itinerary, and
with so many stops, he is always at work.

I think even the youngest children agree that while the
touring isn't easy, it's exciting. We have audiences with kings
and queens, and in the Vatican, the Holy Father, Pope Pius XI,
calls on us to sing "Ave Verum" for him. It's one of the happiest days of my life.

But in Paris something I've suspected to be true since the
start of our trip becomes apparent. Johanna is braiding Rosmarie's hair for our concert when I see it—a bald patch that
Rosmarie has been trying to hide by parting her hair differently these past few weeks. I cross the hotel room in several
strides.

"What is this?" I gasp. It can't be real. "How did this happen? Are you pulling out your own hair?"

Rosmarie begins to cry and I accuse her of wanting to

derail the tour. After all, how can she perform with a bald spot on her head? "We'll have to paint it," I say, and she now begins to wail.

"Mother, she isn't well," Johanna says. "Maybe she should take a night off."

"We're the Trapp Family Choir," I thunder, overruling this suggestion. "The only family where *all* the children sing— not some. And she is nine years old. If Lorli can manage, then so can she."

Except Lorli isn't managing. Not really. She is only six and the late hours are wearing on her. At night, she cries and asks to be carried back to the hotel. And in the morning, she almost falls asleep over her breakfast. *But it's only temporary,* I tell myself. It's the opportunity of a lifetime to see the rest of Europe, and this is what we do—setting off with our dirndls and lederhosen to all the great castles and cathedrals.

So Rosmarie carries on. And so does Lorli. And I ignore the looks the older girls pass among themselves, because someday they'll appreciate all of it. I would have given the world to have traveled across Europe with my siblings and a father who loved me. It may seem hard now, but in a few years the long hours of practice and late-night concerts will all seem worth it.

At Christmas we return to a stack of newspapers piled on top of our dining room table. Family and friends from all across Europe have sent us our reviews, and Hans has sorted them from the longest on top to the shortest. I think of him reading each article and then carefully finding its place in the stack and my eyes fill with tears.

"Happy to be home?" Hans asks.

Georg sighs. "Yes." He misses the routine of our life here.

His morning walk around the estate with Hans, and their evening smoke on the porch, the two of them puffing away on their pipes as the sun dips below the horizon of trees.

We gather around the long wooden table and Rupert does the honor of reading each review aloud. It's more than any group could hope for. *The Guardian* has called us "the most talented family in Europe," and a newspaper in Vienna says we're the "rising stars of musical theater." Most important, we've earned enough money to run the villa for nearly a year, even without boarders.

At Christmas, the neighbors who had turned their backs on us a few years ago now come around to enjoy a concert instead of caviar. And for the briefest of moments it seems as if we might be able to fall back into the same beautiful life we had known before our fortunes changed. If we'd been paying attention, we would have known better. But in February of 1938, when Chancellor Schuschnigg tells Austria that there is nothing to worry about from Hitler and Germany, we believe him.

Then comes March, wrapped in a blanket of sleet and snow. For Agathe's twenty-fifth birthday, Mitzi bakes her sister's favorite chocolate cake, with brown sugar and vanilla, and we gather around the dining room table singing "Hoch soll er leben!" while snow falls over the estate.

"Look how beautiful!" Lorli exclaims, going to the window.

"Should we take the cake into the library and watch the snow fall?" Agathe suggests. The library has always had the best view.

So we all relocate, and while Georg stokes the fire, the room fills with the heady scent of burning cedar. Rupert turns on the radio, and above the crack and hiss of the flames comes an unexpected voice. Everyone freezes and I lower my cake to my lap. It's the voice of Chancellor Schuschnigg.

"What's happening?" Hedwig whispers.

"I am repeating this special announcement. Today, on the eleventh of March, 1938, the sovereign nation of Austria has fallen into the hands of the German government."

Agathe's plate drops to the floor.

"We are yielding to force." The chancellor's voice breaks. "We have chosen the ignominy of surrender over a long and bloody war. Austria—God bless you!"

Ten of us look around the library at one another, in deep shock. Then the German national anthem begins to play and suddenly it's real. We have surrendered our country of six million people to Germany's eighty million—just as they knew we would. Because any war between us would see our people slaughtered down to the last woman and child.

Georg's eyes fill with tears and Agathe's birthday is completely forgotten. Then suddenly the door to the library swings open and Hans is there, his blue eyes bright with excitement. He approaches Georg, who is seated behind his desk, and it takes me a moment to realize what's happening.

"Herr Korvettenkapitän, I feel it is my duty to inform you that I am a member of the Party. I wanted you to know before"—he glances around the room, averting his gaze when he comes to Father Wasner—"before anything might be said or done that I should have to report. Austria and Germany are one. Heil Hitler!"

Hans removes himself before any of us have the chance to respond, then a German voice comes over the radio and proclaims, "Austria is finished. Long live the Third Reich!" A

Prussian march begins to play the "Preußens Gloria," and when I see Georg with his eyes raised to the Austrian flag above the mantelpiece, I begin to weep.

The youngest children, Lorli and Rosmarie, come running, afraid of the silence that's ruined Agathe's party.

"What's happening?" Lorli asks, collapsing into my lap.

"We have a new government," I say between my tears.

"But why is that bad?"

I smooth her hair back behind her ears and make space for Rosmarie on my lap. "Because we didn't choose it," I tell her. "An angry man came and took over our government, and now we have to live with it."

Georg cuts his eyes to me, because Hans is only on the other side of the wall, but I don't care. I rise and ask Father Wasner to lead us into our chapel to pray. As we leave, I hear the bells of Nonnberg begin to ring. I inhale sharply and the voice on the radio joyfully proclaims, "Throughout Austria the people are greeting their liberators. Austria is free from oppression, and right now you are hearing all of Salzburg rejoice!"

I gasp. "Lie!" I scream, and immediately, Rupert and Werner are at my side.

"Mother, you can't—"

But I shake off Rupert's hand. "The nuns would never ring the bells—"

"Of course not," he reasons. "It's the Nazis."

Over the next few days, we discover what kind of influence these Nazis wield. There are stories of protesters being taken into the woods and never reemerging, of Jews being forced from their homes and put on trains. When I ask Georg why the Germans are so interested in the Jews, he doesn't have an answer for me. But when I ask where they're taking them, his face turns very pale.

"I've made a few phone calls," he says, "to some old friends from the navy." We're the only ones in the library, but his voice still drops. "They told me the Nazis are taking them to concentration camps."

I don't understand.

"Prisons where they'll force them to do manual labor," he explains.

I gasp. "What about the women and children?"

His face is grim. "Them, too."

My heart is racing. "We have to warn the Berghoffs and the Allstadts," I say. "And the Stiblers."

Georg motions for me to lower my voice. "Already done."

I glance at the door, hating how secretive we've become in our own house. "How can they do this?" I cry. But that's the thing about war and invasions. The enemy can do whatever they wish.

That afternoon, as Agathe returns with the girls from school, a long black car rolls into our drive and several men in uniform get out hurriedly. I stop beating out the dust from our dining room rug and feel my stomach clench.

The youngest one leads the group to our door. He acknowledges me with the new greeting that all of Austria is now supposed to adopt. "Heil Hitler." He salutes me and I simply stare back, hoping I look too old and stupid to have mastered this. "Is the Captain at home?"

I'm about to answer when Georg walks up and stands in the doorway beside me.

"Heil Hitler!" All three men salute at once.

My husband stands there, clearly too old and feeble to respond as well, and the young one clears his throat.

"Sir, the city is preparing for a visit from the Führer. We expect every house in Salzburg to be displaying the swastika. Yet it's come to our attention that you don't even own a flag."

"This is true," Georg says.

"How is this possible when we have already been here for two weeks?"

"Oh." Georg shoves his hands deep into his pockets. "I'm afraid it's just too expensive," he says. "We barely get by with what we have without buying flags."

The young man marches to the car and returns with two red banners. In the middle is the ancient symbol sacred to Hindus, now turned slightly and made into the emblem of the Nazi Party. "If you'd like, we can help you hang them from the windows."

"Oh." Georg studies them and furrows his brow. "Look at this red. The color does nothing for my villa. But if you'd like me to decorate, I have some lovely rugs." He turns their attention to the one I was beating clean moments before. "Shall I hang that from my window?"

The young man doesn't know what to say, and his comrades are growing impatient. These young Austrian boys aren't soldiers. A month ago, they were shoe clerks and apprentices.

"We have sixty more houses to get to," one of them complains. "We gave him the banners. That's what we came here to do. Let's go."

Georg smiles, as if the visit has been a big success, and we wave as they drive away. But as soon as they're out of sight, he crumples the red fabric in his hands. That afternoon, he calls a family meeting. Rupert is home from university with his new degree in medicine. Under any other circumstance we would be celebrating. But now we join Father Wasner around the dining room table and wait in silence.

"What happened today was a very close call," Georg says. Hans has been sent into the city to find a new tire for the car, so for the rest of the afternoon we can all speak freely. "This isn't going to be the last time the Nazis will make a request of us. And soon these requests will turn into commands." Georg has lived through a war once already and knows. "Father Wasner, of course, can do as he pleases. But I would like the rest of us to avoid the city at all costs."

I start to protest, but Georg holds up his hand. "The whole of Salzburg is hung with red and black, and we'd all sooner end our lives on dung heaps than salute that madman. We can only get into trouble by venturing out."

"Father's right," Werner says. "How long before we run across someone who takes offense at our silence?"

"Even at the university dissent was becoming dangerous," Rupert says. "I'm glad to be out of there."

"What happens when you find work?" Agathe asks.

Rupert shakes his head and answers honestly, "I don't know. But I won't salute their Führer."

We keep away from the city during the next few weeks, thinking that if we simply avoid other people we will be safe. But the children must still go to school, and this becomes our greatest worry. Each day Lorli and Rosmarie have some new heartache to report, beginning with the Nazi Party's view on Jesus. We're arranged around the fireplace mending and reading when Lorli asks quietly, "Is it true what they say in school?"

"And what do they say in school?" Agathe asks. Her voice is light. She is so good with children. Whereas immediately my blood is boiling.

"The teachers said that Jesus was a naughty little Jew who made trouble for his parents. But is that true?"

Agathe glances at me, bracing for the torrent of anger that's about to be unleashed, and soon Georg comes in from smoking his pipe on the porch to see what the commotion is about. When I'm too upset to tell him, it's Agathe who explains.

"Which teacher was this?" Georg asks calmly.

"We don't know their names," Rosmarie says. "All the teachers are new, even the principal—"

Georg and I exchange looks. It's not enough that the Nazis have taken over our government. Now they want our children, too.

"They said we're not to go home and talk about what we learn in school," Rosmarie tells us. "They said our parents are too old to understand. But we are the future," she says. "And we are the ones who will save the world."

I actually feel sick.

The next day, I am called into the office by the new principal. I arrive ten minutes before the children are let out, slowly making my way through the school. Eleven years ago I was a teacher here. The squat wooden buildings are still the same. There are even the same blackboards that Sister Johanna had made for each classroom door, to mark attendance. But the faces inside are unfamiliar. The Nazis have forbidden all nuns from teaching. God is to have no place in their new world.

I knock at the principal's office and a stern-looking woman with thin brows and extremely black curls answers the door.

"Frau von Trapp." As I enter, she holds out her hand. This used to be Sister Gisela's office, filled with potted plants and pretty lace curtains. Now there are no decorations. Of course, the cross over the desk is gone.

I seat myself on a stiff wooden chair and the principal takes her place opposite me. From behind her desk, she laces her fingers and studies me. "Your youngest daughter is a problem," she says.

"That's funny. She's never been a problem for me."

The woman fixes me with her gray eyes. "She is refusing to sing our new anthem," she says. "And when I asked her why, she told the class that her family would prefer to be discarded on a dung heap than sing the praises of their country."

Because it's not our country, I want to say. Instead, I just feel my face go hot.

"You see how this is a problem." She smiles, and I hate everything about her—the red of her lipstick, the giant curls in her hair. "But tomorrow I am sure she will join us in class. It would be very bad publicity for a family like yours to be seen as unpatriotic. Other families have found themselves sent to the camps. But I'm sure that won't happen to you."

CHAPTER TWENTY

MARIA

Salzburg, Austria
1938

STANDING IN FRONT OF the mirror, I draw my shirt tightly around my waist. Then I turn and look from the other side. "Georg!" I shout, but he's shaving and can't hear me over the running water. "Georg!" I cry, and this time the urgency in my voice cuts through the sound. He hurries out and I leave the shirt tight for him, so he can see the tiny bulge.

"Are you—"

I smile, then suddenly my eyes fill with tears until I can't even see him approach.

"Oh, Maria, a baby. Number ten!"

I blink back tears and steady him with my gaze. "Twelve."

"Of course," he whispers. He looks immensely sad for a moment, then I pull him closer and bury my face in his shoulder to cry. I'm thirty-two, and in eleven years of marriage, there have only been two children of my own.

"What if this one doesn't stay?" I whisper.

"Then we will pray," he says, swelling my heart, because prayers have never been his first course of action. "And you will rest," he adds firmly.

I inhale the lingering scent of his shaving cream and nod. "Yes. This time, I'll rest."

The next morning we go to see Dr. Katz. I put on a tea-length dirndl embroidered with silver edelweiss. Dr. Katz is from the mountains, like me, and I know he will appreciate it. But when the nurse comes to see us in the foyer of his little office on the Getreidegasse, the most famous street for shopping in Salzburg, she tells us he's left.

"What do you mean, left? For the day?" Georg questions.

The woman presses her lips together, then folds her hands on the desk as if she's being incredibly patient with us. "Left as in gone. He was Jewish," she says.

"And what does that matter?" Georg's voice is rising. "This is his clinic. I was here when he started it thirty years ago!"

"Is there something I can help you with?" A man in a white coat appears behind the nurse, and the woman turns on her heel.

Georg's mustache is quivering. "Your nurse has just told me that Dr. Katz isn't here."

"That's right," the man says simply. "I'm Dr. Krause. What can I help you with today?"

And just like that, Dr. Katz is gone. I look around the foyer, to see if there are other outraged faces, but the women are either tending to babies or knitting. The men are reading newspapers, undisturbed.

We're taken back to the room where Dr. Katz has always seen us, but everything that once belonged to him has vanished. The framed photographs of his children, his charts, even his little wooden horse on a string.

"Do you know where he's gone?" I ask Dr. Krause.

The man looks over his round spectacles at me. "Where who's gone, Frau von Trapp?"

"*Dr. Katz.*"

"Two weeks ago I was told there was a position to be filled here in Salzburg, so I came. This is all I know. Now how can I help you?"

I stare teary-eyed at Georg, but there's nothing to be done. I can't speak. I can't even look around the office without wanting to cry. So Georg tells this new doctor about my condition. How my kidneys haven't been strong enough to carry a child to term these last few years.

The doctor examines me and confirms what Dr. Katz has said. Then he gives me strict instructions to rest.

"Whether this child can be born will be determined by how well you take care of yourself, Frau von Trapp. Keep to a strict diet of vegetables and broth, don't become too excited, and in eight months there will be a baby."

When rehearsals with Father Wasner are over that evening, Georg calls a family meeting, first to discuss Dr. Katz, then the coming baby. We wait until the children have finished clearing the plates before explaining what happened this morning. It's such upsetting news that I focus my attention outside on the rain, which hasn't let up since we returned from the doctor's office.

"What do you mean, gone?" Rupert echoes our disbelief. Like Georg, he's dressed in a heavy argyle sweater. This entire month has been unseasonably cold.

"No one can tell us where he is. Did he flee? Was he taken to a camp?" Georg lights his pipe and then tosses the match aside. "I've made some phone calls—nothing so far."

"But he can't be gone," Lorli says, climbing onto Georg's lap. "Dr. Katz gave me my wooden horse."

"Yes," Georg says, his voice barely above a whisper. "He loved to make toys."

"So who will be our doctor now?" Rosmarie asks.

"A man named Krause," I say, blinking quickly to keep myself from crying.

"So, no more Dr. Katz and no more Bruno Walter," Rosmarie reflects.

Georg and Father Wasner exchange looks across the table and Georg lowers his pipe. "What do you mean?"

"At school today they told us that Jews like Bruno Walter can no longer conduct Aryan music. Is that true?"

The room goes so intensely silent for several moments that the only sound is the staccato rain on the roof.

"Bruno Walter is a genius," Father Wasner explodes. "And anyone who says otherwise is a fool!" His cheeks are red and his eyes are blazing. I've never seen him so angry. Music is his life's work, and some of the greatest musicians in Austria are Jewish. "What are these teachers doing to the children?"

Rosmarie shrinks back into her chair, and I pat her knee to reassure her that she isn't to blame. Then we all glance at the door, worrying about the imaginary specter of Hans interrupting us.

"You still haven't told us why you were visiting the doctor in the first place," Mitzi says.

Georg looks at me and for the first time that evening I smile. "A baby is on its way."

There are gasps all around the table, then congratulations, which feel inappropriate after such grim news.

Lorli climbs over to my lap and studies my stomach. "So will it be a boy or a girl?" she asks.

"Probably a girl like you and Rosmarie," I say. "We were thinking about Barbara for a name."

The older children appear uncomfortable, but the youngest are excited.

"And if it's a boy?" Rosmarie questions.

"Oh, it won't be a boy," I say. "Your father hasn't had a boy in years!"

This should be our last family meeting for some time. But each day there's some new outrage to discuss that isn't fit for the dinner table, and soon we are meeting every evening after rehearsals, gathering in the library and drawing the doors shut, then dropping our voices to just above a whisper. I don't know what Hans makes of it and don't much care. This man who was like a younger brother to Georg is now a stranger in our house.

On the tenth of May, Father Wasner doesn't wait until after our rehearsals to tell us what's happening at the university.

"They're burning books!"

"What do you mean?" Mitzi panics.

Father Wasner collapses onto the long, cream sofa in our music room, then buries his face in his hands. "Foreign literature, Jewish literature, anything the Nazis are deeming too radical. Even books by the American woman Helen Keller, simply because she asks for fair treatment for the blind." He tugs at his collar. The Nazis have as little sympathy for religious leaders as they have for the disabled. They will come for Father Wasner next. And then us. Because they won't stop until they've rid the country of every last dissenter.

For two days there is nothing much to report. We go for a family walk near the base of the Untersberg and for a brief moment we all feel like ourselves again. The hills don't care about politics. And they're the only thing of any considerable size not draped in the Nazi red and black. I stand with my face to the wind and close my eyes, inhaling the sweet scent of narcissi on the breeze. I feel small flutters in my stomach, the same way I did with the two I lost.

Just let me carry this little girl to term, I pray. *If you let me have this one I'll never ask for another.*

Georg comes up behind me and wraps me in his arms. "How do you feel?" he mumbles into my hair.

"Nervous." But the sturdy warmth of him makes me relax.

"These aren't easy times for a child to be born into."

No, they aren't, I think. But we will do what we've always done. Take comfort in our family. And God. Let the Nazis abandon Him. They will see how well that works out for them.

The next morning, I am praying in our chapel downstairs when the postman arrives with a letter from Vienna. It's addressed to Rupert. My chest tightens, wondering what it could mean. I take it to the library, and when everyone convenes for our evening meeting no one recognizes the address.

Rupert holds it up to the evening light, examining the envelope.

"Here, give it to me," his brother says, and Rupert hands the letter to Werner, who quickly opens it and skims the contents.

"Oh," Werner says, but no one is sure what sort of *oh* it is.

"What? What is it?" I can't bear the uncertainty.

"A job offer," Werner announces, but he sounds confused.

Rupert takes the letter and reads. Then his face darkens, and I have a good idea of what's coming next. "A position in Vienna's largest hospital has suddenly opened up and they are wondering if 'the son of the esteemed Captain von Trapp and member of the now famous Trapp Family Choir' wishes to fulfill it. Suddenly opened up!" He crumples the letter in rage.

"Rupert!" Agathe exclaims. "Don't you have to respond?"

"Let silence be their response!" He rises, running a hand through his hair. "I'm no Dr. Krause."

Father Wasner nods approvingly, and Georg crosses the library to embrace his eldest child. But I hear Rupert sigh. He's twenty-seven and has worked years for this degree, traveling back and forth between his university and Salzburg to juggle life as both a singer and a medical student. This should be a time of excitement and new beginnings. Instead, everything feels like it's ending.

For the next few days we discuss the possible repercussions of turning down the offer from Vienna. The discussion even continues outside at the picnic tables, where Johanna has laid out a simple lunch.

"It's only a matter of time before the Party comes after us," Martina warns. "We don't display their flags, we don't use their salute, the children aren't singing their anthem in school. We should be prepared." She has always seen the glass as half empty. But this time, it really is. She traces her finger over the wood of our picnic table, and no one dares to disagree.

It's such a glorious time of year, with the fields spread out below a blue sky and a bright sun. How long will we be able to stay here? And where will we go if we can't?

"We really must keep our heads down," Rupert says. "We should only go to our concerts and come back. We shouldn't even talk with the neighbors."

I watch Lorli and Rosmarie running through the fields and feel desperately sorry for them. And for little Barbara, who isn't even here yet. How has it come to this? Tearing Jews out of their homes, sending them to camps, burning books, imprisoning political opponents. God will turn His back on Austria. He must if we continue allowing this. But what can we do?

It's late in July when the answer comes in a letter from the Department of the Navy. Hans finds us outside, picnicking on a blanket beneath the evergreens, and his face is lit up.

"From the Reichstag administrative office," he says breathlessly. "All the way from Berlin."

My heart stops in my chest. I look at Georg and see the color drain from his face. He takes the letter and tucks it into his jacket pocket, earning a disappointed look from Hans. The children are with Father Wasner, rehearsing our new songs now that religious pieces by Bach and Handel are forbidden to be performed in public. We wait until we're alone on the blanket to see what it is the Reichstag wants.

There's both wonder and fear in Georg's voice when he says, "It's a new command."

"*No.*"

He passes the letter to me, but the words don't make sense. *We formally request . . . The Adriatic Sea . . .*

"What? What is it?" Rupert asks.

I haven't even noticed that the children have stopped singing.

"Papa?" Mitzi presses.

A circle forms around our blanket and Georg draws a deep breath. "The Reichstag has asked me to take command of the submarine fleet of the German Kriegsmarine."

To take command of the Kriegsmarine is to be set for life. No more troubles with money. No more troubles over anything at all. In 1917 Georg's submarine had held no more than five men at a time and sprang leaks. But according to Georg these new boats are extraordinary, with space for thirty-five men and a dozen torpedoes. To take this command would mean having a career again.

"What will you do?" Werner asks.

Georg folds the letter and shoves it deep into his breast pocket. "Tell them no, of course."

"They'll want to know why you're refusing," Rupert warns.

"Because I'm happily retired and too old," he says angrily.

"Georg." I meet his gaze. "That's not all that was in the letter."

The children wait for him to speak, and he shifts uncomfortably. "They want me to establish a base in the Adriatic Sea."

"But the Adriatic doesn't belong to Germany." Agathe frowns. "What do they mean?"

Father Wasner's voice is somber. "I think we already know."

War is coming.

CHAPTER TWENTY-ONE

MARIA

Salzburg, Austria
1938

IT BEGINS WITH THE Strassers. I open the door the next morning and the entire family is arranged on our porch, as still as actors waiting for the curtain to be drawn. There are Mr. and Mrs. Strasser in the back with big smiles, then their three boys, as tall and confident as their father. I feign surprise, then dutifully usher the five of them inside.

"Look, Georg, it's the Strassers," I say, and we all pretend to be surprised by the wonderful timing of their visit. Agathe brings coffee and cake into the library, and Martina and Johanna join us to exchange small talk with the boys. The children are roughly the same age, all in their late teens, and there should be no shortage of topics to converse about. But the Nazi flags flapping from each of the Strassers' windows down the street means that few subjects are safe.

While Karl Strasser is talking about the summer weather, I catch Leopold, his eldest, trying to impress Johanna. She laughs politely at his jokes, but I know she's been exchanging letters with that boy from Vienna, the son of the former vice mayor, and isn't interested.

"I'm thinking of joining the Party," Leopold says, when none of his jokes seem to impress.

The entire library goes silent.

"It may seem like an opportunity for advancement," Georg says, and he of all people should know, "but what happens when they send all you boys to war?"

Leopold tenses. "If anyone is foolish enough to start a war with us," he says heatedly, "then it will be over in a few months."

His brothers nod in agreement, and I turn to their mother, Christina.

"A war is coming," I say gravely, even though outside the birds are chirping and the jasmine bush smells like endless summer. "And Germany will be the one to start it. You don't want to lose your sons."

Christina lowers the coffee to her lap. She has never dressed in the traditional white blouse and dirndl that most women wear in Salzburg. She prefers whatever is fashionable in Paris. Today, it's a full-skirted redingote in silk jacquard. The pale pink brings out the color in her cheeks, which rises as she answers. "No war is going to take my sons." She laughs dismissively at the thought. "Just look at them."

They are all strapping boys, broad-shouldered with ruddy good looks.

But Georg's voice is serious when he says, "War doesn't care how tough you're built. I've seen boys cut down in the prime of their youth. This isn't the time to be joining any party."

"Says the man who will command the Kriegsmarine!" Karl claps Georg on the back good-naturedly and laughs. "We've all heard the good news!"

Georg is sitting next to me and I feel his muscles tense, and I don't have to meet his eyes to know what he's thinking. Hans can no longer be trusted.

"Well," Georg begins, "you know that I'm retired—"

Karl stares in disbelief. "You can't be thinking of turning it down?"

"Actually, yes."

"But . . . it's the greatest honor they could possibly bestow." Karl turns for confirmation from his wife, who nods fervently. "A new fleet . . ." He can't get over it. "And aren't you still taking in boarders? There'd be no need for stuff like that anymore."

"We haven't had boarders in some time," I say defensively.

"Very well, but you would never have to fear going back to that."

"I'm afraid the matter is settled," Georg says simply.

When the Strassers are finished with their interrogation, the Hofmanns arrive, and by the end of the week we've had seven different families pay us a visit. This isn't the calm the doctor was hoping for, and Father Wasner suggests I focus on finding new pieces for our concerts rather than entertaining our nosy neighbors.

"We can't leave them on our front porch!" I exclaim.

From his position behind the podium, Father Wasner gives a little shrug as if to say *why not?* and I have never felt a greater fondness for him in my life.

To distract from our mounting worries, we begin practicing twice a day. Only Rosmarie protests. The rest of us are more than happy to occupy ourselves with Jodler and Mozart. Georg, of course, remains in the library, grinding his teeth against his pipe as he reads the papers. We all know not to disturb him at this time. So it can't be good news when he appears in the doorway of the music room. He waits for two movements from Sonata in C Major to be finished, then clears his throat.

"I've just had a phone call."

Father Wasner lowers his baton and I place a protective hand across my stomach. *Please don't let it be bad news,* I think. *Please.*

"We've had an invitation to sing at a birthday party."

We all look at one another. Then Werner laughs. "Well, what's wrong with that?"

"Maybe it's for one of the Strassers," Agathe jokes.

"Or the Hofmanns." Rupert rolls his eyes.

"No," Georg says. "It's for the Führer."

I take several steps back and Father Wasner lowers himself into a chair, burying his head in his hands. He's been a vocal critic of the Nazi Party in his university's paper. Turning down the Führer will be the end of his career.

"I don't understand," I begin. "How does he know—"

"He heard you on the radio. His personal secretary was on the phone."

I imagine what the Strassers would say about this. How there could be no greater honor. How everything we'd touch after this would turn to gold. But all I can think is that our success has just been our undoing.

"What did the secretary say?" Father Wasner asks. The color has completely drained from his face.

"That we represent what's best about Ostmark." This is

Austria's new name. "And that our presence would show the world how Ostmark and Germany have united." Georg clenches his jaw. "I cut her off before she could continue."

"Good!" There are flutters in my stomach. Barbara is as angry as I am. Or maybe that's just my own rage. "And what did you say?"

"That we are traveling to Italy and will not be available. She asked that we reconsider our trip." He leans against the doorframe, as if for support. "I said no."

Rupert closes his book. "How long do you think we have?"

Georg takes a staggered breath. "Twenty-four hours," he says quietly. "Maybe less."

Hans has today off. We will have to give him a distant errand tomorrow.

"I want to be clear on what's about to happen," Georg says. "If I don't return the Führer's call tomorrow to say that we've changed our minds, we will need to leave Austria at once."

Rosmarie's voice is shaking. "For good?"

Georg crosses the room and takes a seat, then calls her over. She climbs onto his lap, burying her head in his neck. "Yes." He tucks her hair behind her ears and she begins to sob into his chest. "We'd have only tonight to pack," he tells the rest of us. "And if Father Wasner wants to join us, he would need permission from the archbishop. Understand that this would mean leaving everything. Our city, our friends, this house. If this is what we agree to do, I'll place a call tomorrow to that American manager who asked you to tour overseas. We would need train tickets leaving for Italy no later than tomorrow evening."

It's such a wrenching decision.

"Is there anyone who thinks we should stay?" Georg asks.

Rosmarie is still weeping, but no one speaks. Not even Father Wasner, who will certainly lose his position at the university if he remains. I think of Lorli upstairs, napping while her entire future is being decided. She will never know another Austrian Christmas or hike the Untersberg in summer. Georg passes Rosmarie to Agathe, then comes over to me and kisses my forehead. "It's not the childhood we planned for little Barbara, is it?"

"No." I can't stop the tears. "But God will see we've done what's right and He'll provide."

First thing in the morning, Georg goes to Hans and puts his hand on the younger man's shoulder. "We'd like you to take the day off," he says.

There's no one but us in the kitchen, but Hans still looks around. "Am I being dismissed?"

"No. Nothing like that," Georg says quietly, but the sadness in his voice gives us away. "A war is coming, Hans. Maybe not tomorrow, but I want you to trust me on this. And you need to decide if a party that sends its enemies to death camps is really worth dying for."

The two men watch each other sadly, then Hans turns on his heel and walks away.

The rest of the morning is a blur. Without Hans in the house, we are free to pack. The children are responsible for their own two suitcases, filled with whatever they want to take. The rest of the cases are to be filled with our instruments— a spinet, a virginal, four six-stringed gambas, eight recorders, and my beloved guitar. There is a case for our music books and three others for our costumes. And, of course, a small case filled with baby clothes and toys for little Barbara.

Father Wasner leaves early that morning to speak with the archbishop, and when he returns, I can't tell from his face whether his request has been granted or not. He collapses into a chair in our music room and silently watches as Rupert and Werner shove books of music into a bag.

"Well?" I exclaim, unable to contain myself. Wasner is part of our family now.

"He said that if I didn't go, I would be acting against the will of God to save my own life. They are coming for me," he whispers. His face, which has always looked so young, suddenly seems haggard. "Has Georg booked the train?"

"Tonight at five," I tell him.

He will need to pack at once. He crosses the room but pauses at the door. "I am going to miss this place."

There is no time to say farewell. No lingering in each of our children's rooms or walking in our garden for one last look. At any moment the doorbell might ring and it will all be over.

Georg spends the day on the phone, first booking the tickets, then calling Otto Wagner in New York to see if the offer of coming to America is still good. We will have to leave Austria regardless, and I linger in the doorway to hear what the American says. His voice bleeds through the receiver, loud and strong.

"Yes, but the boat will leave from London. Can you get to England?"

"Of course," Georg assures him. "We will be there in two weeks."

"You'll be on a six-month visa," the man says in German, and Georg assures him that this is fine as well, although I'm certain he doesn't know what a visa is any more than I do. "I'll make your reservations at Hotel Wellington on Seventh Avenue and Fifty-Fifth."

"*Dankeschön.*" Georg begins writing furiously.

"It's all set then. We'll see you in three weeks."

When the call is finished, Georg slowly replaces the receiver. "We have to get to England."

I look down at Barbara, who is due in five months, and a familiar panic begins to settle over me. "What about the baby?" I ask.

"Our baby is simply going on an adventure," Georg says lovingly.

"And the money?"

He actually smiles. "How many times have I complained about my pension?"

I gasp. The Italian government has always refused to let his pension be paid outside of Italy.

"We can collect it in Tyrol and use it to make our bookings," he says.

It's as if God knew all along that we'd need it for this moment. I look outside at the perfect summer sky arching over the meadows and feel my throat beginning to close. No more summer picnics on the grass, no more concerts under the evergreens. When my eyes begin to mist, Georg comes and takes me in his arms.

"And what will happen in London?" I ask.

"We'll board the *American Farmer.* From there, it will be an eleven-day voyage to New York."

I don't ask "What then?" because how do any of us know?

If our concerts go well, we may be able to support ourselves in this new country. If not, only God knows where we will turn. : . .

There can be no tears as we leave the villa. No indication at all that we might not be coming back. We stand on the drive in our billowing sleeves and embroidered bodices, the boys wearing short black Tyrolean coats. Three taxis roll over the gravel and we try to look cheerful as we wedge our cases into their trunks. When one of the drivers asks about our trip, only Martina is strong enough to respond.

"Oh, just a few weeks in Tyrol. We all love to hike."

It's a twenty-minute wait for Father Wasner, who arrives with red cheeks and only two cases. His entire life in a pair of gray bags half the size of Lorli.

"Ready?" the driver chirps as Wasner squeezes himself between Martina and Georg.

No one has the heart to answer. Finally, the man swivels in his seat and Georg gives a silent nod. No family has ever looked more miserable going on vacation.

We roll away from the Villa Trapp and each of us turns to see the house one last time, the buttercup-yellow walls as bright and fresh in the afternoon sun as the day I first saw them twelve years ago. Tomorrow, Georg's sister will come from Korneuburg to supervise as the house is boarded up.

A deep sense of foreboding clenches my stomach, and I can't tell if it's real or just the pregnancy. I turn to Georg and drop my voice to a whisper. "You don't think that Hans—"

He shakes his head swiftly. "I don't know. Let's just get on that train as fast as possible and be gone."

But it's not that simple. At the station, there are fifty-eight bags to unload, and while attendants heave the cases onto the train one by one, familiar faces begin crowding around us.

"Maria!" Ingrid Hofmann shouts from across the station, and the children instinctively close in around me as she approaches. She's fashionably dressed, as usual, in a pretty skirt suit with squared shoulders and a narrow waist. Her blond hair has been swept up into a large bouffant. "Well, look at this!" She sweeps her gaze over our sea of bags. "I had no idea you were going on a trip."

Martina smiles tightly. "A hiking trip."

"And you?" I ask pointedly.

Her eyes linger on our music cases. "Stefan's brother has just come back from Germany. He's been offered the position of a Reichsinspekteur."

I try not to look as revolted as I feel.

"Oh, don't worry. I'm sure if Georg doesn't wish to return to the navy, they'll find something else for him. He served with such distinction. They won't care that your family has fallen on hard times." She glances down at our cases, since hiking in Tyrol is no one's idea of a lavish vacation. Then Father Wasner's voice interrupts us.

"Maria, the bags are loaded!" he shouts.

I smile. "Enjoy your summer, Ingrid."

How long does it take for a train to roll out? We find our seats and I can see Ingrid standing on the platform with Stefan and his brother, the new national inspector. They're all watching the train, us in particular. Georg waves, trying to look neighborly. Then the whistle blows and I catch myself blinking back tears of relief.

"Three hours," Rupert whispers.

I nod, understanding. Lorli leans her head into my chest and I must doze off, because the next moment Georg is shaking my shoulder.

"We're across!" he's saying.

I bolt upright. "What?"

"We're in Italy."

I look out the window for confirmation. A sign in Italian points the way to a *ristorante* and my heart flutters in my chest. But our freedom doesn't feel real until the last bag is unloaded on the platform in Tyrol. We're so concerned that all fifty-eight bags make it out of the train that none of us realize what's happening around us. Finally, an old man approaches me.

"Are any of you searching for accommodation?"

With so much noise in the station I'm not sure I've heard him right. Plus, the smell of the steam and hot oil is making me sick. I stare at him for a moment. Even Georg, the only one of us who speaks Italian, isn't sure how to respond.

"Well, hasn't anyone told you what's happened?" the man asks. We all shake our heads and he raises his walking stick. "You're the last train out!"

I don't understand what this means.

"It's on the radio," the man shouts over the sound of the whistle. "Hitler has shut the borders. Yours was the last train out."

CHAPTER TWENTY-TWO

FRAN

Manhattan, New York
1959

"WAS HE RIGHT?" FRAN exclaims, incredulous. "*Was* it the last train out of Austria?"

From their seats on a bench outside of Saint Patrick's Cathedral, Maria and Lorli nod in unison.

"If we'd waited just one more day to leave, none of us would be here," Maria says, folding her hands in her lap.

Churchgoers are still pouring out from the ten o'clock service. Fran waits for them to leave before asking, "Would they have imprisoned your entire family?"

"Oh, yes, and sent us to one of the camps. After we left, the priests who'd spoken out alongside Father Wasner were taken to Auschwitz." Maria drops her voice. "Only one of them survived."

It's so awful that Fran has to close her eyes. And now she understands the different ending for the play. It's only been fourteen years since Hitler took his own life in Berlin, and with flowers still fresh on the graves of men killed in action, no theatergoer in New York is prepared to hear the Führer's name mentioned onstage.

In some ways, what Rodgers and Hammerstein have done is incredible, taking this story of good escaping from evil and making it palatable for a country still traumatized by four years of war. But one look at Maria tells Fran that it isn't palatable for everyone. And what of their lives after they arrived in America? It's been more than twenty years since the *American Farmer* sailed into New York's harbor.

Fran asks the women if they remember their first time in America, and both of them laugh.

"Our taxis pulled up to the Hotel Wellington and we couldn't even thank our driver. Only Rupert knew enough English to get by," Lorli says.

"What about the manager who sent you the tickets?" Fran asks.

"Oh, without him we would have been utterly lost," Maria says. "He showed us how to open a bank account with the four dollars we had left from our time on the ship. And after we'd earned a little money from our first few concerts, he helped us rent a house in Pennsylvania."

Maria recalls her fear of riding an escalator for the first time, and Lorli remembers her first taste of Coca-Cola. Father Wasner was invited to say a daily Mass in Saint Patrick's Cathedral, and every morning the entire family would make their way to Fifth Avenue to hear him preach.

"It was so exciting at first," Lorli says, "like a family vacation." But her lips turn downward, and whatever happened next is obviously painful. "But in reality, all of us were refugees, and we were here to sing." Fran notices that Maria has chosen to remain silent. "Mother decided that Rosmarie and I were too young to go on tour, so we were boarded at Raven-hill Academy in Philadelphia."

Fran tries to imagine arriving penniless in a new country, then being left at a school where no one speaks your language.

"We weren't able to see them for months," Maria admits. "It was very traumatic. I wish—" Her gray eyes brim with tears and Lorli reaches across and pats her mother's knee.

"You didn't know."

But Maria shakes her head, using her sleeve to dab at her eyes. "The touring wasn't easy," she explains. Not that anyone realized this at first. In the beginning, the bus that Otto Wagner had procured for them rolled through America's rural towns and farmlands and the family thought they had arrived in paradise. At harvest time, the scent of apples filled their bus. The driver would pull over at one of a dozen orchards found along the side of the road and the family would stretch or take a little walk. And wherever they sang, the family met with nothing but success.

Otto Wagner was clever and had booked them in towns filled with German immigrants. When the von Trapps would arrive, the audience experienced nostalgia for a land many of them had never even seen, listening to music from a world only their parents or grandparents had known. Following Otto Wagner's advice, Maria would bring out her guitar and the family would perform folk songs from the Alps. Then winter came and many of the country lanes grew impassable. Concerts had to be rescheduled for larger cities, where the bus could make its way through streets that had been plowed free of snow and ice. Except that audiences in larger cities weren't as enthusiastic about a family choir singing about the Austrian Alps. Finding lodging became a nightly ordeal, and each day that passed brought Maria closer to the birth of her third child. What if something happened to the baby while they were on the road? What if all the stress of these cold nights and long bus rides prompted her to deliver early?

But the baby was fine, and by the time the von Trapps returned for their daughters at Ravenhill Academy, Lorli and Rosmarie had a new sibling. Only it wasn't the little girl they'd all been waiting for.

"Can you imagine?" Maria asks. "We had everything ready. The tiny lace dresses the other children had worn, even a name. But it was a boy!"

"Johannes," Fran remembers. The last and youngest von Trapp child.

"It should have been a wonderful Christmas," Maria says. "A new baby, a new country . . . We'd even learned all the American tricks."

Fran laughs at the thought of Americans needing secret methods for survival. "Tricks?"

"Oh, yes. Like how Americans go to shoemakers to iron their hats."

"And how drugstores sell food—even ice cream!" Lorli adds.

"We'd all learned some basic English by then. We might not have been thriving, but we were living," Maria gushes. "Then our tourist visas expired." Her lips turn down. "And America refused to renew them."

So they packed up their fifty-eight suitcases and crossed the ocean again, this time traveling to the only remaining countries willing to give them a contract to sing. They were all in Scandinavia.

"We thought this might have to be our life, touring from country to country. Then Hitler invaded Poland and we realized we would never be safe in Europe. For you, the war didn't start until 1941. For us, it began in 1939."

So Otto Wagner did one last favor for them. Their family wasn't bringing in enough money for him to continue as their manager, but he arranged for a second visa and procured them tickets on the SS *Bergensfjord*, headed from Norway to New York.

"It was such a kind thing for him to do." Lorli has the same open expression and wide gray eyes as her mother. "At Ellis Island the immigration officer asked my mother how long we planned to stay, and my mother exclaimed that she hoped we'd be staying forever."

Fran gives a little gasp. Even she knows what a mistake that answer must have been.

"We were put in detention straightaway." Lorli draws a staggered breath. "It was a week before we were told what would happen to us."

Fran remembers this from Maria's book. But Maria hadn't made it clear how they were released from detention.

"Otto called a few people he knew at the embassy. Eventually Frances Perkins, the secretary of labor, heard about our situation. When they released us, the press was waiting outside." Maria perks up at the memory. "They wanted our pictures!"

Lorli looks less cheerful. "That's when the real work began," she says. "Touring, publicity, marketing."

"But what did you do for a manager?" Fran asks.

Lorli glances at her mother and both women smile. "Freddy Schang," Lorli says.

"Frederick Schang was the president of Columbia Artists Management," Maria explains. "When Otto said he wasn't interested in being our manager, we took it as a sign from God."

Lorli laughs. "Yes, a sign we should reach even higher. At first, Freddy had no interest in being our manager either," she confides.

"You remember that?" Maria exclaims, and Lorli gives her mother a long look. "But you were only eight," Maria protests.

"He told us he didn't think he could manage a little choir dressed like nuns." Lorli turns to Fran. "So my mother demanded to know what was wrong with that."

Fran is holding back her laughter. The president of Columbia Artists Management! "And what did he say?"

"That American audiences enjoy looking as much as listening, and unless we could miraculously find a little sex appeal, we could forget about ever making it in New York. My mother marched out of that office angrier than I'd ever seen her, then went straight to Macy's."

Fran is confused. "The department store?"

Lorli confirms this with a nod. "Her English wasn't great, but she asked the first salesman she came across where she could find some sex appeal."

Fran roars with laughter, and several women leaving the cathedral begin to stare. "So did he find it for you?"

Maria laughs. "No! He fled and never came back. But we returned to Freddy's office on West Fifty-Seventh. And even though everyone wanted me to leave well enough alone, I told him in no uncertain terms that he'd made a mistake."

"She said if he'd agree to be our manager, we would have more sex appeal than all of his other clients combined," Lorli explains.

Fran is practically crying.

"Eventually, I think Freddy took pity on us," Lorli guesses.

"Did having him as your manager change anything?" Fran asks.

"Oh, *everything*," Lorli admits. "He taught us about appealing to different audiences, and publicity, and marketing."

"We shortened our skirts," Maria adds.

"Only a few inches."

"And started wearing lipstick. It worked," Lorli says.

Then a few years later we were successful enough to buy the lodge in Vermont. We bought it for the land. The actual building was a run-down shack. The children built it into what's there today with their own hands."

It's an unbelievable story, Fran realizes, even more extraordinary than what's written in the play.

Maria rises, brushing off her dirndl, and it's clear that the reminiscing has come to an end. When she returns to the cathedral to use the restroom, Fran brings up the subject of the premiere.

"I will go if she asks, but I doubt any of my siblings will come. I know you're worried about what she might say to the press," Lorli replies.

Fran flushes, embarrassed by how transparent her motives must be.

"If I'm honest, I have no idea what she might say. But you

listened," Lorli points out. "That's really what she wanted. Mr. Hammerstein will have to do the rest himself."

"I'll be completely honest, Lorli. It's unlikely he'll change the play," Fran warns, hating that her boss has put her in this position. When she returns to the office on Monday she's going to let Hammerstein know exactly how she feels about all of this. He needs to be the one to tell Maria that a story is more appealing when a character undergoes a major transformation. And let *him* be the one to explain that Georg was chosen to be this character—the one to hear the sound of music and see the light.

When Maria returns, Fran asks when she and Lorli intend to leave.

"Tomorrow morning," Maria says firmly. "And though I've enjoyed chatting with you tremendously, I am not going to lie. I am disappointed to have come all this way and been denied an audience with Mr. Hammerstein."

"My notes will be ready for him on Monday," Fran assures her. She will have to type them up over the weekend. "I have no doubt in my mind that he will eventually get in touch."

Maria arches her heavy brows. "*Eventually?* The play debuts six weeks from today. Isn't that right?"

"Yes." Fran swallows. "November sixteenth."

"Well, that's not a great deal of time to make corrections."

On Monday morning, Fran is so focused on her confrontation with Hammerstein that she forgets she'll also be seeing Jack. The realization hits her in the elevator just as the operator chirps, "I believe this is your stop." She stands still for a moment, thinking about what's to come, until the operator prompts, "Miss Connelly?"

"Oh. Right." Slowly, Fran makes her way down the hall, her heart beginning to race as she turns the brass handle to Hammerstein's office. She can't see any movement through the frosted glass, but that doesn't mean the place is empty. Today, however, she's the first one in.

She glances around her desk for instructions since Hammerstein is often in the office over the weekend, but can't find a single note from him. No yellow scraps of paper folded neatly at the corner of her desk, not even a hastily jotted line about continuing with the press releases. *He's working on something else*, Fran thinks. *He must be.*

She pulls out the notes on her interview with Maria and takes them into Hammerstein's office. As usual, his desk is cluttered with papers and stacks of dog-eared books. Because there's no chance he'll find the notes on his desk, she leaves them in the center of his chair, then considers penning a letter to him about Maria. She's not sure what more she can add to the notes that would convince him to speak to Maria himself, but she's drafting the letter in her mind when the phone shatters her concentration. She's partway through her usual greeting when a voice screams on the other end, "Where *are* you?"

For a fraction of a second, Fran panics that she's forgotten an important meeting.

"Fran—are you there? Are you there?" Dick Halliday sounds hysterical.

When Fran realizes who it is, her voice goes flat. "I'm here." She cradles the receiver against her ear.

"Well, there's a matter of a missing guitar in the theater!"

"A missing guitar," Fran repeats, somehow doubting this is the crisis that Mr. Halliday believes it is.

"Maria's guitar." Halliday is breathing heavily. "Mary can't play Maria without that guitar and right now it's missing."

"Have you considered asking the stagehands?" Fran suggests.

"Of course I've asked the stagehands! Do you think—" There's an interruption on the line and Dick Halliday grumbles, "They found it." Then the line goes dead and Fran stares at the receiver.

"Something the matter, Miss Connelly?" Hammerstein looks tense as he walks through the door, but Fran just shakes her head and hangs up.

"Mr. Halliday couldn't find Maria's guitar. Not to worry. He handled the situation with his usual calm."

Hammerstein laughs. "Oh, yes. I can imagine it, Miss Connelly. Do you have time to tell me about Maria?"

"Of course." Fran follows him down the hall and wonders if Jack's office will remain empty today. It's been three days since they've spoken. Perhaps he's taken a vacation.

She seats herself opposite Hammerstein's desk and notices that when he lowers himself into his chair, he does so gingerly. *Something's hurting him,* she realizes, and immediately feels guilty. Because it isn't work that's been keeping him away. Something is wrong.

"I can't express enough gratitude for these notes," he says, tapping the pile of papers Fran worked on all night. "I'm sure there's a lot in here to digest."

"She was adamant about wanting to see you," Fran says. "But at least she hasn't acted as if she resents the fact that it's me hearing her story."

"I wanted to see her," Hammerstein admits. "But my doctors forbid it and told me to rest. How do you think she'll take all this?" He waves his hand, and Fran understands that by "all this" he means the musical.

She doesn't lie. "Not well. She's very upset about the way her husband is portrayed, and to be frank, the play isn't accurate."

He sighs. "Doesn't she like what we've done with her character?"

"No."

Hammerstein looks startled. "But she's witty and charming—"

"Yes, and that's what her children remember about their *father*. Not *her*. The German film caused a major rift in the family. Imagine seeing the roles of your parents reversed onscreen and having the entire world believe that? And now it's about to happen again, only with a bigger audience."

"It sounds as though the children might not even want tickets to the premiere."

Fran shakes her head firmly. "They don't. Well, perhaps the youngest daughter might. The rest aren't so close to her anymore."

Hammerstein pauses. "Because of the film?"

Fran considers the question. "I think it all fell apart after Georg died. Remember that Maria was an orphan," she says, trying to rationalize the fear Maria must have felt with Georg gone. "She tried to keep them all together. Even went so far as to lock Johanna in her room to keep her from getting married. But the children were desperate to lead their own lives."

Hammerstein leans forward in his chair. "How old was Johanna when that happened?"

Older than Fran. "Twenty-nine." But if Maria was panicked, she had reason to be. "She has spent most of her life
saying goodbye to things. First her mother, then her father,
then her country, then finally her children."

Hammerstein is quiet. "I'll read through these notes tonight," he says, and Fran feels a surge of triumph, thinking of
all the times Jack had said that Hammerstein would never
even look at them. "I can't change the characters in the play,"
he adds. Is it regret in his voice? Or just exhaustion? "But
perhaps I have one more song to write. Something for all . . ."
He looks out the window and his voice grows distant. "All the
difficult goodbyes."

Fran nods and wonders what he's seeing outside. "Is everything all right, Mr. Hammerstein?"

He turns back to her and smiles sadly. "I'm afraid I won't
be in tomorrow. My doctors have scheduled surgery to remove a spot of cancer in my stomach."

Fran gasps. People like Hammerstein don't get cancer.
He's too young, too robust, too full of determination. "I'm so
sorry," she whispers, knowing the words are inadequate even
as she says them. "Is this—is it public knowledge?"

"You're the first to know here. But it's not a secret. I'll be
fine," he promises. "A few weeks off and I'll be back with new
material. We have a play to put on."

Fran is in a daze when she leaves his office, nearly bump-
ing into Peter in the hall.

"Hey, everything all right?" Peter's face is tanned, as if he
spent his weekend outdoors. It makes his hazel eyes look
green.

"Yes—no."

Peter hesitates.

"It's not me, it's Mr. Hammerstein," she explains.

Peter waits for her to go on, but when it's obvious she isn't going to continue, he doesn't press. It's only when the two of them go to Sandy's Diner for lunch that Fran realizes she wants to talk. She takes a seat next to Peter so they won't have to shout, and the feeling of having him so close makes her feel better.

"Hammerstein is having surgery tomorrow," she confides.

Peter leans back hard against the vinyl seat, shocked. "What kind?"

"Stomach cancer."

He glances over his shoulder to be sure there's no one around from the office, and Fran quickly reassures him.

"It's not a secret. Otherwise, I would never have said anything. I'm sure he'll make an announcement today before everyone leaves." Her eyes well with tears. "Do you think—"

"He's as strong as an ox, Franny. I wouldn't worry."

But Fran blinks quickly. She can hear her mother's admonishing voice in her head: *What good is powdering away your freckles if you're just going to go and cry it all off?* But there's no one like Hammerstein, with his slow smile and quick mind. And certainly no other writer on Broadway with such kindness. She still has the copy of *The New Yorker* that he saved for her, placed prominently on her desk.

"Even if it's serious," Peter rationalizes, "he'll have the best doctors in New York. Did he say how long he'll be out?"

"A few weeks."

At this, Peter sucks in his breath. The premiere is six weeks away.

After lunch, it's clear that the rest of the office has learned about Hammerstein's diagnosis. His assistants file silently out into the hall, clearly fighting the urge to commiserate with one another. Fran notices that Jack isn't there, and later, on the walk back to her apartment, she asks Peter about him.

"He didn't tell you?" They've stopped in front of Sal's, a tiny coffee shop filled with Italian ceramics that Jack always hated. "It's so kitsch," he'd complain. "He went back to Virginia. His father thinks young senators are what the people want nowadays. He's going to help Jack run."

Fran feels a momentary flash of anger that her boyfriend didn't even have the decency to tell her this. But it's replaced by the rush of relief that she realized who he really was, just in time. Imagine if they'd continued going steady and gotten married? The idea feels absolutely ludicrous now. She glances up at Peter and sees that he's watching her.

"May I ask you a question?"

Fran smiles. "Of course."

Peter runs a nervous hand through his hair. "How upset are you about Jack?"

Heat floods into Fran's cheeks, because the truth feels embarrassing. "Not very. What about you and Eva?"

"I was devastated for a while, I have to admit. But then it started to feel less like clouds converging and more like clouds parting. Like maybe I hadn't been seeing clearly up until then." Peter takes a step toward Fran and she realizes that she's been holding her breath.

"So what do you see now?" Fran asks.

Peter takes her hand. "A funny, kind, talented, and truly beautiful woman."

Fran steps into Peter's embrace, and the feeling of her lips against his melts away every other feeling in the world. There's no more worry over Hammerstein's health or anxiety over Maria. It doesn't even matter what happens with her book. She inhales Peter's scent, a mix of soap and cedarwood, and feels her body relax into his.

"Let me walk you home," he says.

"But Eva—"

"Franny, it doesn't matter." He steadies her with his gaze, and she can sense how deeply he means this. There's always been a comfort with Peter that she'd never felt with Jack, and now she knows it's the sense of finally being in the right place.

CHAPTER TWENTY-THREE

T HE NEXT MORNING FRAN wakes with a start. She sits up in bed and pulls the covers to her chest, trying to sort out her dreams from reality. It happened. She really kissed Peter yesterday. Their slow walk to her apartment wasn't her imagination, nor the way they sat together in her kitchen for hours, chatting over instant coffee about the big and small things of life.

She'd learned last night that Peter has no intention of writing his own plays.

"It turns out I'm not particularly passionate about crafting my own work. But helping other people craft theirs . . ." His hazel eyes lit up, then he leaned forward on the table and confided, "Hammerstein thinks I have real talent." In fact, Hammerstein told Peter there'd be a job for him at Rodgers & Hammerstein for as long as Hammerstein remained on Broadway.

They talked about parents—her supportive father and his chain of grocery stores; his accomplished mother, who was a successful writer herself. And they talked about what they hoped for the future. They both wanted to continue living in the city, but relocate to somewhere with more space once there were kids.

Later that morning Peter is at Fran's doorstep with a cup of coffee from Sal's. Fran looks at the paper cup with its bright yellow sun and feels her throat close. *It's just a cup of coffee,* she tells herself. But it's not. It's more than that. She links arms with Peter and the feel of him next to her, solid and sure, somehow makes the world seem more certain.

"It's going to be strange without Mr. Hammerstein," Fran says. Walking close to Peter, her happiness makes her remember how much she loves autumn in the city. The silver birch trees have all turned russet-gold, and with the rain last night, the air is a heady combination of rich earth and wet leaves.

"I don't think he's ever missed a day. He's usually the first one in and the last out."

"Knowing Mr. Hammerstein, he's taken work to the hospital with him," Fran says.

"Oh, he'll be panicking the entire time he's there. Which reminds me, I doubt I'll be seeing you for lunch. Hammerstein's asked us to oversee Halliday at the theater. I don't think he trusts him not to change the script."

"You're kidding," Fran says.

Peter shakes his head. "Halliday wanted the opening scene to feature Maria catching her bloomers on a tree branch. Thought it would give the audience a big laugh."

Fran stares at him in horror.

"It's going to be a long day," Peter admits.

The office is as lonely as Fran imagined it would be without the boss. No voice booming loud and cheerful through the walls, no scent of cigar smoke wafting down the hall. In fact, she's the only person there until just before five, when the door swings open and Peter returns with the rest of Hammerstein's assistants. She thinks the group seems muted, then realizes that a young man is with them who rarely comes to the office.

"Mr. Sondheim." Fran rises and extends her hand, and Hammerstein's protégé shakes it warmly. Hammerstein has always said that Sondheim is the third child he should have had. The two even share the same black hair and dark eyes.

"Franny, always good to see you." He smiles, but the expression doesn't reach his eyes. Two years ago, Sondheim made his mark on Broadway by writing the lyrics to *West Side Story*. Now *Gypsy* has opened and it's turning out to be his second big hit. This afternoon, however, he doesn't look like a man on top of the world. "I've come to collect a few things for Ockie," he says.

"Of course." Fran unlocks the door to Hammerstein's office and leads him inside. "I hope everything went well this morning."

Sondheim remains still for a moment, then his eyes fill with tears. "No. I'm afraid it isn't good news."

For once, Fran doesn't know what to say. Instead, she waits for Sondheim to continue.

"I've just told his assistants that he has cancer and that the doctors removed the tumor. But it wasn't just the tumor. The cancer spread. They don't know how long he has left."

Fran actually feels dizzy and Sondheim takes a staggered breath, like he can't believe the reality of it either. "I'm . . . I'm so sorry," she whispers.

Sondheim pinches his eyes closed with his fingers, then tries to focus on the matter at hand. "Everything will go on. There's nothing he wants more than to finish this play."

"He said he had one more song left to write."

Sondheim confirms this. "Yes. He wants the papers from his second drawer. And he wanted me to give you this."

He holds out an envelope and Fran takes it. She stares at it for several seconds, trying to guess what could be inside.

"I believe he was hoping you would give me an answer."

"Oh." Fran tears it open and is moved by the sight of Hammerstein's familiar handwriting, with its big loops and curls. The paper smells faintly of lavender, like something he might have borrowed from his wife.

Dear Miss Connelly,

I read your notes with great attention and have decided I must meet with Maria in person, despite Mrs. Hammerstein's insistence that I remain in bed. Maria has graciously accepted a dinner at our apartment on the fourteenth, and I wonder if you would come as well, since you are the one who knows her best. Perhaps you might bring Peter? I find him to be a wonderful conversationalist as well as an extremely talented writer. I trust him to tell me the truth about this song before I send it out into the world. And I suspect he would not be averse to accompanying you.

All good wishes.
Sincerely,
Oscar

Fran feels her face go warm at the suggestion that Peter would enjoy accompanying her, then looks up to find Sondheim watching her intently. She can see the question on his face and obliges. "He wants Peter and me to come to dinner."

Sondheim laughs. "Sounds like Ockie. Still groggy from surgery and already making plans."

On the walk home that evening, Fran tells Peter about the letter. It's not until they're almost at Sal's, however, that she tells him what else she's learned. "Sondheim said it's terminal."

Peter stops walking, and in the glow of the streetlamps, the raindrops on his peacoat look like a spray of gold. "That can't be right. This morning he told us it was stomach cancer, but that he'd had the operation."

"Yes, and the operation removed the tumor." Fran shakes her head miserably. "But the cancer had already spread. There's nothing more the doctors can do apparently."

They continue toward Fran's apartment, and she can see how shaken Peter is by the news. "But he's always been so healthy—"

Fran nods. "When he began coming in late, I thought he was working on something else. Maybe something he didn't want Rodgers to know about. You know how they are." Always quarreling, never really getting along. There couldn't be two more different men. While Hammerstein didn't drink, Rodgers appeared to be an alcoholic. And while Hammerstein genuinely believed in love—having found it with his second wife, Dorothy—there wasn't a girl in New York who escaped Rodgers's notice.

Peter wraps his arm around her waist and holds her close for the remainder of the walk. It feels good to have someone to share the devastation of the moment with. Because it isn't fair. Of all the men in the world to be struck down, why Hammerstein?

They stop outside her building and Peter tucks a wet curl behind her ear. In a few minutes the drizzle will turn to steady rain. They should hurry. But he presses his forehead to hers and they both close their eyes.

"See you tomorrow?" he asks.

"Yes." All she wants to do right now is climb under her covers and forget everything.

He kisses her briefly, and Fran can still feel the warmth of his lips against hers when she reaches her apartment and finds an envelope in her mailbox. The return address looks familiar. Then her heart begins to race as she realizes what it must be. In her apartment upstairs, she drops her pocketbook next to the door and tears open the envelope, skimming the letter. She has to read it several times just to be sure.

"There's been an offer!" She can't believe it. "There's actually been an offer!" She reaches for the phone, and a moment later, her father is celebrating at the other end of the line. All those nights of delving into Vinnie Ream's story. The long weekends of research. The writing. And now the world can read *A Northern Wind*, the story of this extraordinary young sculptress who became Lincoln's artist as well as his confidante during the Civil War. Even her mother is briefly impressed.

"So your book is really going to be published," she says. "Oh, sweetheart, I didn't doubt it for a minute. And what does Jack think?"

"Don't know," Fran says lightly. "Jack has apparently gone back to Virginia to run for Congress. But I suspect that Peter will be extremely happy for me."

There's silence. "That Peter Rickman boy from your office?"

"Mmm-hmm," Fran hums into the phone. Fran knows her mother is dying to know more, but her father takes the line back.

"Honey, we are so proud of you. So tell us, when will it come out?"

Fran explains the long process of publication. How first the book will need to be edited, then copyedited, then publicized. "A year?" she guesses.

It doesn't matter to her father. His daughter is going to have a book published.

As soon as Fran puts down the receiver, she dials Peter, and when she tells him the news, he's thrilled.

"Don't hang up your coat. I'm taking you out to celebrate!"

"What?"

"Oh, yes," Peter assures her. "We're going out."

Twenty minutes later, Fran gives a little gasp as Peter appears in her doorway. His shoes are wet and his hair is plastered against his head. "Didn't want to stop for an umbrella," he explains. "Shall we?"

"Would you like to dry off first?"

"And waste good celebration time? No chance." He reaches for her hand. "Let's go."

Jack would never have gone anywhere with wet shoes or wet hair. Fran grabs a large umbrella, and when they make it down to the street, Peter pops it open over their heads. And this is really all the celebration Fran needs. The shelter, the rain, and Peter's solid arm wrapped around her waist.

———

Several weeks later, Fran stares at herself in the mirror and has to remind herself to breathe. In her three years of working for Hammerstein, she can't recall a single occasion where an employee has been invited to the lyricist's home. It's an unthinkable honor. She studies her blue satin sheath with its small bow in the back, then slips on a pair of matching pumps and a white shrug that contrasts nicely with her hair. It's a special night and she wants to look the part.

When she opens the door for Peter at seven o'clock, he steps back and inhales. "You look . . . stunning."

"You don't look so bad yourself." It's true, especially with his curls combed back and his black suit tailored to his broad shoulders and narrow waist. She now knows that he used to run track-and-field in Boston, and since his graduation five years ago he's continued with running. She can feel the muscles of his thighs as she draws close to him and presses her lips against his.

Peter's breath comes faster. "Don't do that," he warns, "or we'll never get out of here."

Fran steps back. "What do you think will happen tonight?"

"With Maria or Hammerstein?"

Fran reaches for her pocketbook on the side table and locks the door. "Maria."

They start to walk and Peter hesitates. Fran can see how the question worries him. "She must know it's too late to change the play," he says. "Do you still think she might cause problems?"

"It's possible," Fran admits. "She's a forceful personality. She's been told that Hammerstein isn't the one who wrote the script, but she also realizes that the final word rests with him."

"Does she know about his illness?"

Fran shakes her head firmly. "Not unless he's told her, and I can't imagine him calling her and doing that."

They reach East Sixty-Third Street and look up at Hammerstein's five-story town house, the tall, glittering windows overlooking the tree-lined pavement below. Fran feels a nervous fluttering in her stomach as Peter rings the bell.

A maid in a simple black dress answers the door. "Mr. Rickman and Miss Connelly?" she asks.

They each affirm with a nod and she shows them into Hammerstein's home, with its sweeping balustrades and heavy chandeliers. Peter passes a look to Fran and she confirms what he's thinking with widened eyes. It's magnificent. Fran has heard a rumor, which may or may not be true, that even though Hammerstein's father had been the wealthy owner of several theaters, he had forced his son to become a self-made man, giving him next to nothing.

The maid leads them past a handsome dining room, where a long wooden table has been set for five, then takes them into a formal living room lined with cream-colored bookcases. Fran can hear Hammerstein's laughter before she sees him, a great bellowing sound that puts her fears to rest.

"Peter, Fran." Hammerstein rises from the couch and Fran conceals her shock at how much weight he's lost in such a short time. His voice, however, is the same. "I want you to meet Mrs. Hammerstein."

A beautiful woman, probably in her sixties, rises from a chair. Her dark hair is swept back from her face in a loose chignon, and there's real warmth in her eyes when she smiles. "Please, just Dorothy," she says. She's wearing an elegant black satin dress, paired with a stunning diamond necklace.

"A pleasure," Fran tells her, and Peter follows suit.

"Fran, you know Maria," Hammerstein continues. But Maria doesn't rise. In fact, from the look on her face, Fran suspects she's interrupted some sort of an argument. "And Maria, meet Peter, my most trusted assistant."

Maria tries for a smile. "And are you working on the script as well?" she asks.

Peter glances at Hammerstein. "Well." He clears his throat. "I'm not sure anyone is working on the script much these days. The play is in rehearsals—"

"Why don't you sit down," Dorothy suggests, indicating the empty chairs.

Everything is a shade of white or cream. The rugs, the walls, even the grand piano in the corner of the room. The maid reappears with drinks, and though Maria refuses, Fran accepts a martini. Then Dorothy tells them about Maria's recent phone call with Mary Martin, who will be playing her onstage.

"Mary hasn't stopped talking about your chat for days. I don't know what you told her," Dorothy says lightly.

"She asked me to teach her how to yodel," Maria says, and everyone laughs, imagining what this conversation must have sounded like. "She has a good, strong voice. But the von Trapps never did yodeling until we arrived in America."

"Is that right?" Dorothy asks, putting down her drink, and Fran can see that she's intrigued.

"Yes." Maria nods. She's wearing a traditional dirndl in blue with an embroidered silver vest. She should look kind and matronly, but something in the set of her jaw gives her the appearance of a disapproving teacher. "I'm curious," she says, "why isn't our time in America part of this play?"

"Well." Hammerstein spreads his hands. "I'm afraid we only get two and a half hours to tell a story."

Maria sits forward and suddenly becomes animated. "But our life in America is the most exciting part!"

"Will you tell us about it?" Dorothy asks.

So Maria takes the rest of their cocktail hour to tell them about her time touring the States. The family met everyone during those days, from famous movie stars to popular politicians. Then in 1942 they bought a piece of land in Vermont. Its only building was a dilapidated shack, and without significant funds the family tore it down and built an alpine lodge with their own hands. Once it was completed and the family settled in, they began hosting music camps there for aspiring singers. When the United States entered the war, the eldest boys signed up with the army. Both were shipped overseas, and both survived. It felt like God Himself was protecting the von Trapps.

Then in 1947 tragedy struck.

"It was from his time in a submarine." Maria's eyes pool with tears. "All those diesel fumes and poor ventilation. Most of Georg's U-boat crew had died of lung cancer years before. Then it came for him." The tears slip down her cheeks, and everyone is silent.

Fran holds her breath and purposefully avoids looking at Hammerstein.

"He was a good man. A kind man," Maria says firmly, eager to make a point.

Hammerstein agrees. "And by the end of the play, this is what we want our audience to take away. That Georg was a wonderful father."

Fran can see Maria struggling to reconcile herself to this.

That perhaps it makes no difference how Georg starts off. It's where he ends up that matters.

"Did your family continue touring after Georg's death?" Dorothy asks quietly.

Maria clasps her hands together in her lap. "No. I tried to keep everyone together, but the girls wanted to go off and get married." The bitterness is still heavy in her voice. "Of course, Rosmarie stayed, but that . . ." She shakes her head at the terrible memory. "She never liked to sing. I should never have forced her."

Hammerstein reaches out and places a giant hand on her knee. "We all have parenting regrets."

"Ha! I see your statue," Maria says.

"What—that?" Hammerstein looks to the plaque above the mantelpiece and the giant "Father of the Year" embossed in gold. Then he laughs. "I keep that there as a reminder. Because when it was presented to me, it couldn't have been further from the truth." Hammerstein sighs. "It reminds me to do better."

"I should have done better," Maria admits. "All that work and now only Johannes runs the lodge. No more singing. No more family Christmases. Everything just"—she snaps her fingers—"changed in an instant."

Fran can see how much this pains her.

"It's the hardest part of being human," Hammerstein agrees, putting down his drink. "Accepting that even the best things will have an end."

For a moment Fran thinks he's going to tell Maria about his diagnosis. In fact, gaining her sympathy might be the only way to ensure that she won't go to the press with her complaints. But Hammerstein remains silent, and Fran realizes that he's not telling her on purpose. He wants her to fall in love with this play as much as he has, to recognize the beauty of its journey and its songs. Not to be guilted into it.

"Fran gave me her notes on your visit," Hammerstein says. "I read them page by page and something stuck with me. A moment you told Fran about, when you were standing on the Untersberg."

"Yes, I remember."

"The whole world around you was changing, but the hills were the same. The flowers were the same." Hammerstein rises and walks to the piano. There's a single sheet of music on the stand. "For months I've felt a song was missing from the play. Then I tried to imagine you on the top of the Untersberg, buffeted by the winds of change while the natural world around you remained peaceful. And this is part of God's gift to us, isn't it? The knowledge that even while our circumstances might change, the world He created is stable and filled with beauty."

He hands her the music, and when she reads the title, her voice trembles. " 'Edelweiss.' "

Hammerstein smiles sadly and takes a seat at his piano. "Would you like to sing it?"

It's the shortest song in the play. Only fifteen lines. But by the time Maria is finished, everyone in the room is weeping.

CHAPTER TWENTY-FOUR

O F ALL THE MOMENTS she'll remember about this night, Fran wonders if the most vivid will be the crush of reporters crowding the red carpet outside the Lunt-Fontanne. It's chaos, with journalists shouting out questions to the stars amid the pop of photographers' flashbulbs every few seconds.

"Madness, isn't it?" a woman asks from behind.

It's Mrs. Hammerstein, dressed in an exquisite black gown topped with an equally exquisite mink stole. She looks like an older version of Sophia Loren, with cheekbones that could cut, and heavily lidded eyes. Oscar Hammerstein is with her, besieged from all sides by reporters with their scribbling pencils and notebooks. He smiles at Fran, but she can read the nervousness in his face.

"It all comes down to this, doesn't it?" he says to her quietly.

Every celebrity in New York has turned out for this night. Marlene Dietrich, Gypsy Rose Lee, Ethel Merman. More than two million dollars in advance tickets have been sold, but none of that will matter if the critics—and Maria von Trapp—are unimpressed. "Is she here?" Fran asks.

Hammerstein uses his chin to indicate a woman in a green satin gown coming out of a white car. Fran gasps when she sees who she's with.

"Are those her sons?" Peter asks.

Dorothy smiles a little. "And two of her daughters. Oscar called each of her children and gave them the same pitch he gave to Maria."

It's such a gamble. Now, if any one of them dislikes the play . . .

"However many changes have been made, this story is still based on her life," Hammerstein explains. "She should be with her family."

Fran looks back at Maria and sees that the smile on her face is one of deep joy. How did Hammerstein do it? Reuniting her family for this!

The play, of course, is spectacular. The theater rings with laughter as Maria tears down her curtains to make play-clothes for the children, then falls silent as Liesl's boyfriend Rolf betrays her family. And the entire audience seems to fall in love with the Captain at the same time as Maria herself. It's one of Hammerstein's most inspirational stories, and Mary Martin is absolutely luminescent as Maria.

But it's the real Maria the front row is concerned about. Fran catches Hammerstein turning to glance at Maria's expression throughout the play, studying her reaction to every song. She's smiling when the nuns are singing about their frustrations with her. But Fran thinks she catches a frown on Maria's face during Rolf's performance of "Sixteen Going on Seventeen."

When the play is finished, the applause inside the Lunt-Fontanne is thunderous. But Maria doesn't move. Then suddenly the curtains swing closed and she rises.

Oh, God, she wants to be the first to leave, Fran thinks. *This is disastrous.* But that's not what she's doing. While the audience is still clapping, Maria turns to them and takes her own bow.

No one applauds louder for her than Hammerstein.

In the glittering lobby outside, Fran overhears Maria's first interview with the *Post.*

"And what did you think, Mrs. von Trapp?" A young man in a suit takes out a notepad and pen, poised to write.

Fran holds her breath.

"Well, it's not exactly our life story," Maria says. There's silence for several moments as she gathers her thoughts. "But our love for God and family was there, and this is what has always been most important." Beside her, all five of her children nod, even Rupert, in spite of being transformed into a girl named Liesl.

Fran exhales and Peter squeezes her hand. Maria has given the musical her approval. Whatever happens after this is in the hands of the ticketholders.

At the after party on the roof of the St. Regis, Maria finds Fran.

"I want you to meet my children," she says. The green of her satin gown—a gift from the Hallidays, with a matching handbag—brings out the color of her eyes. "Rupert, Werner, Johannes, this is Fran." The three men smile. They all have their mother's rosy cheeks. "My wonderful daughter, Agathe. And, of course, you know Lorli."

"I'm sure you've heard this throughout your lives, but it's truly a pleasure," Fran says. "Your mother has told me so many wonderful things about all of you."

"Fran is a writer." Maria beams. She's almost unrecognizable without her trademark dirndl. "And this here is her good friend, Peter."

Lorli grins at the expression "good friend." "It was a wonderful play," Lorli tells him. "If I try to forget that it is supposed to be about our lives, I would say it was one of the best musicals I've ever seen."

"The music was fantastic," Rupert agrees. "Even if I did get turned into a swooning sixteen-year-old girl."

"Well, at least you were in it," Johannes jokes.

Everyone laughs, and it's a relief that none of them seem to hold a grudge. Perhaps the shock of the German film has taken the edge off seeing their father portrayed as some strict disciplinarian. Fran knows how she would feel if a musical turned her mother into its star and her father was made the dynamic character, there to transform into a more open and loving person throughout the play. At first she would be hurt, then she would be outraged.

"Do you think Papa would have liked it?" Lorli asks.

The family falls silent. An orchestra is playing music on the far side of the roof, and Fran imagines that the von Trapps can probably identify the song. They've had an extraordinary musical education.

"He would have loved the music," Rupert admits, and everyone agrees.

"Especially 'Edelweiss,'" Werner says quietly.

Maria glances across the rooftop at Hammerstein, who's surrounded by a circle of friends. He catches her eye and leads the group over. The night is surprisingly temperate for November. Most of the men are dressed in only tuxedos. But Hammerstein is wearing a peacoat over his.

"Congratulations, Mr. Hammerstein," Rupert says.

Hammerstein actually looks bashful. "Well, this wouldn't exist without your family. Your mother was adamant that your father be shown in a gentler light. So please don't hold any of the Captain's personality against her. She told us what a wonderful man he was."

"I suspect he would have enjoyed the show," Rupert says.

Dorothy sounds genuinely surprised. "Really?"

"Well, the music anyway."

Dorothy smiles wryly. Then a man approaches their group and immediately Hammerstein stiffens.

"The reviews are in," he guesses.

The man nods. He appears to be about Hammerstein's age, with dark hair, round glasses, and a cleft in his chin. He looks at home in this crowd. "Herbert Mayes," he introduces himself.

Peter and Fran both shake his hand. The von Trapps smile.

"Herbert's my neighbor," Hammerstein explains. "Also, the editor of *McCall's*." He looks anxious. "Well?"

"The *Times* thought it was absolutely wonderful." Next to Herbert, Dorothy exhales. "And the *Post* called it your best work yet."

But Hammerstein's not impressed. "I have friends at those papers. What about the *Tribune*?"

Herbert hesitates. "Not as glowing."

"Just read it."

The editor takes a piece of paper from his coat pocket, and it looks to be an early copy of a review that must now be going to press. He nervously adjusts his glasses, then hesitates.

"Well, go on," Hammerstein says.

The man clears his throat. "'A show not only too sweet for words, but almost too sweet for music.'"

Dorothy inhales sharply and Hammerstein clenches his jaw. "What about Kenneth Tynan?"

Herbert's voice grows quiet. "From the *Observer*?" He hands Hammerstein a paper, and Hammerstein reads it aloud. "'A show for children of all ages, from six to about eleven and a half.'"

There's silence in the small circle around Hammerstein.

"Don't listen to them." Maria takes Hammerstein's arm. "They're only reviews."

"Yes," Hammerstein agrees, and for the first time since his operation, Fran thinks he looks as unwell as the doctors say he is. "But they're the reviews of my last play."

Maria glances at the faces around her, and while Dorothy steps away, too devastated to listen, Hammerstein explains.

For a brief moment, Maria looks deeply distressed. Then her resolve returns and her grip tightens. "Do you know what our manager said after we performed for him here in New York? He told us we'd be sure to sell out every nunnery from Manhattan to Chicago." She smiles at the memory. "He thought only priests or nuns would want to come and hear us. But you know who convinced him otherwise? The people. Agents, critics, managers . . . None of them buy tickets." She dismisses them with her hand. "Only the people do. You wait."

AUTHOR'S NOTE

Defying critics, *The Sound of Music* went on to run for another 1,442 performances. A week after the premiere, the cast recorded an album that would sit at the number one spot on the *Billboard* music charts for sixteen weeks, while the show itself would go on to win five Tony Awards, including Best Musical in 1960.

As the doctors had predicted, Hammerstein didn't have long to live. Nine months after the show's premiere, Hammerstein succumbed to stomach cancer, passing away at his farm in Pennsylvania. On Broadway, the lights went dark in tribute to the man who'd written the lyrics to some of the greatest musicals of his time: *South Pacific, Show Boat, The King and I,* and—of course—*The Sound of Music.*

Tragically, Hammerstein didn't live long enough to see the release of *The Sound of Music* by Twentieth Century-Fox. He would have no idea of the kind of devoted following the movie—and his lyrics—would eventually inspire. But the film would go on to become the highest-grossing film of its time, nominated for ten Academy Awards and winning five, including Best Picture.

I spent a great deal of time debating whether I wanted to tackle the life of someone as famous (and, more important, beloved) as Maria von Trapp. As a child, I'd been enchanted by *The Sound of Music*—the scenery, the hills, the upbeat songs. As an adult, however, I was intrigued by the film for entirely different reasons. I was curious about what might inspire a girl to enter a convent at the height of the Roaring Twenties—or in Austria, the Weimar years. Had something happened to her that she was hoping to escape? Was this a path her parents had pushed her toward? I was curious as well about her relationship with Georg's children. The film had made it seem as if the transition from love interest to full-time mother of seven had been easy. Was this true? Were times somehow simpler back then? But my decision to finally write about Maria came during the pandemic, when I found myself watching the film with my children and these questions remained. Who *was* the real Maria von Trapp?

It turns out that the real Maria was every bit as fiery as the woman depicted in the Broadway play. Over her eighty-two years of life, she was the author of seven books, beginning with her 1949 autobiography *The Story of the Trapp Family Singers*. It was this autobiography (she wrote a second one) that served as the basis for *The Sound of Music*. Some of the more unbelievable scenes in this novel—Maria's list of infractions at the convent, her hilarious request to buy sex appeal, the family's escape on the last train leaving out of Austria into Italy, and even the bow Maria took for the audi-

ence at the Broadway premiere—truly happened. As did
some of the sadder moments, unfortunately, such as Maria's
abuse at the hands of her uncle, her loss of several children
during pregnancy, and, later, Rosmarie's mental health de-
cline.

Toward the end of her life, Maria seems to have lived with
a great deal of guilt over how she left her youngest children in
boarding schools when they arrived in America. "The parting was always a very bitter moment for all of us," she wrote
in her first autobiography, "but at that time I still thought
children had to go to school, and everything else had to be
sacrificed to this fact. Later I should learn better." She had
similar guilt over her inability to see how years of touring
would later affect Rosmarie.

But when writing a historical novel (and this is indeed a
novel, with artistic license taken with respect to both dia-
logue and characters where necessary), overreliance on auto-
biographies can be risky. There were chronological errors in
Maria's book, for example, and although she often describes
her parenting style as tough but fair, modern readers might
feel otherwise, as did her own neighbors, who recalled how
life for the von Trapp children was one of much work and
very little play. Thankfully, many written sources exist about
Maria, including a memoir penned by her stepdaughter Agathe. I found Agathe's recollections particularly useful when
trying to verify some of the more unbelievable scenes from
Maria's life, such as Georg's marriage proposal, which really
did happen the way it's described in this book, with the children unintentionally acting as intermediaries. "I really and
truly was not in love," Maria wrote in her autobiography. "I
liked him but didn't love him. I loved the children and in a

way was really marrying them. However, I soon learned to love [Georg] more than I have ever loved, before or after."

Given this statement, it came as little surprise that Maria would be upset about the script for the Broadway play. By the time she approached the production about changing the characters to more accurately reflect real life, however, rehearsals were already underway. Even if she'd known about the play earlier, the fact that she'd sold the rights to her story gave her little recourse. Yet the risk was real that she might complain to the press, and the three-eighths of a percent given to her by the Hallidays is true, as well as the gift of the satin dress and matching handbag.

Some of the most entertaining research I did concerned the theater world of the 1950s. The near-hysterical phone calls Dick Halliday used to make to Hammerstein's office, and his suggestion that Maria catch her bloomers on a tree limb, are all actual events. And while Fran and Peter are fictional characters, they are based on two of Hammerstein's most dedicated employees, both of whom worked for him while he was writing the lyrics to *The Sound of Music*. I owe an immense debt to biographers like Todd S. Purdum, whose book *Something Wonderful* helped me to re-create pivotal moments from the last year of Hammerstein's life.

Tragically, the lyrics to "Edelweiss" were indeed the last that Hammerstein would ever write. Yet as a testament to Rodgers and Hammerstein's enduring popularity, the song became so synonymous with Austria that in 1984, President Reagan used the lyrics in a toast to Rudolf Kirchschläger during the Austrian president's state visit. Kirchschläger's reaction was supposedly one of resigned bemusement.

Even Maria seems to have made her peace with the script

by the time the movie was being filmed, going so far as to make a surprise visit to the film set in Austria, where she stubbornly remained until the director finally offered her a cameo (you can see her walking by an archway during the song "I Have Confidence"). The film's actors recall her being larger than life, someone who absolutely knew what she wanted and went after it. But after spending time with Maria on the set, the director refused to send her tickets to *The Sound of Music*'s film premiere at the Rivoli Theatre in New York. His concern would certainly have been different from Hammerstein's, as by this point she (if not her children) had come to embrace the script. Perhaps he was concerned about being upstaged. After all, Maria knew how to win over an audience.

WHATEVER HAPPENED TO . . .

RUPERT: (1911–1992) After serving in the U.S. Army during WWII, Rupert practiced medicine until the 1980s. He had six children.

AGATHE: (1913–2010) After the family stopped singing together in the 1950s, Agathe worked as a kindergarten teacher in Maryland. She didn't marry or have children.

MARIA "Mitzi" (1914–2014): Mitzi spent nearly thirty years working as a missionary in New Guinea. On her return, she helped to run the Trapp Family Lodge. She didn't marry or have children.

WERNER (1915–2007): True to his childhood passions, Werner became a farmer in Vermont. He went on to marry and have six children.

HEDWIG (1917–1972): Hedwig worked as a music teacher until she died at fifty-five of an asthma attack while in Austria. She didn't marry or have children.

JOHANNA (1919–1994): After being locked in her room to prevent her from getting married, Johanna eloped with the vice mayor of Vienna's son, Ernst Winter. After the war, Johanna and Ernst returned to Austria, where they had six children.

MARTINA (1921–1951): After marrying in 1949, Martina died during the birth of her first child.

ROSMARIE (1929–2022): After years of touring, Rosmarie worked as a missionary, eventually settling in Vermont, where she owned several thrift shops. She did not marry or have children. She died at the age of ninety-three.

ELEONORE "Lorli" (1931–2021): Two years after she stopped singing with her family in 1952, Lorli married and raised seven children.

JOHANNES: (1939–) After graduating from Yale with a master's degree in forestry, Johannes is currently the president of the Trapp Family Lodge in Vermont. He has two children.

MARIA (1905–1987): After Georg's death in 1947, Maria did missionary work with her children in New Guinea, only returning to Vermont to manage the Lodge. Her life after *The Sound of Music*'s cinematic debut was never the same, and she enjoyed making publicity appearances alongside members of the cast. By the time of her death in 1987, she was the author of seven books.

FRANZ WASNER (1905–1992): Portrayed as the character of Max Detweiler in *The Sound of Music,* Father Wasner toured with the von Trapp family until the 1950s. After fifteen years of missionary work, the Vatican appointed him rector of the Anima in Rome, where he remained until 1981. He retired in Salzburg.

THE VILLA TRAPP: During the war, the Nazi leader Heinrich Himmler used the von Trapps' villa as his summer residence. When the war was over, Austria returned the villa to the von Trapps, but the family no longer wished to live there, given who had occupied it. Subsequently, it was turned into a hotel, and today it is used as a house of prayer.

ACKNOWLEDGMENTS

I owe a deep debt of gratitude to a number of people for helping *Maria* along its publication journey. First and foremost, I must thank my truly inspired editor, Susanna Porter, whose keen eye for detail and way with words are simply unsurpassed. To my agent, Dan Lazar, who believed in this book even before the first word was written, my eternal thanks. And to the fantastic people at both Writers House and Random House who helped make this book a reality, my sincerest thanks as well, especially to Victoria Doherty-Munro, Maja Nikolic, Peggy Boulos Smith, Kate Boggs, Sofia Bolido, Anusha Khan, Carlos Beltrán, Lorie Young, Megan Whalen, Katie Horn, and Kimberly Hovey. I must also show gratitude to those who read the book while still in its infancy. Sarah Parker and Claudia Zaira—your early advice was invaluable. I also could not have gotten through the pandemic without your friendship, or the friendship of Nicole Anderson, Mari Jose-Ferrer, or Saida Ortega. The five of you were the reason I emerged from quarantine sane enough to be able to write. A very sincere thanks as well to fellow author Allison Pataki, for putting me in contact with someone who met Maria while staying in the Trapp Family Lodge in Vermont. And finally, my eternal love to Amit, Liam, and Colette, who came with me to Austria and endured an untold number of trips to the places Maria went during her life in Austria, including the top of the Untersberg.

MARIA

MICHELLE MORAN

A Book Club Guide

DISCUSSION QUESTIONS

1. What is the most shocking difference between Maria von Trapp's real life and her life as it's portrayed in the movie?

2. Why do you think the writers made so many changes to Maria's life story? Were they effective?

3. What would have happened to the von Trapps if Georg had married the princess? What would have happened to Maria?

4. Was Maria a good stepmother? If so, why? If not, why not?

5. How would you feel if your own life was turned into a movie and major events were altered? Would you care? Should the people who've had this happen to them care?

6. Does Broadway/Hollywood have a right to change the story of a person's life? Or do they owe it to the subject to remain as faithful as possible?

7. Assuming you've seen the movie or the play, what is it about Maria's story that appeals to audiences? Would her real-life story as told in this book have had similar appeal?

8. What does Hammerstein's music add to Maria's story both on stage and in film? Would *The Sound of Music* have enjoyed the same success without it?

9. After signing away the rights to her life story, Maria was offered three-eighths of a percent of the musical's profits by Richard Halliday. Was this fair?

10. Would Maria have remained in Nonnberg if she'd turned down Georg's marriage proposal? Why or why not?

11. Did Maria love Georg in the end, or did she remain married to him because of the children? What do you think her stepchildren felt about her marriage to their father? Did their feelings change over time?

MICHELLE MORAN is the internationally best-selling author of eight historical novels. A California native with a master's in education, she was inspired to write historical novels by her experiences on archaeological digs. Her novels, translated into more than twenty languages, include *Nefertiti, The Heretic Queen, Cleopatra's Daughter, Madame Tussaud, The Second Empress, Rebel Queen, Mata Hari's Last Dance,* and *Maria.* A frequent traveler, she currently lives with her family in England, where she is researching her ninth book.

michellemoran.com
IG: @authormichellemoran
Facebook.com/AuthorMichelleMoran